OLIVER GREEVES

Nelson's Folly

First published 2020 by Oliver Greeves

Produced by Independent Ink
independentink.com.au

Cover design by Daniela Catucci @ Catucci Design
Edited by Sabine Borgis
Internal design by Independent Ink
Typeset in 12/16.5 pt Adobe Caslon Pro by Post Pre-press Group, Brisbane

Cover images: Detail from a portrait of Miss Bertha Eccles, a direct descendent of Fanny Nelson; Nelson Statue at Trafalgar Square, London, UK, iStock.com; an engraved illustration image of Nelson boarding the San Josef at the Battle of St Vincent from a vintage Victorian book dated 1886 that is no longer in copyright, iStock.com; part of British Postage Stamp depicting HMS Victory, circa 1982, iStock.com; King George III guinea coin, public domain; Classical Numismatic Group, Inc. www.cngcoins.com

A catalogue record for this book is available from the National Library of Australia

NATIONAL LIBRARY OF AUSTRALIA

ISBN 978-0-6450237-0-1 (paperback)
ISBN 978-0-6450237-1-8 (epub)
ISBN 978-0-6450237-2-5 (kindle)

This book is dedicated to the memory of my grandmother, Bertha Eccles, the great-great-great-granddaughter of Fanny Nelson.

CONTENTS

CHAPTER ONE
December 1792

Fanny awoke, shivering. She gritted her teeth and, careful not to wake him, got out of bed and hastily pulled on the shawl that lay on the chair and a pair of thick woollen socks. She returned to bed, pausing at the chamber pot before climbing beneath the covers. Undisturbed by her movements or the light of the frigid moon, Horatio slept on, mouth open and snoring. Twenty years in the Royal Navy had taught him to sleep soundly anywhere.

The old grandfather clock chimed in the parlour, as a cold Norfolk wind whined through cracks in the window sash. The sigh of the draught reminded her of years gone by in Nevis, where Caribbean trade winds blew soft and warm all year. She drew the bedclothes tighter, an ember of resentment glowing.

How her life had changed since then – she had once been mistress of Montpelier and now she found herself in a borrowed frozen rectory in Norfolk! When they'd first arrived, Edmund – Horatio's father and a clergyman – had moved to a smaller rectory at his second church so they could have this place to live. They survived on a penurious budget, one that did not stretch to include a coal fire to heat their bedroom.

She rolled over to find a more comfortable position on the mattress. It was only ever intended to be temporary. Everyone had expected Horatio to get another command in the Home Fleet and they'd planned to buy their own house with money Fanny was due to inherit. But that hope dimmed. The inheritance was still in probate. And Horatio had never been given another command. Fanny had put two and two together. She recalled Nevis merchants complaining about the officious British captain who'd interfered with their American trade. Horatio claimed he'd done nothing but enforce the law. And then he'd made more enemies by writing home about corruption in the dockyard in Antigua. He always had an answer: he'd merely been doing his duty. She tried to look on the brighter side. She was still young. There would be more children. He would get his ship and the prize money for a new house. She fell back to sleep.

The day dawned with a feeble sun and grey sky. It was still dark at eight when the maid brought in the bowl and a jug of hot water and woke her up. Horatio had risen and she could hear him washing in the adjoining room.

He called out as he heard her stirring. 'Fan, I'm walking to the village to meet the mail. I want to get the latest on the war situation. Are you coming?'

Although they lived half a mile from the centre of Burnham Thorpe, with Josiah away at school now – he'd begun boarding the prior year when he'd turned twelve – they had picked up the habit of walking along the river to Burnham Market where the London to Norwich coach stopped. They would pick up mail and buy produce in the market then walk back along the field path to Burnham Thorpe, returning in time for dinner, which, in England, was served after midday.

'Yes, dear,' she responded to him. 'At least it looks like a clear morning, for a change.' She poured the water into the bowl and started to sponge herself.

War was on people's minds. Another war with France. More taxes to pay, more men pressed for service, horrible threats of invasion. When Fanny was growing up, they had fought the Seven Years' War with the French. How glorious the victory had been, but when the American colonists rebelled, back came the French for revenge. But now they were revolutionaries like the Americans, spreading the poison of their ideas to England. There was no doubt in her mind that war would break out again – and very soon.

She met Horatio at the breakfast table in the parlour, which was warm at least, the maid having banked the fire and prepared scrambled eggs, bread, butter and conserves which were waiting for them. Fanny sipped her hot tea while Horatio drank a small glass of beer. He was dressed in the style of a country squire, she noted approvingly. New breeches, stout shoes and a woollen tweed coat to keep him warm. He looked so chipper, his eyes bright and clear. He was happy. There might be news.

'We'll be back before dinner!' she called out as they left the house.

Their route took them down the gravelled driveway to Wallsingham Road, where they turned onto the path to the Burn and then followed the winding river to Burnham Market. January rains had swollen the murky stream to its banks, the lower branches of the weeping willows which lined it now swept up in its current. On the other side of the river, grey fields stretched to the horizon, the fallow ground, whitened by frost, blending into the leaden skies. Tramping along, their breath evaporating in long trails, they walked in companionable silence for five or ten minutes until Horatio turned to her. 'Fanny,' he said intently, 'my command simply *must* come soon.'

'Yes, I know,' she replied, a sudden wave of anxiety hitting her at the thought of him leaving. She took care to turn away towards the river and carefully compose herself as he talked on.

'I am convinced that providence will have a special role for me to play in this war and I will do that to my utmost.'

'I have lost my mother, my father and my first husband and I cannot bear to think of losing you!' she exclaimed, the words out of her mouth and tears welling before she could regain herself. In the silence that followed, she continued. 'But I am most happy you will have a command. Perhaps we will be able to afford a house after this is over. I will look after Josiah and your father and your interests while you are gone.'

'Fanny, we need to talk about Josiah.'

'What do we need to discuss, Horatio? Josiah is comfortable at his school. He will flourish there. Then soon enough, he will study at Cambridge or Edinburgh.'

'No, Fanny. He's to come with me. I intend to take five or six local lads with me when I go. One will be Josiah.'

Her heart beat faster. She held her breath and tried to keep her voice light. 'Horatio, after all this time, what's caused this ... this change of plan?'

'I think this will be good for Josiah. He will grow up to be a real man. So long as he works hard and has a good spirit, he'll do well in the navy. He's a good lad and he listens to everything I say. He's a bit quiet but he'll learn to be a sailor.'

'But we have already agreed that my family in Edinburgh will article him in their law practice.'

'Fan, you know better than I, we've got no money for Cambridge or to article him with Lockhart. Nisbet's trust is still in probate – and we were counting on that money from your late husband to pay for his son's education. And we never received the support I counted on from your uncle, either.'

'Horatio, we will find the money. Josiah might even win a scholarship. And I promise you, I will get that money.'

'Fan, listen to me. The fathers of the other boys I take with me will each pay me a stipend to take their son. That money will cover the cost of Josiah too until he gets his midshipman's ticket.'

'But what about his education?' Her voice was shrill now.

'And what about mine, Fan? I myself am the product of an education on board a ship.' He stopped and she turned to face him. 'I went to sea at twelve and studied my three R's, and I challenge anyone to find a better mathematician, writer and commander of His Majesty's vessel than I am. I know that a naval career is uncertain, and nothing would please me more than Josiah becoming an attorney, perhaps even a judge or distinguished barrister. But we simply cannot afford it.'

He fell silent and they trudged on by the river, the path eventually veering off and crossing through a spinney while the river continued to flow north. The conifers closed over their heads and the path became dark with shadow. Fanny felt the weight of sadness descend. Although his argument was sensible, he was going to take her baby boy away. Horatio strode along, absorbed in his own vision. She tried to gather herself, as she knew he was not a man who would want to acknowledge her feelings.

Finally, Horatio broke his own silence. 'And you, Fanny, have a role to play for me and for Josiah. I want you to be my representative in England. You will move up in society as I am promoted. I will have money then. You will buy good dresses and fine hats. And visit London and Bath and great country houses. We shall write to each other about everything.'

Fanny's heart melted. 'I ... I will certainly do my best, Horatio, but are you sure about Josiah?'

'I know that you fear for his life, but our lives are in the hands of the divine providence. Josiah could die of smallpox or consumption or have an accident on our terrible roads or take a common cold and perish. Nothing is certain. In his early years on board, he will be safe – even in battle. I will protect him as if he is my own son, for I regard him as such.'

'But what about me? I'll be here alone.'

'No, no, you'll be fine. You have the family – father, William and Sarah, your friends. You'll get used to it. Then it will be over and we will be together again. You'll see.'

They followed the path behind the cottages of the village and out on to the high street. The walk had warmed her up, but she was still upset. The carriages of the better-off gentry were parked on the grass verge. Farmers and merchants were tending stalls and women were buying produce and exchanging greetings. It was the same as ever. The smell of fresh bread and the song of a fiddle would normally have lifted her heart. But it was not the same today.

At the inn, they paused for coffee and cake. As they sat there, Mr Coke of Holkham Hall bustled in, followed by his steward. He paused when he saw them and doffed his hat to Fanny who acknowledged him with a polite inclination of her head. Horatio stood to greet him.

'Good morning, Mr Nelson,' Mr Coke said loudly. 'How does this news from France find you? Eager to do battle with the enemies of the nation?'

'Yes, ready when called, Mr Coke. Soon they will need men who really know how to fight.'

'I look forward to renewing our acquaintance with you, Mr Nelson. Call on me, if you would! Mrs Nelson!' He tipped his hat and moved off to join an older man who was seated at another table.

'What was that about?' asked Fanny.

'No doubt he wants something. Now excuse me, Fanny, I must go see if the mail is here.'

He was gone only a few minutes and when he returned, he had a bright smile and, with a little jig, he waved a letter in the air.

CHAPTER TWO
January 1793

The yellow carriage, courtesy of the Admiralty, drew up at the parsonage. After all the penny-pinching years, Horatio experienced a momentary frisson of pleasure at the thought someone else was paying. He gave Fanny a farewell kiss while the driver stowed his cases. Then they set off for Kings Lynn Road. His elation grew as he leant back on the firm leather seat, stretching his legs and savouring the rattling pace. It was the first time in five years he had received orders to attend the Admiralty but by no means the first time he had visited. On those other occasions, he'd travelled uninvited by his own shilling on a crowded public coach and, once at the Admiralty, he'd had to wait his turn for meetings which were invariably perfunctory.

It was dark by the time they stopped at the Crown Inn at Hockerill at half past four. As Horatio waited for the driver to unload his luggage, a troop of army recruits passed by, their recruiting sergeant bellowing and their shambling attempt to march a testimony to their lack of training. Cannon fodder.

The inn was crowded with gentry and Horatio was given a shared room with three other gentlemen. 'On their way to London to seek commissions in the army and navy,' the innkeeper explained.

'Younger sons without prospects.' Horatio muttered as he paid for his room.

He was hungry and sat at the crowded common table. The man next to him was recounting a recent journey through France, describing with enthusiasm the guillotine's fascinating efficiency. A fashionably dressed man reported that his London hotel was jammed with French refugees and claimed that he had bought a number of oil paintings from them at knockdown prices. The discussion at the table soon turned to parliament. While Fox was supporting the French Jacobins, Burke, who had sympathised with the American revolutionaries, was fearful of the revolutionary spirit. War was on everybody's mind.

Horatio was asked about the navy and said a few words. There was a polite question or two before the conversation turned back to the regiments the men were planning to join. *Wealthy young fools* thought Horatio contemptuously.

The carriage reached his uncle's house, on the summit of a hill overlooking Kentish Town and the spread of the metropolis beyond it, early the following afternoon. Other than the view of London, the house might well have been in any village. It was the home of a successful servant of the crown. Though modest in size, it was a comfortable double-fronted house built from grey flint and framed by red brick, with a roof of blue-violet slate. Its fruit trees and borders had been pruned and tidied for winter, but elm, sweet chestnut and beech trees lent the house a quiet park-like dignity. The driveway was lined with rowan trees, now without their leaves and berries. Horatio remembered visiting and playing in this garden as a boy, climbing the trees and imagining he were a sailor looking out to sea. The carriage stopped in the turning circle and Horatio got down and approached the heavy oak door, which opened before he reached it. Uncle Suckling, diminished by age but still very much himself, vigorously gripped Horatio's arms and welcomed him with a smile.

Uncle's cook had prepared a supper and they enjoyed cold roast beef and garden vegetables, taken with a delicious spicy wine. When they finished, Horatio and Suckling moved to a pair of wingback chairs by a warm fire in the old brick fireplace. They exchanged news of the family and shared memories of Horatio's boyhood visits. At length, Horatio steered the conversation towards his upcoming meeting at the Admiralty and enquired after Uncle Suckling's remaining contacts.

'My dear boy, most of my friends have retired or passed on. Between the two of us my brother and I, held sway in the navy and customs but we are now long out of office and we were never at the centre, you understand. We were people at the edge. Our leaders needed our administrative skills and rewarded us with promotions and a little patronage.'

He paused and poked at the sputtering fire. He sat back in his chair still holding the poker. 'My advice, for what it's worth, is to go in with an attitude of humility – hard though that may be for you. My enquiries on your behalf have led me to understand that you offended their lordships on your last visit. It seems that they believe, perhaps rightly, that you have a sense of being wronged and indeed of being "owed things", and wouldn't see there was another point of view.'

Horatio flushed and stirred in his seat restlessly. He felt his temper rising and recalled Fanny's advice not to succumb to disappointment and feelings of injustice. She had said it would not sit well, even among friends.

'Uncle, I see the matter very differently. I was doing my duty, which is all that I ever consider. Politics has conspired to bring me down. They have passed me over despite my seniority on the captains list. I often ask myself what I need to do to prove my worth.'

Suckling picked up his clay pipe and lit it, nodding his head slowly as rings of blue smoke drifted upwards. There was a long pause.

'Life in a bureaucracy like our great navy necessitates patience, my boy. Eventually, when there's a need, names resurface and men rise from their obscurity – yes, sometimes beyond expectations. There is usually no rational explanation other than a need has arisen for a man's particular skills. Assistance from someone helped in the past or from a family member is always handy, though. And it is always better to have fewer enemies than you have.' He returned the pipe to his mouth, scratched his thinning hair and chuckled.

Uncle Suckling was right; Horatio knew that he'd had made a rod for his own back. But it was damnably unfair. 'Uncle, I hear your lesson and will try to be less indignant and more accepting without sacrificing my honour.'

'That's the spirit, Horatio! Let me tell you a thing or two about the lay of the land at the Admiralty. In short, as you have said, there is going to be a hell of a fight and they are short of captains with the stomachs for battle. Play your cards carefully and without sounding reckless and, with your reputation as a fighter, you will get the ship best for you. When they tell you what it is, don't cavil – you hear me? Now, tell me about young Josiah. How is he doing at school?'

After he said goodnight and began to make his way with his candle to his room, Horatio thought about the conversation. It was good advice, he admitted to himself. There was no use dwelling on yesterday's grievances. He had endured a setback and he might as well start from there. They didn't owe him anything and he would simply have to prove himself again.

The next day, they left early for Whitehall. After several hours of heavy traffic, they reached their destination near the Admiralty. Horatio climbed down and instructed the driver to return for him later in the day. He took his pocket watch from his waistcoat – it was almost ten. He waited as the carriage rattled away, looking up at the great building emerging from the morning mist like a magnificent country house. It seemed even bigger than before. Its splendour signified the Royal Navy was the great power at the heart of the nation. Even now, as he stood here in the dappled sunlight, inside the masters of this great institution were sending hundreds of warships and thousands of men to the very ends of the earth!

'Please sir, please sir, a penny for some food, a penny is all.'

The thin voice interrupted his thoughts. Whitehall was crowded and families of beggars crouched in the shadows, their children running beside the pedestrians. An urchin was holding his sleeve as he stood looking at Horatio, to the building and then back.

Horatio reached into his pocket and thrust a coin into the child's hands. It felt like an offering to the gods. He made his way through the gates and the courtyard, his confidence growing. He felt like an officer again as he straightened his back, adjusted his wig and climbed the steps to the vestibule beyond the tall pillars and classical pediment.

'Captain Nelson!' The warrant officer on duty had recognised him. 'Welcome to Admiralty House! Their lordships will wait upon you.'

'Lordships? I thought I was to see only Lord Hood.'

'No, no, sir. You are to meet Mr Middleton, the Comptroller and Lord Hood and then the First Lord, Earl Chatham. I trust you have made the time?'

'I am, most obliged, I … er …'

He was at a loss for words, his heart rising but then on further consideration, falling again. They must be interested in seeing if he was still the fiery man he had been back in 1788 when they dismissed him. It was a test.

To his relief, the meeting with the Comptroller was a pedestrian discussion about new procedures and changes in ship design. Sir Charles Middleton described the new technique of sheathing the hulls of battleships in thin sheets of copper. It kept the worms at bay and made the ships faster. He mentioned the refit of a third-rated vessel, *Agamemnon*, as an example.

The meeting with Hood, now First Sea Lord, followed an hour's wait. When the door opened and Horatio was admitted, Hood was polite but distant. All he would say was that Earl Chatham, the First Lord of the Admiralty and brother of the prime minister, William Pitt, wanted to see him personally and, following that meeting, he and Horatio would have a longer conversation at dinner. Hood's glowering eyebrows seemed to be sending an unspoken message – be civil, be humble.

Sprawled in a rococo armchair while cooling his heels in the antechamber again, Horatio nervously reviewed his situation. Another thirty minutes passed before the door opened and a servant bade him enter the First Lord's State Room. The Earl was seated behind his elegant Chippendale desk. As Horatio came in, the Earl rose and with elaborate courtesy took Horatio's arm and steered him to a sofa and took a seat beside him, at a friendly but not uncomfortable distance.

'Very good of you to visit today, Nelson,' said the Earl, as if Horatio had been passing by his estate and happened to drop in.

'My lord, it is my privilege to be invited and I am most anxious to assure you–' he began his apology, but was interrupted.

'Captain Nelson, what kind of ship shall we find for you? I am thinking that a second-in-line battleship would be right for your seniority, but I fear that we have none ready for sea at the moment.' He consulted a list for a few moments, then looked up. 'We have *Agamemnon*, a third rated, but she is only a sixty-four. Surely we can find something better than that?'

He looked enquiringly at Horatio, who felt his cheeks redden. Now he understood why the Comptroller had mentioned *Agamemnon*. It was a signal.

'My lord, *Agamemnon* will be a fine command. She will be a fearsome warship when she is ready. I am more than content.'

The Earl broke into a wide smile.

'Nelson, we need fewer placemen and influence peddlers and more men like you. I've had a line of unqualified and frightful braggarts with me all morning. It's a pleasure to see a quiet fighting man, at last! And now I am afraid I shall have to pass you back to Lord Hood. May God go with you and with all your men. I shall look forward to hearing about victories.'

The Earl stood and led him to the door. Horatio's heart pounded. He was back! Thank God for Uncle Suckling's counsel. How easily he might have stood his ground and refused the sixty-four only to be assigned a broken-backed frigate! *Agamemnon* was a new class of ship as big on the waterline as a first-rated but cut down to two decks. With fewer heavier guns and her new copper sheathing, she was a ship fast enough to be in the van and big enough to take out the best enemy opposing her. And the Earl seemed to be apologising ...

Back at Lord Hood's office, a line of captains and other officers were being ushered in and out, each dealt with quickly – and leaving either with smiles or disappointed faces. Hood's servant approached to say the First Sea Lord was busy and begged Captain Nelson's indulgence to have dinner at two o'clock that afternoon at White's clubhouse in St James's Street. Horatio readily agreed.

Horatio walked the short distance, arriving at White's fifteen minutes early. The club, unobtrusive by the standards of London, had a mixed reputation – its exclusivity contended with its claim to be the venue for the country's greatest gamblers. He entered the lobby nervously aware of his old uniform among so many well-dressed and polished men. A servant seated him in the parlour, where three young men were discussing a gambling debt in a corner. Horatio listened idly as he waited. He couldn't help but wonder where these two young men found the money to make such huge wagers.

The front door opened and out of the corner of his eye Horatio saw a slight figure taking off his coat. He looked familiar. Something about the florid cheeks, narrow mouth and bright intelligent eyes reminded him of someone he had known long ago.

The man handed his coat to the servant and was headed for the stairs when he looked in Horatio's direction. He spun and walked towards Horatio, his arms outstretched.

'My God, Nelson!' His Scottish accent gave him away. It was Alexander Davison, who he had last seen years ago in Canada.

'Allick, how good it is to see you again!'

'The last time was ten years ago in Quebec City. I rescued you from the arms of a bonny lass whose father would have killed you or ended your career!' the man said, putting his hands on Horatio's upper arms and squinting, as if to take the sight of him in.

'Allick, indeed, you saved my life,' Horatio replied, laughing.

'What are you doing here, Horatio?'

'I am hoping for a new command. My host, Lord Hood, will be here in a moment. Can we meet again while I am still in London?'

'My dear friend, I insist that you stay with me in Bloomsbury tonight. Here is my card with the address. Shall we say at five?'

'There you are!' The booming voice of Lord Hood interrupted their conversation.

'Dinner time, Captain!'

Horatio hastily shook his old friend's hand and accepted his kind offer. Hood merely nodded at Davison dismissively before taking Horatio by the arm and escorting him to the dining room.

Dinner was wild salmon, gulls' eggs, potted shrimps and smoked eel; then grouse, partridge – accompanied by a bottle of Champagne to wash it down. But despite the glories of the menu, Horatio hardly noticed the food or the wine. Hood was delighted by Horatio's meeting with Earl Chatham and his swift decision to take command of *Agamemnon*. It was as if a different person were sitting opposite him. He was no longer the sarcastic admiral of less than two years ago. Horatio burned with curiosity. And he didn't have to wait too long before Hood answered his unspoken question.

'My dear fellow, two years ago the navy was in a massive cutting exercise to save the Exchequer. It was all about keeping our finest ships and our dockyards. In that setting, what use were you? You'd offended everyone from the King down, including me, and wherever I went in the Admiralty, one of your victims was there to complain. The situation is different now. The French navy is equipped with the best armaments and ships known to man. They are formidable and will commit everything to invade this country. Now we need every fighting man with experience.'

'But why was I called so late?' asked Horatio.

'You are the better for it. You are repentant for your mistakes and will likely not repeat them. And, more importantly, you are hungry. We must bottle up the French and destroy them – before they invade us. God knows Lord Moira's army in Belgium is merely a stopgap. Let me fill you in on your next step.'

Later, seated by the fire at Allick's mansion in Bloomsbury nursing a glass full to the brim with port, Horatio recounted the conversation to Lord Hood. The young lawyer Horatio had known in Quebec City still had a nervous energy and intensity he remembered so well but now he also had the assuredness that came with great wealth. He had his own merchant ships now and he had just equipped a fleet to carry more convicts to New South Wales.

'Horatio, never forget that it's the people in this town who hold all the cards. This time around, make no enemies – only plentiful friends with good connections. Don't ever believe success depends on your talents alone. And never make the mistake of neglecting the interest of others.'

Early the next morning, Horatio rose and set off through the early traffic across London Bridge towards Gravesend before the sun showed its pallid image through the smoky air.

As the carriage rattled and swayed over the cobbled streets and dusty unmade highway, Horatio thought about Allick. How could he have made so much money in such a short time? While Horatio had been languishing in Norfolk, Allick was getting things done here. *By God*, he thought to himself, *I will have a house like that, and a fortune and a title.* He owed it to Fanny and to his family. And he'd got his start now. He had great plans for Allick, too: he would make the merchant his prize agent, his eyes and ears in London.

Agamemnon was in dry-dock when Horatio arrived at Chatham dockyard at noon. The moment he saw her, he knew what a great decision he had made. She was sleek and the fresh copper sheathing nailed to her hull glowed. He explored the ship with the yard foreman, who explained, 'She was launched in 1781, sir; fought the French and Americans and now her refit is almost done. She's fast and true in a big sea. She's well made, I'd say.'

They had both taken off their jackets and were crawling through the bilges and interior spaces, examining the hull. Then they both climbed the top mast to review the ship from aloft. She was a lean and hungry beast. No wonder she was fast, her huge but elegant frame was built for speed. She had no guns aboard yet and there was no furniture in the spacious great cabin. That would all be done by the time Horatio returned. He imagined her in a rough sea, her decks crowded with sailors and marines, balls and bullets flying, sails billowing and the enemy at his mercy. Could he manage a vessel like this with 600 men on board? Could he earn their respect without being a flogging captain? Yet as he asked the question and even as his doubts mounted, he felt a sense of peace, as if he were finally at home again.

The road home was long and tedious. He was anxious to be back with Fanny and to share everything with her and almost as anxious, he admitted guiltily, to join his new ship. The carriage took him to Greenwich where they ferried over the Thames to the Cambridge road. The rain of the previous day had created a sea of mud and it was not until late in the afternoon of the second day that they reached Burnham Thorpe. By then, he had digested everything and was prepared for the next step. He was ready to go.

Fanny greeted him warmly. She had news of her own. A messenger from Mr Coke had come to the rectory to request Horatio visit at Holkham Hall upon his return. 'He sent us a brace of partridge, Horatio. He has been most friendly. He has something to ask you,' Fanny explained as Horatio freshened up from the road.

Horatio's father, Edmund, joined them for a cele-bratory supper that evening. Fanny had polished the silver and found a bottle of claret in the cellar, and their merriment was only somewhat subdued by the knowledge that it would soon be time for Horatio and Josiah to depart. Father Edmund had lost none of his dry wit and, aware of the tension in the air, kept the conversation flowing. Horatio was reassured that he was leaving two strong friends behind. Nevertheless, the matter of Josiah's future sat uncomfortably between him and Fanny. He would try to make as much prize money as possible and buy her a decent house. They would be rich. It would be painful for her in the short term, but there really was no choice to be had.

CHAPTER THREE
March 1793

B riar stick in hand, Horatio tramped through the fields towards Holkham, the shining sun, the dew-flecked grasses, budding trees and fresh yellow gorse announcing winter was done.

Mr Coke, lord of the manor of five Burnham villages, including the parsonage where Horatio lived, owned 10,000 acres of arable farmland and had his residence at the heart of the estate in Holkham Hall.

It was curiosity and a half-formed idea of a deal that prompted Horatio to make the visit. Some years earlier, when he was newly returned from the West Indies, Horatio had been invited to an evening at Holkham. When he'd arrived, he had been shocked to find that his fellow guests were gentlemen of few means and no significance. He had been mortified and had stiffly declined subsequent invitations.

Coke's success had always grated on Horatio – though, if he was honest, he knew it was the result of damn hard work and agricultural know-how. But even that didn't alter the fact that Coke's opportunities were only possible because of the loyalty and service of families like Horatio's. The Walpole family on his mother's side had been first ministers of the King since the 1750s. The Nelsons, too, had served the Crown in the church and navy. His family were royalist Tories through and through. Coke was Whig, and while the Walpoles and the Nelsons built the nation's wealth and prestige, Coke and his Whigs tried to restrain royal authority while they profited from the very stability provided by Tory policy. He remembered Uncle Suckling's advice, and before his resentment could blossom, Horatio contained his anger. He took off his coat, flung it over his shoulder and picked up his pace towards the house.

Coke sat in his office, a well-positioned room with an expansive view over his gardens and lake. His fields, farms and woods stretched to the horizon. Framed sketches of agricultural implements and drainage designs covered the walls from floor to ceiling. Coke looked up as Horatio was announced. He was a short chubby man, casually dressed in country flannel that compared unfavourably with Horatio's tweeds.

'Ah, Nelson, good of you to come. I caught a glimpse of you through the trees,' Coke rose to greet Horatio, a convivial smile playing on his lips.

'Indeed. It's a fine day for a walk.'

There was an uncomfortable pause.

'Sit down, sit down. Let me order you something.'

They sat. The door opened and a servant with a silver tray silently handed the two men dishes of coffee.

'I hear good things about your prospects from my friends in London, Nelson,' Coke began after the servant had left the room.

'Yes, they have offered me the command of *Agamemnon*, a sixty-four,' Horatio replied, wondering where this was heading.

'Yes, it's your new ship which I wish to speak with you about, Nelson. I have friends with young sons.'

Favours.

'*Agamemnon* is not a great ship for youngsters,' Horatio served back. 'And it has no schoolmaster. There will be a risk to life and limb. Sea battles are deadly. I don't think it is such a good idea.'

Coke smiled as if to agree.

'Nelson, I have two families to whom I am obliged. The Hostes and the Weatherheads, you know of them of course. Parsons like the Nelsons.'

'I simply can't afford it,' Horatio said flatly.

'I have talked to both men and they will pay and, if they don't, I will.'

Horatio took a sip of his coffee. *Aha, now we get to it.* 'I'll not offer credit. The money must be provided ahead of time,' he said slowly, as if considering it deeply.

'Yes, yes. I'll take care of that. Render the accounts to me and make sure your bills cover everything, won't you? They're good boys and will be a credit to their families.'

'Very well, so long as the finances are understood.'

'Most excellent,' Coke said triumphally. 'Now, is there anything else that I can do?'

Horatio thought quickly. 'If I take these young gentlemen, I would be obliged if you would do your best for Fanny. She will be lonely once Josiah and I have left. My brother William, the rector, enjoys your agricultural meetings, too.'

'Nelson, we are indebted to you. Count on me.' He stood, holding out his hand.

Horatio shook his hand, adding, 'And many thanks for the game you sent over. Most enjoyable.'

Back at the house over dinner, Horatio listened half-heartedly as Fanny described the farewell party she was planning.

'Norfolk is not much given to parties beyond the assembly room balls, Fanny, and it will be another expense.'

'I want a party for all the village – a thank you to the neighbours, gentry, servants and all, and a grand farewell to you! The men will be entertained at the Plough Inn while the women will visit with me at the rectory. We will have fiddlers and a marquee and country dancing after dinner.' Her eyes were sparkling.

'How are we going to pay for it, Fanny?' Horatio asked, a tang of annoyance in his voice.

'With the distribution from my uncle's estate. There will be more than enough.'

He gave it proper thought. Though his penurious instincts cried out, it couldn't be denied that a grand party would demonstrate his new standing very effectively. 'I am pleased to agree, especially since you have agreed that Josiah will come with me.'

Fanny looked away.

'Have you decided where you will live?' he asked, the subject of the party closed.

Fanny didn't answer.

'Are you planning to stay here?' he enquired again.

'No,' Fanny replied hotly. 'I will take rooms in Swaffham while I work out what to do. It's not too far away and close enough to William and Sarah.'

There was no more discussion.

On the day before the party, Fanny and her friends decorated the Plough in red, white and blue bunting and set up a small platform and chairs in the forecourt. The following day rewarded them with blue skies. The trees in the rectory garden were now clad in blossom and played host to dozens of swallows and wood pigeons returning from winter's migration. Fanny's borrowed marquee had been erected in the garden.

At noon, gentlemen gathered at the Plough until the forecourt of the pub was crowded. Coke arrived punctually and spoke first, telling the villagers to rejoice in Nelson's new command and to celebrate the men who would sail with him. The five boys joining Horatio were then paraded. They stood on the stage awkwardly, looking mightily unsure of themselves. Josiah stood at one end, still a weedy lad with tousled brown hair and ruddy cheeks. The Hoste boy, scarcely ten, was a beautiful child who barely reached the elbow of Weatherhead, who towered over them all. They were all given a hearty cheer. Seven farm labourers who had volunteered were next up. As Horatio mounted the platform, another small boy standing with his father had a tantrum because he couldn't go with the others. Horatio laughed and renamed the urchin 'Valiant', before beginning the address he'd prepared.

'I thank all my friends these five years.'

There was applause and cries of 'Hear! Hear!'

'I fought the French in the Seven Years' War when I was Josiah's age. Then again in the American war. Now, once more I go to fight our implacable foe! France despises us. They envy our prosperity and our freedom. They have killed their king, in the name of liberty! I ask you: what kind of bloodstained liberty is that? We must annihilate them, but I warn you: it'll be a fight to the death.

'Wives and sisters, cherish our memory and pray for our safe return! I give you farewell, relying on the goodness of providence to return us laden with glory and honour! Wherever *Agamemnon* takes us, Norfolk will ever be in our hearts!'

There was loud applause and cries of, 'God save you, Nelson.' After which every man there crowded into the Plough for a dinner of poultry and game, free-flowing beer and bumpers of wine.

At the rectory, wives, daughters and children were entertained by Fanny, who had set up borrowed tables and chairs in the sitting room, the parlour and the dining room. She dispensed Madeira and sherry wine while a maid poured ginger beer for the children. There were pies, sandwiches and homemade fruitcake. Before too long, several ladies were tipsy and the house was full of chatter and laughter and children running amok. Later in the afternoon, the men returned from the pub with the fiddlers for country dancing and the party continued until the wee hours.

~

The next morning, tired villagers gathered at the Plough once more to wave farewell as the travellers boarded their two coaches. Horatio and Fanny had barely slept – Horatio, knowing he might not see Fanny for several months, was loving and attentive to her until it was time to go.

After another toast to the King, the villagers gave three times three cheers for the departing sailors. Josiah clung miserably to Fanny. Dogs howled as a platoon of local militia fired their muskets. Then the coaches set off, followed by dogs and small boys, with Valiant leading the pack.

As the coach turned the corner and took the road to Kings Lynn, Horatio considered the years he'd spent at Burnham Thorpe. It were as if he'd been a ship becalmed in the doldrums; day-to-day routines had continued but life was listless, torpid and dull. And, yet, he realised that resolute calm and his determination to be hopeful had helped him survive. It occurred to him that while the sails of his ship were filled and he was on the move, Fanny's was still stuck. He resolved she would never regret marrying him.

He had Josiah to look after now and Josiah's success would be the reward for Fanny's faith in him.

One of the men began to sing, and Horatio and the others joined in. At last, he was back!

CHAPTER FOUR
April 1793

It was an easy walk to *Agamemnon*'s dock from the captains' lodgings where Horatio had enjoyed a comfortable couple of weeks while the ship's preparations were being completed. Each morning, as he approached, he could see her new copper bottom greening in the moist air and her masts towering above the dockyard buildings. On this morning's brisk march to get to her, Horatio thought about his first time at Chatham, when he'd been only ten years old. He remembered the deafening sounds, the smells and the overpowering size of everything. The yard's docks, warehouses and factories had seemed to stretch forever along the Medway – almost a city in its own right.

He looked on with interest as thousands of workers poured through the main gates. Heavy drays loaded with bales of canvas and barrels of pitch rumbled over the cobblestones. The air rang with shouts, the thud of hammers and the high-pitched whine of the sawpits. A gritty furnace smoke mingled with a smell of brackish water and sewage. Seagulls on spars and rooftops fluttered about. Horatio loved the yard – and its craftsmen, whose handiwork would soon be tested by storms and cannon fire. This morning, however, he was preoccupied with delays in getting *Agamemnon* ready for sea trials.

Yesterday, he had called on Captain Proby, Commissioner of the Yard, to request more carpenters and blacksmiths be put to work. The captain had been helpful and Horatio, newly aware of the need to be diplomatic, refrained from commenting on the slackness he saw everywhere. Nor did he mention the yards in Norfolk which were twice as efficient. He thought about the complaints he had made about the Antigua dockyard – the complaints which had held up his being called back up for service. He wasn't about to make the same mistake again. His priority was to get to sea.

He focused on the ship instead. It could be years before another refit. Storms would test rigging and masts. Gunnery and sea battles would shake it to pieces if beams were rotten or joists were weak. Together with his team of warrant officers, Horatio inspected, negotiated and occasionally threatened. The boatswain worked on the sails and rigging while the first lieutenant begged, borrowed and stole the guns Horatio wanted. They found a stock of carronades, which were deadly in close action. He'd been told there were French spies operating in the yard who were fed misinformation about the inferiority of the English long guns. But the carronades, less impressive to the eye, represented a new weapon that would soon be tested in battle.

Crewing was his biggest headache. He started at the top with his senior commission officers, assembling a passable combination of experience and zeal. For the position of purser, Horatio had already earmarked Thomas Fellows, who had been recommended by his old mentor, Captain Locker. The contentment of the crew rested on Fellows' shoulders. The quality of food and drink and other comforts made a great difference – no small task with 600 men on board. His warrant officers, the backbone of the ship's day-to-day management, were already aboard when he'd arrived. The master, the boatswain, gunner, carpenter, cook and surgeon were specialists who kept the ship going. Without them, it would be impossible to maintain order or even sail. They were all good.

But finding enough seamen to make up the complement seemed to be impossible. London and nearby towns had been picked clean. Horatio ordered an expedition to Whitby in Yorkshire, the home of Captain Cook, and another to Newcastle, as well as the smaller towns in Norfolk he knew personally, but even after this exercise he still fell short of his tally by almost 200 men.

He found himself growing irritable and forgot his recent decision to remain calm. When he fell silent, the officers knew something was brewing. A chance word or expression could set him off.

'Hinton, you are usually up to your job, but I can see that when it comes to mustering men you're as incompetent as a fresh-faced midshipman!' he'd barked at the first lieutenant upon hearing of the lack of success of the expedition.

Hinton, unable to endure the taunts, had responded defensively. 'With respect, it is not my name that lacks currency, Captain, nor are my promises discounted by virtue of years on the beach.'

There was a long silence, before Horatio backed down. 'I see your point, Hinton. I am coming to terms with my reputation. We will have to make do.'

Fortunately, a week before they were due to sail, the yard manager, with whom Horatio had developed a good rapport, gave him eighty seamen from ships in the reserve. His patience with Proby had paid off and, although this still left over 100 more to be found, he was optimistic.

Orders from the Admiralty commanded *Agamemnon* to join Lord Hood's Mediterranean fleet. He had mixed feelings about this – he'd worked for Hood before and he could be difficult. He was also the man who'd blocked his career and although he had made peace with him on that score, there was little trust between them.

He broke the news to Hinton over dinner. 'In the Med, we will be nowhere near the rich hunting grounds of the westerly approaches to France.'

'True,' Hinton said thoughtfully, 'but those block-ades are the living death. Day in and day out, back and forth and then, in a trice, a slack watch and the enemy slip out. It's hell! There's definitely more chance of action in the Med.' Hinton took a mouthful of stew and chewed it slowly. 'I was in the Med on my last ship. We were based in Leghorn. Such a good time. Great food, wonderful social life.'

'I think you are a trifle optimistic, Hinton,' Horatio cautioned. But beneath his sternness, he had a sense that this would be the best opportunity he would ever get. He knew that he would be away from Fanny for one, two or even three years. But he would work hard for prize money and they could buy a decent house and some land with it.

By the first week of April, the trees were in full leaf and *Agamemnon* was ready to be towed from her dock to the ordnance depot where her guns would be swung aboard and stowed. Powder and fuses followed. That complete, the officers and the captain of the marines came aboard for a briefing. The crew were marched up the gangplank to the sound of the ship's band. Josiah and the other young boys came aboard and were taken down to the lower deck.

The next morning, *Agamemnon* was due to be piloted by the yard manager down the Medway to Sheerness – the manager's knowledge of the currents, depths and hazards of the Medway River would be essential in successfully guiding *Agamemnon* through it and into the North Sea. Upon his arrival that morning, Horatio shook his hand vigorously, thanked him profusely and gave him a note of appreciation for Captain Proby. Horatio had witnessed a frustrating amount of slackness since he'd been at Chatham, but he hadn't a bad word to say about the yard manager, who was a man who really knew his stuff and who this morning, after a quick briefing with Horatio, climbed into the pilot yawl and was gone.

It was a fine day, with blue skies and an easy south-westerly breeze blowing. The sales were hoisted, Horatio wincing at the clumsiness of the crew. Then *Agamemnon* pointed her bow eastwards, the banks of the estuary widening until there was nothing to be seen but the cold brown waters of the North Sea. Horatio called Lieutenant Hinton over and told him to muster hands on deck. Hinton signalled to the marine drummer and eventually the men assembled below. Gruffly, Horatio addressed them from the rail.

'Men, that was the slowest muster I've ever seen! We will practise that until you are seamen. On my ship, sailors jump to. For the next few days, I will be drilling you until you can run up the masts and take in the sails like navy men. We will work at this until you are "ready men". Men who have been with me before know that I am not a flogging captain, but don't thwart me or you will be the worse for wear!'

Horatio surveyed the rows of upturned faces. He saw blankness and raw resentment. He turned to Hinton. 'Give them an extra round of grog. They are going to need their strength and their wits over the next few days.'

He returned to his cabin and lay on his bunk. The damp North Sea chill wrapped its clammy hands around him. The vessel was alive with the sounds of the ship – the creaks and groans of rigging and men. He lay awake. Five years of idleness had reduced him to a shadow of the commander he had been. His earlier euphoria had disappeared. The aching truth was that he felt lonely. He had left behind the person who loved and cared for him the most. It would be perilous to pursue fellowship aboard the ship. The first thing to do was to get used to being alone – even though only a few inches of bulkhead separated him from the 600 other men aboard.

CHAPTER FIVE
May 1793

Fanny folded her sheet music, closed the lid of the piano and pushed the bench beneath the key bed. She had been practising a Mozart sonata. How wonderful it was to play a piano after years of harpsichord! Not that she disliked or discarded the latter. Its tinkling precision and silkiness rendered Mr Bach's preludes perfectly.

At first, it had been unnerving to play her sister-in-law's instrument – its sound was so clear, so loud. But she'd become used to it, and now she knew she would get one when she settled in her new home – wherever that would be. Music had always been her sanctuary, a place she sought out on her own, but where she was never lonely. The conquest of a challenging piece of music was a great source of satisfaction, especially if she had a performance to prepare. And she did: tonight, she would play for Horatio and the family.

She rang the bell and asked the maid to serve tea in the garden. She made her way there, enjoying the mellow aromas of her in-laws' house – fresh flowers, old oak panelling and furniture polish.

It was a bright May morning. Butterflies were haunting the well-tended flower beds and bees hummed amid the rhythmic call of the wood pigeons. White magnolias, violet camellias, and plentiful hydrangeas dotted the garden with colour, while great oaks shaded the lawn. It was tranquil, peaceful, artless beauty and it caused her anticipation of seeing Josiah and Horatio again after two months to soar. They would be arriving from Portsmouth and would be here for two nights.

The sound of footsteps and the excited chatter of the children signalled that the family was back from church. Two of Horatio's brothers, William and Suckling – who was named for his uncle – and Catherine and Susannah, his sisters, had come with their families; only Maurice hadn't been able to make it. Fanny walked down to the summer house at the bottom of the garden to admire the view, which is where Catherine found her a few minutes later. The two women wandered the gardens together, Fanny asking Catherine all about the house and how she'd gone about creating its present glory.

An hour later, a coachman's horn heralded Horatio's arrival. Fanny could hear the jingling of harnesses and the wheels on the pebbles of the driveway. By the time the carriage stopped, she was waiting. Josiah jumped from the coach and ran to her first. She held him at arms-length, already seeing changes. It was only two months, but his chest was broader and his face was bronzed – he looked so handsome! Horatio was only steps behind, and embraced her affectionately. How dashing he was, with his dark lustrous hair and kind eyes, his new uniform unbuttoned at the neck. He shook hands with George Matcham, kissed his sisters and swung little George in the air and then, with his arm around Fanny, he moved with the rest of the party into the house.

As Fanny helped him unpack, she listened to Horatio describe the shakedown journey from the Medway to Portsmouth.

'*Agamemnon* is not just good, Fan, she is great. But I am so rusty. I have forgotten all I knew about command. I feel like a midshipman again! Fortunately, I have marvellous warrant officers running things. My crew is inexperienced but are as keen as mustard!'

'How is Josiah?' Fanny asked.

'He was seasick like many of the sailors, myself

included. He is learning to be a seaman. He climbs
the rigging and takes in the sails and is in charge of
the ship's boat. He is doing well in his studies, too.'

'He *looks* different – bigger, older and perhaps a
little tougher,' she said, with a sigh.

'No doubt! He is learning more than he ever
learned before. His boyishness will be the first thing
to go. To be a seaman in the Royal Navy is to be ready
and willing for any order and to jump to. He is earning
the right to give orders.'

'Horatio, I miss him so much.' She went to him,
clasped his hands in hers. 'Promise to look after him!'

'Of course I will, my love. Now, I have some news
of my new posting.'

Her heartbeat raced as he described the destination – Toulon. So far away! Weeks of sailing and no
promise of an early return.

'Fan, I thought I would be in the Channel Fleet,
but Toulon is in the hands of the French royalists and
we are sent to support their fight against the Jacobins.
Maybe this will turn the tide in France.'

'But when will I see you again?'

'I don't know,' he answered honestly, holding her
gaze. 'Perhaps a year. Maybe longer.'

She scrambled for a solution. 'But can I travel to
see you? Will you and Josiah get leave to come home?'

'This is the navy, Fan. We will be away until

they give us leave. I'll let you know as soon as I do. Meanwhile, we'll write. I want to know every detail of your life. And I'll do the same.'

She gathered herself. 'You're right,' she said, attempting a smile. 'I signed up for this when I married a handsome captain. I have been lucky to have you with me every day for the last five years!'

'That's the spirit, Fan. Come here.' He kissed her. Then he turned back to unpacking his box, talking as he worked. 'What do you think of this house? What a fortune George must have! Catherine's done nicely for herself with him.'

'We had an interesting conversation yesterday. For the first time, I understand *why* he has done so well. You remember those conversations we have had about the fighting captains and prize captains?'

'Yes, I have been a fighting captain and have nothing to show for it!' He laughed with tinge of bitterness.

'Yes, dear. Well, it seems George was something of a prize captain with the East India Company. As the resident of Baroche, he was powerful. It was a remote place but famous as a trading emporium. He was the Rajah's advisor, collecting the taxes and selling business licences.'

'I can imagine how much he might have made on the side,' said Horatio.

'It seems so dishonest!' added Fanny.

'From what I know, the Company is perfectly happy for their people to make money from trade. India's a dangerous place to live – few survive.' He paused before going on. 'Fan, as we talk about his success, I feel I have done a poor job of looking after us ... No, listen to me ... There will be plenty of prize opportunities for me and you will be the mistress of a home much greater than this. I promise you.' He took her in his arms again. 'We'll seal that promise tonight!'

Fanny blushed and looked him in the eye. 'Whatever you do, Horatio, remember your reputation. The Nelsons are not wealthy, but they are honest. In Nevis, there were so many greedy, cruel and shameless people – people desperate to make money from the slave trade, from the poorest people at the bottom of the heap. I was ashamed of what we'd done to make our money.'

Horatio cleared his throat. 'Fanny, my duty and my men will always come first. Only after that will I take every opportunity I am legally entitled to. Those are the conditions of the navy. Some captains prosper mightily and live a long life. Some die courageously in battle. We have to be ready for either.'

A dull boom from a bronze dinner gong sounded throughout the house. Fanny quickly finished dressing and together they descended the stairs to the dining room.

When the men rejoined the ladies in the sitting room after dinner, Fanny sat down at the piano to play the sonata she had practised. The piece was marked 'Simplecente'. The movement developed into a complex of scales culminating in a triumphant coda. She forgot her fears, her misgivings and her doubts, and immersed herself in the passion and the power of the music. Horatio, sitting by her side, turned the pages when she nodded and whispered words of encouragement. But she was unaware of him. She was alone.

When she finished, the family stood and applauded, none more vigorously than Josiah. Fanny curtsied playfully, blushing from the enthusiastic reception, and especially touched by Josiah's response. Shortly afterwards, Fanny pulled Josiah aside, and asked him to accompany her on a walk.

'Tell me about your time on the ship,' said Fanny, slipping her arm through Josiah's.

'We live in tiny quarters in the stern of the ship below the waterline, mother. We can't stand up without crouching, so short it is. Weatherhead and I are the seniors and the other three boys do as we say. Our officer is the master of the ship. He has a proper cabin next to ours. We are learning to be good seamen. I'm not afraid of climbing the masts even in bad weather.' He was eager to get it all out.

'How do you get along with the other sailors?' she enquired.

'There are 600 men on board, so it's always crowded; everyone's always pushing and shoving. The officers have everything under control. Only ...' He hesitated.

'Only what, darling?'

'Only I don't like punishment muster. I hate it! There was a boy my age who was flogged along with an older sailor. The blood ran down his back and he blubbered like a baby!'

A flogging! And her boy, watching and fearing. Oh God! And Horatio. He must have ordered it. She recalled the horrific beatings she had witnessed on the plantation.

'He must have done something bad to deserve that?' Fanny checked.

'No, he was just too scared to climb the mast in a storm – like Bolton was and I was. But we went.'

Fanny heart sank. Her son in a sailor's cruel world.

'Don't worry, Mama, I'm a good sailor. One day, I'll have my own ship. You will be proud of me. 'Eggs and bacon', which is what we all call *Agamemnon*, is much better than my school boarding house.' He turned and gave her a wide grin, as their short walk brought them back to the house. Fanny kissed him with a sudden sense she would not see him for a very long time. What would he look like then?

Later that night, Fanny and Horatio made love. He was tender and passionate and fierce.

Two days later, the men all prepared to leave together. Horatio's father, Edmund, his brother William and his brothers-in-law George Matcham and Tom Bolton were all to travel with Josiah and Horatio to Portsmouth where they would all stay overnight on *Agamemnon*. Maurice, Horatio's brother who hadn't been able to make the house party, was to meet up with them on the ship.

It was very quiet after they had gone. The women sat together in the parlour drinking tea. Catherine was tired. Sarah, William's wife, was mindful that Horatio was now the more successful brother and was sullen. Susannah, the farmer's wife, was talkative while Fanny, glowing from her night with Horatio, felt conflicting emotions of joy and sadness in constant interplay.

'And now that Horatio has gone, how are you going to spend your days? Playing the pianoforte with your wealthy friends?' Sarah asked, quite rudely, her bitterness startling Fanny. She realised Horatio's promotion had changed the balance of power. She smiled.

'Things have changed, yes, but it is for the better. I will miss him desperately, but I know the family will benefit from his achievements. He is such a great man and has such a generous heart.'

But even as she said the words aloud, she asked herself how well she really knew Horatio. Josiah's story raised questions in her mind about the ruthlessness demanded by the job. Would she ever have to face that side of him? And how was she to survive without him and without Josiah? The pleasures of this house were fading fast and the prospect of returning to the silent rectory in Burnham filled her with misery.

CHAPTER SIX
June 1793

A steady north-east wind carried *Agamemnon* through the English Channel. The Bay of Biscay, usually so rough at this time of year, was calm sailing too. At Cádiz on the south-west coast of Spain, Admiral Hood, now the commander of the fleet, made a courtesy visit to the Spanish admiral, and Horatio along with Hood's other captains were invited aboard the huge flagship, *San José*. Horatio was fascinated by the ship and noted how well built it was compared to the British battleships. Even the French did not have these. But the skill of the shipbuilders was not matched by the quality of the Spanish officers. 'With a barge of my sailors and a few marines, I could take the *San José*,' he wrote to Fanny later that night.

In the officers' mess room where Horatio dined

every two weeks, he found excitement and optimism in plenty. 'With this fleet like this, we will easily outgun the French; keep them in port bottled up and raid their merchant ships,' he heard the fourth lieutenant say.

'Believe me, Allison, the French are never a pushover,' Horatio counselled. 'In the past, their ships were better than ours, with more disciplined crews and undeniable courage. Their problem now is discipline. Being an officer on a French ship is at the will of the crew and not by virtue of commission. In these conditions, why should an officer risk his life? Our advantage lies in our discipline – and our gunnery. If we engage them at close quarters, we will take them nine times out of ten.'

From Gibraltar, the British fleet sailed for Toulon in the south of France, the home of the French Mediterranean Fleet. As the fleet entered the outer harbour, Horatio was taken with the natural beauty of the port. Rocky islands and peninsulas were scattered like pearls on a green cloth, while surrounding hills enfolded the city in their hollow embrace. It was a great harbour for a fleet, he realised, but he wondered if it could be defended on the landward side.

Royalist rebels had taken the city and welcomed them. Lord Hood went ashore and negotiated with their leaders. An agreement was reached for the

British to stay and help defend the port against the Jacobin army.

Agamemnon anchored in the outer harbour. The humidity was stifling. Around the ship were dozens of Spanish, British and French battleships, as well as merchantmen and troop carriers. On dry land, marines were digging in, installing cannon and filling sandbags. On the heights to the west, Fort Mulgrave was under construction – a formidable mass, like Gibraltar, built to resist attack from land and sea alike. Still, Horatio had grave misgivings about the fleet's overall strategy.

That first evening in port, Captain Troubridge, of *Culloden*, paid a visit to Horatio, who received him enthusiastically. He and Horatio had known each other for most of their careers. Troubridge was also outside Hood's circle of advisors and he too could see the weakness of the situation.

'I just don't see how occupying Toulon will advance our cause,' Horatio said. 'Our presence will unite the French, who will view it as occupation by their traditional enemy. We don't have enough troops to defend it. If I had my way, the first thing I would do would be to insist the French ships join the Royal Navy or else seize them.'

'But that would be sure to alienate our new allies,' replied Troubridge.

'Well, we will pay now, or we will pay later. It's a dilemma we have faced before and we'll face it again. We'd be better to take the punishment today while we have the upper hand.'

The following day, orders came through to find officers who spoke French for shore duties. *Agamemnon* lost two lieutenants and 100 or so men were detached. Horatio boiled with resentment – he had just managed to get *Agamemnon* up to fighting capacity only to now lose a goodly chunk of the crew to a cause he couldn't support.

To add insult to injury, a number of other captains were given positions in the occupation forces while Horatio, unable to speak French with any fluency, was passed over. If only he had taken up Fanny's offer to teach him the language on those long walks! But he'd had no interest in learning a foreign language back then. And now he was paying the price.

At last, six days later, Horatio was summoned to the great cabin of *Victory*, the Royal Navy's flagship. He was expecting an order that would allow him to demonstrate his fighting skills. But the job at hand was to carry dispatches – to British ministers in Italy.

'*Agamemnon* is a fast ship and you have some experience dealing with civilians from your days in the West

Indies. Take this letter to Sir William Hamilton. I am requesting the King sends reinforcements,' instructed Hood.

'Are you sure someone else can't do this? I have a lot of experience in land operations. Would I not be more use here?'

Hood turned away. 'Take your ship out on the next tide, Captain.' Hearing the steel in Hood's voice and remembering previous disputes with him, Horatio quickly decided not to go against him. 'And, Captain, try to stay out of trouble. No skirmishing! Go there and come back, immediately,' Hood added.

'Aye, sir.' Cool obedience despite Hood's shabby treatment. Horatio knew it would do him well not to expect too much while Hood was in charge.

Within twenty-four hours, *Agamemnon* hauled up her anchor and set off with a good following north-west breeze behind her. The days were becoming shorter as autumn overtook summer and the hot and sticky weather in Toulon had given way to cooler winds.

Horatio settled into a routine. He would go to bed early with instructions to be awoken if anything unusual happened. Usually, he slept undisturbed and rose at dawn, ready for the day. Paperwork and inspection followed his breakfast. He met with his warrant officers before dinner to discuss their departments. Dinner was at two in the afternoon. He ate alone or with the midshipmen or Josiah. Then he would sit at his portable writing desk, complete the captain's log and write a letter to Fanny.

While he enjoyed the independence, he couldn't shake the feeling that he was missing out on opportunities for promotion in Toulon. His humble role as a messenger made him long for a skirmish. He needed to test the crew. There was regular gunnery practice, speeding up broadsides and testing the firing angles of the guns and the new firing pins. If the broadside was ragged, the offending crew would be punished. When the ship performed, Horatio rewarded them with extra rations of grog.

'If *Agamemnon* can get three broadsides for every two of the enemy, we will have the same fire power as a 100-gun battleship,' he explained to the wardroom officers, over port in the great cabin. 'And we can use our carronades to devastate their gun decks.'

Agamemnon arrived in the Bay of Naples late in the afternoon. They dropped the anchor and the ship swung around to point into the breeze. A heavy swell was surging in and Horatio realised that he could not easily resupply the ship – it would be a short visit. The sky was turning dark and Mount Vesuvius, which had been smoking when they arrived, was veined with lines of glistening red lava, with small explosions shooting sparks into the night sky.

An invitation from Sir William Hamilton returned with the cutter, which Horatio had dispatched with the message as soon as *Agamemnon* had anchored. Horatio called for Josiah.

'Josiah, it looks as if we are dining with the ambassador and his wife tomorrow,' he said.

'But, Papa, the other boys will expect me to go with the lieutenants out on the town,' Josiah protested.

'That's the problem of being the captain's son. You'll come along with me!'

Josiah's eyes were downcast briefly, before he looked up again, a new sparkle in them. 'Papa, is it true that Lady Hamilton is a lady of ill repute?'

Horatio laughed. 'What on earth are you boys talking about? Who told you that?'

'Well, is she?' Josiah persisted.

'Hmm, I suppose you will get to know the story one way or another. Yes, she has a colourful background. She was what we would call a Dolly in her early years. But she has been here for ten years. And Sir William married her, so we will treat her with all respect tomorrow!' He sent Josiah off, and turned back to his paperwork.

Dismissive as he may have been of the boy's enquiry, the following day Horatio found himself paying more attention to his dress uniform, his curiosity piqued by Josiah's remarks. He wished he had a star – but he had to be satisfied with his dress sword and new cocked hat. The cutter, commanded by Weatherhead, rowed them ashore, where Sir William's carriage was waiting. At the palace, he was met by Sir William and Sir John Acton, the King's first minister. Both were of the same age, and were suave, affected men, clearly used to power and independence. Acton, despite the English name, seemed to be a native Italian.

The meeting with King Ferdinand and his ministers took most of the morning. The King promised 4000 men would go to Toulon. Horatio was impressed and delighted with his success. *I am good at this diplomatic work*, he thought.

Then they went for dinner at the Hamiltons' Palazzo Sezza – a strange house perched on the cliffs overlooking the Bay of Naples. A collection of magnificent tapestries, paintings and statues adorned the old building, creating a sense of gloomy grandeur rarely seen at other embassies Horatio had visited.

But as impressive as the palazzo was, Lady Hamilton was more of a surprise. She proved to be an excellent hostess, anticipating every need of her guests. She seemed to intuitively sense that having been at sea for weeks, they would enjoy care and hospitality.

She urged them to take off their jackets and relax while she plied them with drinks and delicacies, listening to their talk with attention so keen that a practised hostess in London could not have done better. She spoke with a northern English accent mingled with polished London tones. She was forthright and funny. Horatio drew her aside.

'Do you miss England?' he asked her.

'Oh no. I miss England not at all,' she replied, with a polite smile.

'I suppose not,' acknowledged Horatio. 'After all, I see you have a magnificent house and a grand view of the Bay. And Sir John said there is a budding friendship with the Queen?'

'I owe all to Sir William, Captain. Without him, I am nothing. He has taught me everything he knows. I speak Italian in the Neapolitan dialect, which pleases the Queen since that is the only language her husband, the King, will use.'

'My word!' said Horatio, impressed by how accomplished she was.

'And you, sir. Are you married?'

'Yes, my wife is a lady – from a West Indian plantation family.'

'I suppose she is very good-looking – to attract

61

someone like you?' Lady Hamilton said coquettishly.

Horatio began to feel uncomfortable. 'Yes, indeed, I am married to a woman of considerable beauty, culture *and* learning. Like you, she has a facility with languages – French, in particular – and she is a musician, a pianist of repute in our part of England. I miss her very much.' And in that moment, almost more than ever.

'Perhaps you can invite her here to visit. I should like that. We have so many great British lords and ladies, drawn here to meet the "strange wife" of the ambassador,' she said, giving a little giggle.

His eyes strayed to a portrait on a wall nearby. In the painting, a teenage girl sat sedately in a nutmeg-coloured chair. She wore an extravagant straw hat wrapped in stylish black silk – the sort of hat worn by women much beyond the years of the girl pictured. But she wore it confidently. The hat shadowed the subject's strawberry and cream complexion and drew attention to her red Cupid's bow lips and her very pretty eyes and face. One of her hands rested innocently beneath her fine chin and the other casually supported her elbow. Her white silk dress was a sophisticated mix of shades and textures. She seemed provocatively naive, her expression too curious, and her pose too mature for one so young. It had an erotic charge.

If Lady Hamilton noticed his gaze lingering on

the portrait, she didn't show it, but simply waited for his attention to return to her. When he did look back to her, it was unmistakable; the lady standing before him was older, but it was indeed the woman in the portrait. Momentarily, Horatio pictured her naked. A wisp of desire aroused him.

'I love to meet sailors,' Lady Hamilton went on, without any irony. 'They are plain-spoken and know what they want and where to get it.'

Horatio looked at her sharply. Was there a hint of flirtation?

'Madame, our work makes us so. We speak few words in the heat of battle. Much hangs on those we do use,' he answered cautiously.

'I think the world would be better if people said what they meant. Sir William and I tell each other the truth and he says that makes me a useful person. Do you have anyone to confide in?'

He looked at her face, to try to determine whether she was teasing him, but she returned his stare innocently.

'Most of the time, Madame, our thoughts remain our own. For a captain on a battleship, it is futile to pretend he can be anything other than commander. And to be a good commander, he has to guard his heart lest desire for companionship compromise his authority.'

He looked at her for a long moment and then affected to take his watch from his pocket. He stood up and bowed.

The King of Naples invited Horatio, Josiah and the officers to hunt that afternoon, but two frigates had been spotted in the bay flying the tricolour. Horatio, sensing an opportunity, sent apologies to the Hamiltons and set off in pursuit. But by the time he made it back down to the harbour, the frigates had disappeared over the horizon and were nowhere to be found.

It was a wet autumn day when they arrived back in Toulon, and the city was bustling with troops, merchant ships and allied navies. Ominously, the batteries around the city were firing continuously. A new Corsican colonel had taken command of the French artillery and was stepping up the pressure on the royalists and their allies, the British.

'Dashed good work, Horatio,' Hood greeted him, pleased. 'Knew you could be relied on. And now I have another piece of work for you.'

'A shore role here in Toulon, your lordship?' Horatio asked, his anticipation rising.

'No. Another dispatch. We are short of grain and we need the Barbary States to support our side. They were mighty offended by the murder of King Louis, but they are traders and feel in a position of power. They have much to lose if the revolution reaches their shores. Get them to sign a contract to supply grain and, if there are any French ships there, see if you can take them.'

Unimpressed, Horatio wrote to Fanny.

I hardly think this war can last, for what are we at war about? Next winter I think will send us home. I long to have a letter from you. Next to being with you, it is the greatest pleasure I can receive. I shall rejoice to be with you again. Indeed, I look back happily on that part of my life united to such a good woman and, as I cannot show here my affection to you, I do so doubly to Josiah who deserves it as well on his own account as on yours, for he is a real good boy and most affectionately loves me …

These days, Horatio thought as he signed and sealed the letter, *the most pleasant part of the day is when I can get to write.*

When *Agamemnon* made way to sea again, Horatio was in the fighting top, perched on the main mast. To the north, he could see allied forts bristling with men and guns. To the west was the pinch gut peninsula, with Fort de l'Éguillette protecting the sea approach and the massive stone fortifications of Fort Mulgrave – the key to the defence of Toulon – creating a bottleneck between the inner and outer harbours.

'If I were the French commander, I would dislodge the allies there,' he said to Hinton, pointing at the fort.

The cruise to Tunis was as uneventful as the earlier voyage to Naples. The crew were fighting fit and Horatio reckoned the gunnery was approaching a level that satisfied him. Martin Hinton was an excellent lieutenant and he now had five good lower-level lieutenants, too. Wilson, King and the other warrant officers had bedded down the crew skilfully. Malcontents pressed from their former occupation as thieves were the only headache. There had already been a theft and the man had been given three dozen lashes.

The meeting with the Arab ruler was as difficult as Hood had suggested it would be. From the moment they anchored in Tunis, they were hassled, cheated and robbed and then offered eternal friendship when the deal was settled. The Bey was happy enough to trade but he would not give up the French ships in the harbour.

'I should cut them out myself,' Horatio said to Hinton, but he knew that this would be fatal for ongoing business with Tunis.

On the way back, Josiah, on watch at the masthead, sighted an enemy ship and alerted Horatio, who ordered the ship to clear for action.

Horatio debated with whether to engage. He remembered Hood's command to stick to his mission. But he was confident he could deal with two small frigates. He had speed and armament. It would be good for the crew to skirmish and it could be profitable if he captured one. As the light faded, he made the decision to follow them through the night and engage at first light.

But when first light dawned, the sky revealed a French squadron – four frigates and two corvettes. They turned towards *Agamemnon*, knowing they had her outmanned and outgunned.

Horatio buckled on his sword and sent Josiah and the other boys to the safety of the lower deck. *Agamemnon*, with the advantage of the wind at its quarter, closed on the nearest Frenchman. Horatio ordered a round from the carronade as they passed the stern. And then the starboard guns opened fire.

Twenty minutes into the battle, amid the whine and deafening smash of cannonball on timber, there was a loud crack and *Agamemnon*'s forward mast and rigging collapsed over her side. She slowed while the larger of the French frigates manoeuvred to engage. This would be a fight to the death. There would be no surrender.

As the frigate approached, there was a flutter of signal flags. The second frigate was already damaged and hoisted sail. After a moment, the remaining three broke off too and the squadron sailed over the horizon.

'Bloody cowards! No spirit in that navy. Anyone who was any good has been guillotined,' Horatio muttered gratefully to Hinton, his sense of relief palpable despite his effort to conceal it.

With a strong sense of a narrow escape, Horatio set course for Sardinia where they licked their wounds, replacing the damaged mast, burying the dead and patching up the wounded. Then he mustered the crew and praised them and promised them extra grog. In his cabin he completed his log, not sparing himself. He realised he was foolish and fortunate. To have lost his ship this early in the campaign would have spelt the end of his career. And Josiah. He remembered his promises to Fanny. Such rashness! He fell to his knees and gave thanks to Almighty God.

The wind blowing from the south sped them on their way, weeks behind schedule. It was winter and the fierce wind made the rigging sing. There was a storm in progress as they arrived back at Toulon, with flashes of lightning in a black sky and rolls of thunder clapping as they neared the outer harbour. As they reduced their sails to a minimum, they saw smoke blowing into the stormy black clouds. A massive explosion. Amid the smoke and mist, they could make out boatloads of soldiers and refugees rowing to the anchored ships. It was an evacuation.

It took Horatio a time to realise that Fort Mulgrave was no longer in British hands. The enemy had taken it and were firing heated shot at the allied ships. A giant tricolour streamed from a flagstaff on the ramparts. The rain slashed down and the town and the hills beyond were lost from view. The city had fallen.

As Horatio and the crew helped soldiers and sailors to climb aboard, he realised the full extent of the catastrophe. British admirals were woefully ill-prepared for total war. This would be the end of Lord Hood. Perhaps there would be more opportunity under the next admiral.

CHAPTER SEVEN
December 1793

Wolterton, the magnificent home of Lord Walpole, Horatio's godfather, was in East Norfolk, a day's travel from Swaffham. It was surrounded by gracious parkland and overlooked an ornamental lake. Although winter winds had stripped the leaves from the trees and the lake was frozen, Wolterton's grasslands were still green and its forested slopes wore the fading yellows and reds of autumn. On a distant horizon, a folly stood proud against a blue sky.

Fanny had been asked to stay for the Christmas season, an invitation which she had immediately accepted. She felt at home from the moment she arrived. The house was warm and welcoming and grand; its huge lobby, state rooms, artworks and family portraits redolent of social standing and permanence. It reminded Fanny of her years as the hostess of a great house.

Izzy, Lord and Lady Walpole's youngest daughter, was five years older than Fanny, and took her immediately under her wing. Izzy certainly didn't look or act the old spinster, though – her face was sweetly expressive, animated by her bright eyes. She always wore her thick black hair up, and it contrasted nicely with her smooth pale skin. She was thoughtful and a little reserved until she warmed to conversation. There was nothing artificial about her, no airs and graces and, though the Nelsons were 'poor relations', there was no condescension to her manner. She was Fanny's soulmate and although their relationship had been conducted chiefly through lengthy correspondence, Fanny had relied on Izzy's friendship these past lonely months.

The day Fanny arrived and after she'd settled in, the two women met in the cosy parlour to enjoy some coffee and reacquaint themselves. Izzy had politely enquired after what Fanny had done since Horatio's departure, and Fanny was wondering how honest to be about how difficult it had been.

'I moved to Swaffham a few weeks after Horatio left Portsmouth. I needed some company but I thought it would not be proper to set up house with

Edmund, given his role as the Burnham parish priest. And I was very glad to leave the rectory as the weather worsened – it's such a damp house.'

'Do you know anyone in Swaffham?' Izzy asked.

'Reverend Best was with my brother-in-law William at Cambridge. But, apart from him and his wife, no one.'

'But, surely, being a member of the Nelson family?'

'Everyone knows *who* I am, Izzy, but I am not Norfolk-born. I am an outsider – no matter how long I live here. No one knows the West Indies. And even though my husband is a sea captain, women can be very withholding, as if I am not to be trusted. Morning tea with the children is a highlight of my social life!'

The two women laughed. Izzy was still single. Her sister had shocked everyone by marrying into an old Irish Catholic family. Izzy had been courted by many 'younger sons' – usually clergymen or soldiers – but, under no financial pressure to marry, had preferred to remain single.

'How are you spending your time?' Izzy asked.

Fanny sighed. Months of emptiness. Some days it was hard to get out of bed. But she couldn't put it like that, not even to Izzy.

'I have a routine,' she said as brightly as she could muster. 'I shop for supplies, keep my rooms tidy, visit the poor and sick in the parish and go for long walks.

Occasionally, I visit Hilborough to see William and Sarah – usually when Edmund is visiting. But not often – William is so self-centred, you see, with a patronising male air that is truly annoying. And Sarah is ambitious and sarcastic. I wonder whether being married to William has caused a bitterness to grow in her. Saturday is my worst day. Monday to Friday, I have things to do and on Sunday, there's Church. But on Saturdays, I have no more tasks and I know everyone else is doing *something*.' She regarded Izzy, trying to conceal the worst of her desperation.

Lady Isobel leant and put her arms around Fanny and held her. There was a short period silence. Fanny feared she might begin to cry at the kindness she was being shown. But she knew she mustn't do that to Izzy. So she sniffled and patted Izzy's back, gently pulling away from her embrace and trying to adopt a placid expression.

'And how is dear Josiah?' Izzy asked after a minute or two had passed.

'Oh, Izzy, I was just so grateful Josiah wasn't in Toulon when it fell. What a catastrophe! He wrote me a letter that described a battle he fought at sea. It was so full of blood and gore I could scarcely read it. Of course, he loved to describe how heroic he and Horatio had been!'

'And Horatio?'

'He was worried his first fight would be viewed unfavourably by his admiral, Lord Hood. They have a history, those two. But Hood overlooked the matter.' Fanny reached out and put her hand on Izzy's. 'Thank you,' she said, 'thank you so very much for listening.'

～

Later, reclining in the bathtub which her maid had put next to the fire, Fanny thought over the conversation. While she worried that the outpouring of her heart was a trifle excessive, she was glad to have shared her feelings with someone so sympathetic. She sighed and sank further into the hot water. How peaceful it was here. The Walpoles drew their guests into their lives effortlessly. Scarcely a day passed when they were not entertaining. Local gentry, politicians, writers and Whig aristocrats arrived in a steady stream, yet it never felt crowded, was never noisy. There was never any pressure.

Isabel's grand piano was a joy to play. The Broadwood was bigger and better than Catherine Matcham's German piano. It could be played as delicately as a harpsichord yet muster huge sounds when she used the 'forte' pedal. Its long walnut case on three legs presided majestically over the drawing room. She dedicated hours to pleasurable practice.

Technique was the foundation but playing the piano also demanded creativity and courage. The women in the audience loved to see strength in another woman. Men, expecting practised inconsequence, were always startled by her powerful renditions. Audiences motivated her to work hard. Their enjoyment gave her pleasure. But best of all was the ability to demonstrate who she really was.

On Christmas morning, they walked through snow to Wolterton's chapel, where Edmund conducted the service. In the days following, when the men were hunting, Fanny and Izzy took brisk walks through the frozen woods. As New Year's Eve approached, the house was gaily decorated in bunting and evergreens for the ball. A small orchestra and a dance caller from Norwich were engaged and invitations to the party were sent out to neighbouring gentry, tenant farmers and their families.

The New Year's ball reminded her that she would soon be returning to Swaffham. Providentially, Edmund – who had come to Wolterton for Christmas and would leave after the new year had come – said he was of a mind to give the Burnham Thorpe living to his youngest son and to take a long holiday in Bath.

It sparked an idea – and the more she thought about the possibility of a stay in Bath, the more she liked the idea. She and Horatio had had a memorable holiday there when they were first married. The climate was warmer and there would be naval officers and their wives for company, as well as the Pinneys, who were also West Indians and lived nearby in Clifton.

She decided to ask Edmund if he would be interested in sharing a house in Bath for a period. He was delighted, and immediately agreed. She and Edmund discussed sharing expenses: he proposed that he could pay for the rooms and servants if Fanny could cover food, wine and any other household items. She did her sums and agreed.

Considering how she would find the money, she thought about her legacies – from her late uncle and Nisbet. Legally, they were Horatio's property and not hers to spend. But there was an obligation attached to his ownership. She would write to tell him her decision. She hoped he would not be unreasonable.

The New Year's ball proved to be more fun than she thought it would be – dancing made her feel young again. The gaiety of the guests was fuelled by a vast consumption of heady punch and by lively music. But she kept her dance card short and enjoyed the spectacle and the gossip, as well as admiring the handsome young men. This was the first year of the war and everyone knew things would never be the same. It made them all even more determined to enjoy the party. She stole away to her bed as the clock struck one in the morning, feeling rather more enthusiastic about the year ahead than she had expected to.

A week or so later, Edmund, who had returned to Burnham, wrote to say he was leaving for Bath earlier than expected. Reluctantly, she said farewell to her friend and returned to Swaffham to pack. She was eager for change. She had accepted that Horatio would be in the Mediterranean for at least another year, but *she* was no longer 'on the beach'.

As the coach breasted Box Hill, Fanny saw the honey-coloured city basking in pale winter sun below, the river carving a liquid path through the valley. She could make out the Royal Crescent, the Abbey and the Roman Baths.

Why is Bath so appealing, she wondered? Was it the clean air, the spa and the waters? Or was it the great Abbey or the hilly countryside of the southern Cotswolds? Or the climate? It was all of these things, she decided, but the engaging society of Bath was foremost.

The apartment at number 4 Milson Street was above a large shop selling draperies. It was well located and had a dining room, a living room, three bedrooms and a maid's quarter under the eaves. Fanny was sceptical about living above a shop – even if it was a millinery establishment – but there was little noise below, so she relaxed and set about making it her home. She was delighted to find letters waiting.

My dear Fanny,
Please have no concern about moving to Bath for the rest of the winter. If you need additional funds you have my power of attorney with Marsh to whom I shall also write.

Her heart was moved. She read on.

We have been supporting landings in Corsica where the local population have turned against the French. This will help replace Toulon as our base.

There followed descriptions of sieges and operations with the army – Horatio's knowledge of using block and tackle to haul cannon had proven to be of vital importance.

Nevertheless, my efforts are not receiving the atten-tion and recognition they deserve, as I have come to expect from Lord Hood, who is both my patron and my worst enemy. Josiah is doing well. He has been

studying for exams and learning to be a good seaman.
The youngsters are a good crop who will all do well
when the time comes.

Oh. What does he mean? she thought. And at the
bottom of the letter following Horatio's affectionate
farewell, there was a note from Josiah:

Mama, I happy and busy working with Papa. I miss
you but I cannot be in a better place. Josiah

She read through the other letters, which were less
remarkable but even the mundane details made her
feel closer to them. Then, in the most recent letter
from Horatio, she read:

The best news was the report that Lord Hood is
returning to England shortly to take his seat in the
House of Lords and he and his wife will settle in
Bath. Please welcome them when they arrive.

Horatio's long and difficult relationship with Lord
Hood would soon be over. He could pass that troubled
relationship over to Fanny to heal, right here in Bath!
She reflected on how often Horatio had complained
about the admiral, yet the two of them were more
than similar. Both had fathers who were rectors. Both

were impatient and bold. Both were judgemental but loyal to those they liked. Lord Hood had sent Horatio into exile, but he had brought him back. And he had taught him a valuable lesson. She looked forward to seeing Lord and Lady Hood in Bath. It would make her feel closer to Horatio.

A few days later, Fanny saw a figure in the distance she recognised. It was a lieutenant who had served under Horatio on *Boreas*. He had visited Montpelier when she was living there with her uncle. They took tea and reminisced about Nevis. Another captain paid Edmund and Fanny a visit at the apartment the following day, and his wife asked Fanny to call the next day. These two encounters so close together confirmed that Bath would be the ideal place to settle.

Edmund met old friends who had abandoned provincial rectories for retirement in Bath. He joined a society promoting the abolition of slavery. For the first time in many years, he was no longer tied by Tory prejudices. She had not thought much about slavery herself but overcame her hesitancy and Horatio's views on the matter and attended the meetings with Edmund. It was a very different set; these were people passionate about moral necessity rather than unquestioningly supporting trade and privilege.

Ten days into their stay she and Edmund were sitting in the sunny living room after breakfast.

'Fanny,' her father-in-law said to her kindly, 'we have so much in common. You lost your first husband and I lost my wife. Both of us are deprived of the company of Horatio. We must stick together and cherish each other.'

She discussed this with a friend at the assembly rooms when they were taking coffee later that day.

'Is it possible outside of marriage to have a soul-mate, someone who understands you completely and whose experiences are so similar to your own that you know what they are thinking?' she asked.

'Since I have never been married, I do not know the depth of marital understanding. I so want that. But I do believe that a level of common feeling, unity of mind and purpose can be reached – even with the opposite sex,' her friend responded thoughtfully.

'Perhaps it is a feeling like that that keeps sailors from going insane. Months and months on ships – cold, stormy and dangerous. Perhaps it is being part of a band of beings who understand each other and will sacrifice themselves for each other – if necessary.'

But there were other times when Fanny felt that she had little in common with Edmund. Their discussions about the High church party and the Low church party, the theological issues, the politics of the local diocese and of Canterbury and York were often dull. But she listened carefully, learning much about the church, and about Edmund's father and family in the process.

Unfortunately, invitations to social occasions were few and far between. The great parties in the Royal Crescent did not include Fanny and Edmund, who were ranked too low to elicit an invitation. Instead, tea and coffee at the assembly and visits with naval and church acquaintances were the stuff of their social life.

Fanny wasn't really seeking 'admittance' to society, knowing how expensive and stressful it could be. Nevertheless, when the advertisements for the spring ball at the assembly rooms were posted around the city, it prompted Edmund to insist they attend and to cajole Fanny to have a new dress made for the occasion.

As she expected, it was a very grand affair. The octagon-shaped anteroom with its lofty ceiling was decorated with flowers and artfully lit so the long mirrors converted the assembly into a vast sea of people. In the ballroom, an orchestra played, while around the perimeter tables decorated with hothouse flowers were set up for dancers to sit and refresh themselves. Side tables held iced pitchers of punch and waiters roamed with them, topping up the thirsty guests. Fanny's fear that they would know few people at the ball turned out to be wrong. They quickly formed a table with their navy friends and Fanny's dance card was as full as she could wish. She was an accomplished dancer and in demand from naval officers both junior and senior. Nonetheless, she felt Horatio's absence keenly.

At one point in the evening, her friend Mrs Pinney introduced her to the Countess of Bath, the patroness of the ball.

'Lady Mary, may I present Francis Nelson, a friend of mine, formerly of Nevis where her father was a senior judge, and her uncle, Mr Herbert, was the President of the Council. She is married to Captain Nelson, who is currently serving in the Mediterranean.'

'I can't say I have heard the name Nelson when I have visited Norfolk,' the countess responded. 'Are you acquainted with the Cokes or the Walpoles?'

'Indeed, I am. Lord Walpole is my husband's godfather.'

'I am gratified to meet you,' said Lady Mary.

Fanny was pricked by the condescension in the countess's tone. How polished these ladies were and how clever they were in assessing a person's station within moments of an introduction! How finely tuned their ability to put a person in their place – all while maintaining a veneer of excruciating politeness.

'Thank you for your kindness to my friend Mrs Pinney, who has told me of your generosity.' This was intended as a genuine expression of thankfulness by Fanny for the treatment of the Pinneys, who had been injured in a coaching accident and taken to Lady Mary's town house to recover.

'Just so, just so,' said the countess dismissively.

Fanny curtsied and moved away with her friend.

By late spring, Edmund and Fanny decided that they would go their separate ways for a while after agreeing that, longer term, they would establish their home in Bath. With this in mind, she and Edmund took a modest detached house in New King Street. With the lease signed, they agreed to meet again in Bath when summer was over, and Edmund returned to his parish in Burnham for the rest of the summer while Fanny visited the Pinneys in Clifton and then travelled to Ringwood to visit Catherine Matcham.

While at Ringwood, as autumn colours invaded the lovely garden, Fanny received two forwarded letters – both from Horatio.

My dearest Fanny, he'd written in a letter dated July.

> *I continue as well as usual and, except for a very slight scratch on my right eye which has not been the smallest inconvenience, I received no hurt whatever ...*

Without reading the rest, except to confirm that Josiah was safe, she tore open the second letter, dated August. Scanning quickly through Horatio's preliminary comments, she read:

You may hear from others. Therefore, as it is all past, I may now tell you that on the tenth of July last, a shot, having struck our battery, caused splinters of stone from it to strike me most severely in the face and breast. Although the blow was so severe as to occasion a great flow of blood from my head, I most fortunately escaped by only having my right eye nearly deprived of its sight. It was cut down, but it is as far recovered as to be able to distinguish light from darkness, but as to all the purpose of use, it is gone ...

At Bastia, I also got a sharp cut in the back ... You must not think that my hurts confined me. No – nothing but the loss of a limb should have kept me from my duty ...

Mrs Moutray's son, who was on shore with me, I am fearful will fall a sacrifice to the climate ... and poor little Hoste is also extremely ill and I have fears about him. Bolton is very ill; Suckling, that giant, is knocked up and 150 of my people are in their beds. Josiah is full of health. Never say he does not have a great constitution. Of 2000, other than me, he is the healthiest ...

Now the cost of the war was apparent. Would he recover from his wounds? What did this mean for their future? Everything suddenly closed in. Her losses overwhelmed all the progress of the last few months. A summer of touring and then settling back to Bath now all seemed so frivolous, so naive. She scolded herself for thinking that life could go on as usual.

That night she dreamed about her mother and about Nisbet. She woke up in tears, the grief of the past heavy in her heart. Catherine tried to encourage her and keep her spirits up, but it was hard to sit and wait for more news knowing that her worst fears had already almost been realised.

CHAPTER EIGHT
March 1794

The soft morning light woke Josiah. He was lying on a bed of straw in the crude shepherd's hut together with thirty of the crew. He donned his dirty trousers and vest, washed his sunburnt face and combed his tangled hair. He was excited. At last, he was near to the action. He stroked his sparse beard as he thought about the day ahead. Today, his crew was going to move the guns to the ridge above them and then bombard the walls of Bastia – the town a sitting duck in the valley below.

They had cut trees, made rudimentary sleds and lashed heavy guns to them. They secured ropes to outcropping rocks using leather straps. The boatswain calculated the number of blocks to move the sleds and they were secured to trees and, step by step, they hauled on the ropes, heaving the guns up the steep slopes until they had them on the summit. They built breastworks and secured the guns in their carriages. Powder and balls took additional journeys. The work was backbreaking; muscle and sinew challenging gravity. But it was also different from their usual roles and an opportunity to master new skills.

The next day, with the guns in place and the powder and the ball loaded, they prepared for the fight. Far below, in the bay where they had come ashore, lay *Agamemnon* and *Victory*, toy ships in the emerald sea. A red flag was set at the main top of the flagship, signalling the order to open fire. Josiah turned his back and put his fingers in his ears as the gunner lit the match.

The booms of twentypounders echoed off the hills and the guns recoiled against the restraining ropes.

The French tried to return fire, but the elevation of their guns made the task impossible and their shots fell well short. Josiah spent the day hefting cannonballs from the hoist to the gunner. It was hot, heavy work and he would sleep well that night. By the afternoon, the heavy pounding set fire to the town and after some hours a white flag was waved, announcing the city's surrender. Horatio, pleased beyond measure with his work, put his midshipmen at the head of the victory parade through the town a few days later.

To the thump of drums, Josiah led the ship's crew through the bomb-blasted streets.

~

A year passed by, a year of many advances and retreats, but no sea battles. Josiah's father now took orders from Hotham, an excessively cautious man. As a result, there was a sense of stagnation, a sense of idling by as the French advanced into Italy. It was that year Josiah that grew into a tall midshipman. He didn't write to Fanny as regularly as he hoped to, the distraction of war was hard to compete with. But he tried to when he got the chance, even though he never knew quite what to say.

Leghorn 1795

Dear Mama,
It has been a long time and I am sorry that my letters never have anything to say. At last I have enough time to write a letter again. Thank you for all your letters. I always enjoy getting them and hearing about Grandfather and Bath and the family.

Father had me and Hoste for breakfast yesterday and commended us both for our courage under fire and for our seamanship. He seems to be happy with my progress towards being an officer. I work hard to earn his trust. The trouble is that he seems to like some of the other midshipmen better than me – Hoste especially, and also Weatherhead, who is my friend. I think he feels that as my father, he needs to show distance with me and is often ready with criticism, where he can be playful and friendly with the other boys.

We were in a fight with Ca Ira, a French battle-ship, the other day. It was carrying 1000 troops to attack our position in Corsica. Admiral Hotham, the nervous Nellie, at last agreed we must take action and Agamemnon together with Inconstant attacked her. Captain Freemantle lost three of his men and took a beating from Ca Ira's guns, while we blasted away at her stern and swept their deck with grapeshot. From that quarter, it was impossible for them to get off a broadside at us. Inconstant sank on the way back to Leghorn and Ca Ira got away. Papa said I had showed no fear, which is almost true.

I know that Papa is tired of working under men like Admiral Hotham. He feels other people are taking all his credit. And I agree, but I must say that Captain Freemantle showed courage when he was so outgunned.

Tomorrow, we arrive in Leghorn after a stormy night. I will end now and send this letter with Father's mail to you. I hope to make you proud of me.

Your loving son,
Josiah

A hint of spring was in the air. Josiah could smell new grass and blossom in the breeze blowing from the Italian coast. He loved these quiet hours before dawn. In the darkness of the quarterdeck, lit only by a flickering lantern, he could just see the helmsman. He liked the feeling of being alone, free of the noise, smells and discomforts of his packed quarters.

The master, John Wilson, was navigating and keeping a quiet eye on everything. The resonant 'clump, clump' of his sea boots on the ladder announced his approach.

Wilson carefully put his instruments on the binnacle and surveyed the sky. 'Aye, there she is. Beautiful view. Another rare opportunity.'

Josiah took up his telescope and turned towards the south-west, where Jupiter blinked in a warm haze. The ship was steady, the breeze drawing her sails smoothly with little roll and a creamy wake.

Wilson took up his octant and adjusted it, sighting the instrument on the four moons. 'Aye, sir, a good night for visibility. Would you check my readings?'

Wilson passed over the octant and Josiah sighted Jupiter and adjusted the instrument. He looked over Wilson's careful handwriting and compared the readings he'd recorded to his own flowing script.

'I have the same readings, Mr Wilson,' Josiah said.

'In which case, I will plot our course,' Wilson said, packing his instruments and papers up.

'Aye, sir. I'll see you later,' Josiah replied, as Mr Wilson clumped back down the companionway.

Silence followed his departure. At length, Josiah gave the order to arouse the ship for breakfast.

'Mr Smith, wake up the new watch and beat to quarters.'

'Aye aye, sir,' Smith answered.

Shortly afterwards, Josiah heard the sounds of running feet as the watch went below.

'Give the order!'

Drums began thumping and loud voices rang throughout the ship, as the crew poured on deck to get to their stations. A seaman climbed the mast to ensure no enemy ship was in the vicinity.

'Good morning, Mr Nisbet,' Horatio addressed Josiah.

'Good morning, sir.'

Josiah stepped back from the binnacle. Horatio looked at the bearing and then took the telescope and scanned the horizon. Josiah smiled. There was nothing out of place on his watch. Father could take pride in him. He saluted the lieutenant who took over his watch and retired below to wash and prepare for breakfast.

Agamemnon berthed in Leghorn, Britain's base on the Tuscan coast. It would be the last chance for shore leave before they returned to England for a refit. Josiah and Weatherhead were in their favourite bar, a plate of polenta and prosciutto before them.

'Listen, Weatherhead, I want to tell you something confidential, but I don't know all the facts,' began Josiah to his friend.

Weatherhead looked up expectantly.

Josiah hesitated, his face flushed. 'I think my father is having an affair with his landlady in Leghorn,' he said finally.

'Are you talking about the woman who owns the house where he's lodging?' asked Weatherhead.

'Yes. Signorina Correglia. Papa tells me she has all sorts of information. You know, spy stuff. She introduces him to the local gentry, the mayor and so on. Knows everyone.'

'Sounds harmless. Why are you suspicious?' Weatherhead said.

'I overheard the boatswain and the carpenter talking. They didn't know I was there. My father was walking down the gangplank and one said to the other "He's off to see his fancy woman". And the other said: "She's a fair dolly!"' Josiah explained.

'Oh … I see.'

'Weatherhead, don't say anything, will you? I've

been stewing on this. I had to tell you. You understand? I feel terrible. If it's true, I'll never believe anything he says to me. Perhaps it isn't true. What do you think?'

There was silence.

'Look, forget I told you this. I just wanted to get it off my chest,' he added.

'Jay, I'm not sure. Your dad is a very good man. You don't know the facts of the matter. But I agree it's a terrible thing if it's true …'

'Thanks for listening.'

'Drink up and let's get going,' Weatherhead said, finishing his drink and getting to his feet.

Josiah swallowed the remains of the beer. He felt better for getting it off his chest and perhaps it was only rumour, an especially ugly rumour.

Agamemnon's refit complete, the crew returned from the bars, brothels and boarding houses. Provisions were taken aboard and the command to up anchors was given. Josiah was a guest in the wardroom that night – an occasion when the Captain was also invited for dinner. The port bottle had already made several revolutions of the table when Horatio addressed the group.

'We have been on our station a very long time and while we've been able to give her some attention here, *Agamemnon* desperately needs a complete refit in England. I have a letter from our new commander,

Sir John Jervis. He wants us to delay our return to England. What do you men think?'

Hinton, the first lieutenant, spoke up first. 'The men are as tired as the ship. They all need to go home and *Agamemnon*'s hull and joints on the larboard side below the waterline are very weak. I'm not sure we should fight with the ship in this condition.'

'Sir John told me he will refit the fleet starting with the officers and ending with the ships,' said Horatio, which was met with hearty laughter.

'Is he as tough as his reputation?' another man enquired.

'Yes, he is tough. He'll go through this fleet like a dose of salts. The French leaders have sorted out their differences, appointed a new Generalissimo and made a peace with the Spanish. We have to take the fight to the new enemy.'

'Sir, does that mean I will be able to take my lieutenant's board before we go home?' Hoste's question lightened the atmosphere.

'I propose to stay with the fleet and take a ship in better condition. I need each of you to consider whether you will stay with me. If not, then go home to your loved ones on *Agamemnon* with my thanks. Now let's fill these glasses and raise a toast to a new commander-in-chief!'

Josiah was summoned by Horatio.

'Admiral Jervis has me slated for promotion to flag rank, but I have to earn my stripes. There will be some ugly battles ahead. You may go home too – if you choose. I'm letting you make your own decision,' Horatio told him, as he poured them tea.

'Father, why would I do that? I am approaching my exams and getting every opportunity to advance – from you,' Josiah replied. There was no way he was going home now, just as things were heating up – not if he could help it.

'Your mother needs one or both of us. She's been alone for three years,' Horatio said.

'I love mother. But how can I serve my country sitting idle in Bath?' He took a sip of his tea, the hot liquid searing his tongue, and tried to stay calm.

'You could opt for another career. A lawyer, perhaps – you'd be more certain of wealth and rank. The war could end tomorrow and then what?'

Josiah considered this carefully. His father seemed genuine enough. He thought of his mates, his exams, the fun he was having. Did his father want to get rid of him? 'I want to stay and fight,' he said resolutely.

'That's what I thought you would say, Josiah. You may have a future if you navigate the politics of the navy as well as you handle the ship. But I need you to stay alive for your mother's sake, as much as mine.

Now, I will say good night and we will talk soon.' He stood and nodded, indicating that the conversation was over for now and Josiah was to leave.

The night was warm and Josiah had difficulty falling asleep. His mind turned the situation over and over. His father may have said otherwise, but Josiah knew that deep down, he wanted him to stay. He had seen how father could be ruthless, selfish and unfaithful, but he still modelled himself on him. In the ways that counted the most, Horatio was still the man he wanted to become. He knew what his decision would be and knew that, in the end, Horatio would support it.

Within a week, they moved to *Captain*, a ship the equal of *Agamemnon* and fresh from Chatham dockyard. Saying farewell to the warrant officers who had taught him everything was unbearably hard. But there was little time for emotions. They were aboard a new ship, with new warrant officers and crew. And, within weeks, as they settled in, they received the news that Spain had declared war. Orders were given to proceed to join Admiral Jervis's fleet in the North Atlantic off the Spanish coast to prevent the Spanish and French invading England. This time there would be a full-scale sea battle. His apprenticeship over, Josiah was prepared to play his part.

CHAPTER NINE
May 1796

Unlike his brother Horatio, William was stocky. His broad face had a purposeful expression and his paunch and thinning hair lent him an air of gravitas although he was not yet forty. When he and Horatio were together, people often thought William was the fine figure of a naval captain and Horatio the reserved country parson.

William was thrilled that his brother's career was moving in the right direction – Horatio had been promoted to Commodore and had a new and lucrative sinecure as 'Colonel of the Marines'. And those emoluments were added to the regular prize money he was earning. If only William could harness some of Horatio's patronage to secure his bishopric! He had made some progress by becoming an honorary Canon of Canterbury Cathedral, thanks to Uncle Suckling's connections, but nothing more had happened yet. He was still just a rector with two parishes and the chaplain of Wolterton's chapel – a post that had no compensation. His career was foundering while better connected alumni of his Cambridge college were already Suffragan bishops. He was stuck!

All Saints, Brandon Parva – barely thirty miles from his birthplace at Burnham Thorpe – had been his church for fourteen years. He also owned the Living at All Saints Hilborough, his father's old parish. He and Sarah had lived there for a time, but he made up his curate to vicar and visited the church only on holy days.

His Brandon Parva church was a mere half-mile away from the small village, not a pretty little place; rather, it was a ramshackle sort of village built untidily around a green. And the rectory was a distance away from the church. William preferred to see himself as a gentleman with a small estate rather than a rector. His house was a spacious early Georgian set in pleasant gardens with a glebe land of ten acres surrounding it.

It was this acreage that he was strolling through now, the day darkening and the damp mist sticking to his coat. Smoke from surrounding chimneys hung in the air. Cows looked at him curiously, and a few ravens fluttered above the leafless elms. Occasionally, he greeted a passer-by – usually one of his congregants.

He counted his responsibilities: in addition to the church with its twelve services a week, a large Sunday school and a congregation of over 200 souls, he was also responsible for the tithe. His barn was a medieval building, often admired by visitors to the parish. He managed the village school, too, and the village's twenty almshouses.

In a way, he thought as he marched along, *my life is more complicated than that of a captain in the navy.*

Opening the front door of the rectory, his confidence evaporated. Sarah was in a bad mood. He could hear her berating the parlour maid. Her harshness grated. As he hung up his coat, he noticed damp patches radiating from cracks in the plaster and felt the sighing draft of cold air through aged window frames. In summer, the view from the drawing-room windows over the expansive lawn was magnificent. But today it was an uninspiring view of leafless trees, clumpy grass and unkempt bushes. The house was in bad repair and there was no budget to fix it.

He took off his clerical stock and donned a threadbare woollen cardigan. Thankfully, the disagreement in the kitchen seemed to be over.

Sarah was vigorously polishing the silver when he entered. The kitchen was the only warm place in the house at this time of the year and William enjoyed the heat on his face and shoulders as he moved to stand by the old iron cooking range. It was kept alight all day, fuelled by coal – one of their few luxuries. Sarah looked up. She hadn't aged well, her greying hair fell over a heavily lined face. Her life was not the easiest, even though she had only two children.

'There you are, Mr Nelson,' she greeted him, a sharpness in her voice. 'I heard the front door and knew it would be you. I've just told Betty that unless she is more attentive, she will have to find herself a new occupation. She should have been at the door the moment you walked up the path! How was the meeting with the magistrates?' She was putting the silver back in the drawer noisily.

'They were interested in hearing what people in the parish were thinking.'

'Did you tell them about the chapel?'

'Yes. They said that this man Wesley and his followers are harmless. I told them the chapel is taking our people. They are keeping their eye on radical preaching, but they say the Methodists are keeping the peace!'

'You must do something! You could start by improving your sermons.'

'You know how to hurt a man, Sarah. My colleagues consider my sermons to be very insightful. And now I must go. I have work to do, as do you.'

He turned his back and left the room, closing the door firmly and feeling the sting of her criticism. In his freezing study, William sat down to write to his brother for assistance in buying another parish.

The last letter from Horatio had offered hope – he had taken more prizes that even now were being sold. Fanny's inheritance had come through. His brother was a wealthy man. Surely, Horatio would not neglect him, his older brother, serving at home? His future depended on Horatio, William thought grimly, struggling with contrary currents of self-pity and resentment.

An invitation arrived one morning a few weeks later. The envelope was unmistakable and the inn-keeper handed it to William with a sardonic glance at the crest which was beautifully and simply embossed on a creamy envelope. William pocketed it without comment and, after exchanging pleasantries with the farmers quenching their thirst in the snug, he mounted his horse and rode home, his excitement rising. As he trotted up the drive, he could see Sarah busy at work helping the gardener clear dead leaves from the herbaceous borders. She spotted him, and sat back on her heels and watched as he dismounted and tied the aged piebald pony to the limb of a convenient tree.

'You look excited,' she called to him.

'Yes, my dear, we have a letter from Mr Coke.'

It was not the first. Since Horatio had left Burnham Thorpe, Coke had invited William to a number of gatherings with other gentlemen. It was a pleasant break from his duties in the parish and an opportunity to meet the county families. He tore the envelope eagerly and read the letter inside. A Holkham weekend! The Walpoles of Wolterton were "old money", but the Cokes were fabulously rich – and connected to the beating heart of the Whig Party. Their home estate of 30,000 acres of prime land was, one had to admit, the very centre of society in the county.

'But what shall I wear, William?' Sarah immediately wanted to know once he'd shared the news with her. 'I can't be seen in the silk mantua that I wore on our two previous visits. I don't think we can accept.'

'Nonsense, Mrs Nelson! I would rather we forgo the visit to Bath than miss out on Coke's house party. Get yourself the dress you wanted, or else borrow one from a friend. We are definitely going. The children are invited too – won't young Horatio and Charlotte be pleased to hear it!'

Visibly pleased, Sarah's attitude softened. The forthcoming visit meant a great deal to her too.

❧

The public coach dropped them at Wells-next-the-Sea where the Cokes' carriage awaited. They drove through pleasant lanes leading to the handsome gates of the estate. An impressive plantation of oak and elm and early spring flowers followed the drive on either side until, turning a bend, the lake and Holkham Hall appeared amid lush gardens and lawns. The butler met them at the door with casual familiarity. William was insulted, complaining to Sarah once they were in their rooms.

'This war is spoiling the country. People of all ranks are feeling they can abandon old customs, proper manners and courtesies,' he grumbled.

'Actually, I think people are becoming more human,' said Sarah, surprising William by her lightness. 'I'm going to enjoy myself and I'm not going to think about anything else!'

Coke's other guests were a mix of county gentry, clergy and military men, all of whom spent the following day hunting.

As William disrobed for his bath after the hunt, he described his afternoon to Sarah. 'I'm not cut out for fox-hunting, Sarah. Fortunately, I had a huge white mare with a stride twice that of my pony. *She* was in charge and carried me over gates and hedges without any encouragement from me at all, thank God! Without her, I'd be in a ditch. No, I am not a hunter and never will be. But I was able to talk with his Grace, the Bishop of Norwich, while the huntsmen tried to raise a scent. I've not seen him since last Mothering Sunday. It was a good chance to catch up and to suggest a slot in the close or even the Dean's job if it comes up. And how was your afternoon, my dear?'

'While you were out, the ladies had an afternoon at cards. Naturally, I did not play, but I spent pleasant hours talking with Mary Weatherhead.'

William knew Mrs Weatherhead –the wife of the rector of Titlesham.

'John, her son, is on *Captain* with Horatio. John told his mother that Josiah is the apple of Horatio's eye. He can do no wrong. It turns out that Josiah, John and young Hoste, Dixon Hoste's son, are the very best of friends. They care for each other and all of them are growing rapidly into handsome and distinguished young officers.'

'How are they faring?'

'John's letters say there have been many battles over the last three years. But perhaps more worrying has been the illnesses. Last year, when they were in Leghorn, the whole ship was sick apparently – John and Hoste, too. The only person not struck down was your nephew.'

'It sounds like Horatio is looking after him. What's wrong with that?'

'Your brother is the only way for your advancement. Don't you see? Do you want to be stuck in Brandon Parva forever? If Horatio is favouring Josiah Nisbet and if he decides to adopt him, as he has often threatened to do, what will that mean for our Horatio and Charlotte?'

'I am going to take my bath now. I'll think about your remarks.'

That evening there was a grand dinner to celebrate the close of the fox-hunting season. There was also a party for local farmers taking place in the stables, and faint sounds of a square dance could be heard floating up on the breeze. Dinner was over and before the ladies withdrew, Mr Coke was proposing toasts.

'To His Gracious Majesty the King!' toasted Coke. Everyone stood and drained their glasses and then resumed their seats around the table.

'It's been a wonderful fox-hunting season and I want everyone to raise their glasses and toast our success today.' Glasses were emptied and quickly recharged.

'And now I would most especially, among all my guests, like to raise my glass to the Reverend William and Mrs Sarah Nelson, brother to our noble Commodore currently serving his country off the coast of Spain.'

Surprised and shocked, William felt himself blushing and he brought his napkin to his mouth to conceal his confusion.

'I have a special reason for toasting them on behalf of all of us, because this afternoon while we were hunting the fox, my butler received an urgent message from my London agent. This was the news of a glorious victory over the Spanish Fleet at Cape St Vincent. Sir John Jervis, gallant admiral and commander-in-chief, took on a fleet of over twenty Spanish ships with only fourteen ships, ten of them battleships, and though outgunned and with a much inferior complement of ships, defeated them soundly.

'Prominent, or should I say in the vanguard of our attacking column, was our dear friend Horatio Nelson, who personally led the attack and divided the Spanish Fleet, thereby allowing our ships to surround and cut off many of their battleships. He personally led a boarding party which captured the mighty *San José* and the *San Nicolas*. With immediate effect, he has been promoted from commodore to rear admiral. The gratitude of the nation has yet to be expressed but I anticipate that our dear friend will be rewarded suitably by the King.

'And now, pray be upstanding. I give you Admiral and Mrs Nelson, the Reverend William Nelson and Mrs Sarah Nelson!'

There were cries of 'Hear! Hear!' from the other guests and spontaneous wholehearted applause. William had never been the centre of such illustrious attention before. He felt weak in the knees.

He pulled himself together as he heard Coke continue. 'And now let's hear from the Reverend

Nelson. What do you have to say, my dear sir, on this marvellous occasion?'

William rose to his feet, groping for words. 'My lords, your Grace, Mr Coke, dear friends. On behalf of myself and my wife and on behalf of my dear brother Horatio, I am most pleased to receive this news and your kind words of thanks.'

He paused to see their reaction and was pleased that all conversations had stopped and eyes were on him.

'My family are descendants of an old county family. We have served in our churches or aboard His Majesty's ships for generations. Such is England! When I think of my dear brother, I have one word that captures his heart and all that both he and I stand for: it is "duty"! It inspires all he does and the sacrifices he makes for our country. Thank you.'

Blushing with pride and surprised with his eloquence and ability to be brief, he reached for his glass and took a great gulp of claret. The applause was astonishing.

Later, in the bedroom, wine and praise melted inhibition and for the first time in many months, Sarah's sighs and moans called for his attention. But, he decided as he disrobed, with Horatio's success becoming the stuff of legend, he must head off any prospect of Fanny or Josiah usurping his position as Horatio's rightful heir.

CHAPTER TEN
July 1797

Horatio was on the ferry from the fleet to Gibraltar, where he had a meeting with his Admiral Lord Jervis, now Earl of St Vincent. He spent the idle hours thinking about the dismal turn of events that had led to the battle and the subsequent sudden victory in which he had played a central role.

As the French advanced into Italy, Jervis had lost the ports he needed to resupply and repair his ships. When the Spanish joined the war on the French side, the threat of invasion was so serious that the London politicians insisted Jervis abandon the Mediterranean. All the gains of the previous years had been lost. And there was a mutiny in the Home Fleet and a threat of it spreading. The fleet had reformed off Cádiz where the Spanish had risen to the challenge and come out ready for a fight.

Horatio recalled the critical moment in the battle. The Spanish line of battleships was too spread. There was an opportunity to break through. The winds were favourable, too. He wore from the British line and smashed through the centre of the enemy fleet. His squadron followed and the divided line was turned and crushed, ship by ship. He admitted to himself that his manoeuvre disobeyed the doctrine that a captain should always await an admiral's signal before departing from the planned attack. But in consequence of his initiative, the Spanish fleet was out of the war and he had captured two of their best battleships.

Yet the personal rewards were meagre and disappointing. Horatio was offered a baronetcy, an inheritable title for a man with no one to inherit. He declined it in favour of a knighthood in the Order of Bath. Although he was promoted to rear admiral, he contrasted his small pickings with the fortune lavished on his commander: an earldom and 3000 pounds a year, as well as 18,000 pounds in prize money! It was his initiative that had won the battle. It was totally unjust!

The small packet boat approached Gibraltar, her white sails luffing as she tacked, the magnificent Rock towering above. His campaign for more recognition had eventually borne some fruit, he admitted to himself. The news of the victory travelled by official dispatch and private letter. Jervis's account naturally emphasised his own strategic brilliance and his favourites' tactical contributions and had not mentioned Horatio's crucial role in the battle. But Horatio had found a wily supporter – Sir Gilbert Elliot, a Scottish diplomat and well-connected insider and, until recently, the Governor of Elba. Sir Gilbert had been on his way home on the frigate *Lively*, which had also been in the battle. He had witnessed the battle firsthand. Sir Gilbert had been dazzled by Horatio's brilliant manoeuvre. He also knew about Horatio's shore battles in Corsica and the downplaying of those achievements by Lord Hood.

Well versed in the art of conveying unofficial as well as official versions of events, Sir Gilbert coached his aide, Colonel Drinkwater, under whose name and eyewitness account the newspapers reported the event. The story was so dramatic and convincing that it became the version widely accepted by the public, if not the Admiralty. Sir Gilbert had taught Horatio another valuable lesson – to manage his own press and to cultivate powerful people in London.

Stepping ashore, he found the admiral's carriage waiting to take him to Jervis's house high up on the Rock. He enjoyed the short journey, the horses straining up the steep road above the Strait of Gibraltar, the shores of Africa faint on the horizon. The great wrought-iron gates, guarded by marine sentries in red uniforms, were thrown back and the carriage crunched up the gravel path. Ahead was a magnificent white house amid shaded lawns and purple bougainvillea. The air was heavy with the scent of lilies.

The carriage halted, the horses lathered and steaming. A servant opened the door and placed a step for Horatio to alight and the butler deferentially escorted him through the vaulted lobby and up the sweeping staircase to the second level, out to a shaded veranda overlooking the sea.

The commander-in-chief was slumped in a deep-cushioned wicker armchair, his bare feet resting on a stool and the sleeves of his cotton shirt rolled up to his elbows. He looked utterly unburdened by the world. As Horatio approached. he put down a book and looked up.

'Ah, Horatio, do come in. Take a seat, my good man. Take a seat!'

Horatio, surprised by the cordiality, took off his coat and admired the splendid view.

'Can we get you a drink, Horatio? How about a small beer? It's too early for whiskey.'

Horatio nodded noncommittally and sat down. The beer arrived. The old bear was in a good mood – which meant he wanted something.

'I want to talk about the Canaries. I've given more thought to the idea we discussed. Your suggestion that we take Santa Cruz de Tenerife and intercept Spanish ships from the Americas before they reach the coast of Spain makes sense. Once through the Strait, they have too many options.'

'I have more experience in shore landings than anyone else in the navy: San Juan, Long Island, Bastia, Calvi, Cappria, Elba–' started Horatio.

'I know, I know!' Jervis interrupted his flow. 'You are a virtuoso in blowing your own trumpet. And talking about trumpets, I did not appreciate you going behind my back to tell the press about your exploits at the Battle of Cape St Vincent.'

'It was Colonel Drinkwater that gave the report you are referring to,' Horatio countered.

'Yes, I know, and I also know Colonel Drinkwater is the right-hand man of your friend Gilbert Elliot, who has access to everyone who counts in London. Also, you are a good writer. I recognised your style instantly!'

'But your lordship surely knows that ...'

'Horatio, I was a sitting member in the Commons for years. I understand the system. I know how people leak their version to the public. But remember this: I am the commander-in-chief. I am the one who takes responsibility for what happens here, and I control the publicity. Let's get that straight, Horatio.'

A heavy silence followed.

'Now, one of the reasons I support this campaign in the Canaries is to rebuild morale. Our withdrawal from the Med and the mutinies on *Blanche* and *Theseus* are symptoms of unrest. I want to exercise our men, get them out of Cádiz.'

Horatio cleared his throat, as Jervis continued.

'My belief is that these mutinous situations get out of control quickly and it takes a special type of captain to deal with it.'

'Yes, I am also aware of your "legendary" ability to win the support of your men, too, but you and I disagree on methods. As the Chinese say, it's better to kill the chicken to scare the monkey. The mutinies at Nore and Spithead prove proper discipline must be applied *before* mutiny occurs.'

'I agree severe measures are called for, but these disturbances have simple causes which can be remedied,' said Horatio. 'In the recent case, I moved to assume command and that act alone changed the dynamic of the situation.'

'You and I disagree on that point. I have two rebels and two sodomites to deal with at the very moment and they will hang from the yardarm the instant sentence is passed. Yes, an expedition to Santa Cruz will be very timely. This expedition will exercise the fleet. They'll return triumphant and invigorated and pass on their enthusiasm to their fellows in the blockade. You will have command.'

Horatio felt excitement overwhelm him. The pitch of his voice rose. 'I will not disappoint you. The Spanish treasure ship, *El Principe*, will be in Santa Cruz. I believe we can cut her out at the same time as we seize the island.'

'I am happy for it, Horatio. You will make us both very rich. Your share of our recent battle will exceed 5000 pounds, by the way. I hope that your squadron will be able to add a zero to that with *El Principe*. Just be mindful to have good anchorage before you engage and always remember we cannot afford to lose our ships!'

'I am absolutely aware of the risks, but I am equally confident of success,' Horatio assured him.

'I am sending two of my very best men, Troubridge and Bowen, with you, Horatio. Bowen is as dear to me as a son and Troubridge is unparalleled in skill and courage.'

Troubridge, the admiral's favourite. Horatio's resentment rose. Troubridge had received more favourable mentions than Horatio had in dispatches after Cape St Vincent. John Jervis's 'my way or the highway' attitude had prevailed again. The man had no subtlety.

'I am grateful,' Horatio replied simply.

'Send the plans to my secretary and I will approve them. Now let's have dinner,' Jervis said and stood from his armchair.

After the sun had sunk, Horatio set off to return to the packet boat. The road seemed twice as steep, the horses straining to hold the carriage back while the driver heaved on the brake. As they descended, he replayed the meeting in his head. Jervis admired him – that much was clear – but it was also clear that as long as Jervis was around, Horatio would be operating in his shade.

He thought about the Spanish treasure ship and the prospect of huge wealth. Only a short while ago, one had been seized – with the lucky captain and Sir John sharing a prize worth over 30,000 pounds. If peace came soon – as it surely would – Horatio would need enough money for himself and Fanny to live on for the rest of their lives. There would never be another opportunity like this!

Josiah, in his new lieutenant's uniform, greeted Horatio as he came aboard. Horatio noticed how much he had grown.

'Did you get Santa Cruz, Father?'

'I did indeed, Josiah,' Horatio replied.

'Father, what prospects is there for Weatherhead's promotion to lieutenant?'

'That is in the hands of Sir John and the navy board, but I intend that Weatherhead be posted immediately as an acting lieutenant for this expedition.'

'You know he is twenty-two years old – five years my senior and with the same experience I have. There's no reason I should be lieutenant and not he,' pressed Josiah.

'Yes, a good man. But what I can manage for you – with the help of your uncle at the navy board – cannot be afforded to all my middies, I'm afraid, even if I plead their cause.'

'Can we all be on the shore party, Father?' said Josiah, moving to his next priority.

'We'll see about that.'

CHAPTER ELEVEN
August 1797

He opened his eyes. He was in his berth. Pain seized his shoulder and he gave a roar. The cabin door flung open and the surgeon and Captain Miller rushed in. He took the laudanum on a small teaspoon of honey and the waves of pain ebbed. He fell into some dark, distant, comfortable place. On the fourth day, the doses were reduced, and Horatio realised that though he could feel every sensation from shoulder to finger, he had no right arm.

He groped in the mist of memory. He recalled setting out from Gibraltar. A brisk easterly wind had been blowing. *Theseus* and the other battleships passed the Strait and ploughed through lumpy seas along the African coast. Ahead, to starboard, was Troubridge's *Culloden*, a mighty seventy-four

Collingwood commanded at Cape St Vincent, and a few miles astern to larboard was *Zealous*. The others followed.

Horatio's captains had gathered around his table to discuss the plan. Troubridge was critical of the intelligence and Sam Hood had pointed out that with the strong current and lack of protected anchorage, the ships could get caught in contrary winds and tide. They agreed the frigates should arrive first and land field guns. Troubridge and his crew would haul them to high ground and fire on the fort to draw away the enemy, like Horatio's successful attack on Bastia. The main body of the fleet would land on the breakwater and take the town.

Why had he underestimated the Spanish so drastically? He'd been so confident that a charge by British seamen with muskets, cold steel and resolute determination would surely prevail against a people who fought at St Vincent with little skill or courage.

Trickles of memory soon became a flood, amplifying Horatio's sense of failure. First, Troubridge had underestimated the distance from his frigate to the beach; and the Spanish military, alerted to their approach, had seized all hilltops within range. Troubridge and Miller tried dragging the heavy guns over the mountains to outflank them. But they had failed and retreated, abandoning the guns and straggling back to the beach, where they were rescued. All surprise was gone. What could have been if he had taken charge of the landing instead of Troubridge?

Another memory. The bullet in the arm was like a blow from a hammer; Josiah stemmed the flow with a tourniquet and rowed him back under the Spanish guns. He had been pinioned lest he resist, and the surgeon amputated his arm while Horatio bit down on India rubber.

As he lay there, he began to feel a little better. He ate some breakfast with one hand and took a bath. His stump was still a livid red with discharge from a suppurating wound. He slept some more. Now he was in his great cabin, sunlight streaming through broad windows. Clean sheets. Smells of tar and sea water. A servant knocked and entered.

'How long am I lying here?' Horatio asked him.

'You've been out cold, sir, for eighteen hours,' the servant answered.

'Can you call Captain Miller and say I am ready to see him?'

'I'll pass the message, sir. They've all been to see you, sir.'

'I have no recollection of that …' Horatio mumbled as the servant left to summon the other captain.

A short time later, Miller entered the room, closing

the door behind him. 'Hastings says it will take weeks for you to recover. You were lucky to survive. The decision to amputate your arm made the difference between life and death,' Miller said.

'Tell me, Miller, who have we lost?'

'The final tally is 150 killed or drowned and 113 wounded. *Culloden* lost thirty-nine and we lost forty-six. Richard Bowen has died and Weatherhead is desperately ill – wounded in the stomach. Captain Thompson and Captain Freemantle were both wounded and are recovering.'

Horatio groaned. Bowen, as close to Jervis as a son! Weatherhead! What would he tell his father?

'I'm dazed and sick, Miller. Remind me.'

'Yes, sir. Do you recall on the first day that Troubridge led the landing party? It was very badly done. Troubridge misjudged the current and the distance to the shore so the enemy knew they were coming.'

Horatio nodded – that much he could remember.

'We all supported your decision to land again the following night,' Miller continued, 'but Colonel Gutierrez concentrated his force. Our feint towards the fort was never believed by the Spanish and they were ready for Bowen and his men. A carronade carried him and several others off. Then you were shot. Josiah saved you and took you to the ship.

Troubridge and I managed to make it to the town but without reinforcements we were surrounded. The cutter received a direct hit in deep water and 100 men who could have supported us were drowned.'

'And Troubridge?'

'He had a clever negotiation with the Spanish colonel, who allowed us to retreat. They could easily have taken us prisoners.'

'What a disaster! This is the end of my career, Miller.'

A week later, though steadily recovering himself, Horatio found himself in Gibraltar Hospital. Warm sunshine played patterns of light and shade on the bed. His stump ached. His heart ached even more.

Weatherhead had died in great pain that morning from his stomach wound, vomiting blood and green and yellow fluid. Horatio had sat at his bedside with Josiah, holding Weatherhead's hand while the hospital chaplain read the twenty-third Psalm.

Pride comes before the fall, he thought. He cursed his unwillingness to reconsider the whole venture back when he could have. He knew very well that overwhelming force was the only foundation for a landing, and he'd known they didn't have the intelligence. He'd been impetuous!

He pulled himself together and read the recom-
mendations for gallantry. Prominent among them,
Josiah. His son had saved his life!

Back at his quarters after the sad events of the day, he
began to write, thinking all the while that he would
have to learn how to write properly with his left
hand – as it was, it looked scratchy and juvenile. He
persisted.

He practised on his private mail, giving Fanny a long
account of the disaster. Being one-armed was tricky in
other ways, too. Pulling up his drawers and stockings,
fastening the buttons on his breeches and coat, cutting
up his food – at every turn, a new frustration. At the
same time, he was determined not to be weak. Better
to go hungry than have someone cut his food.

He visited Lord St Vincent in Gibraltar.

'A left-handed, half-blind admiral is of no value
to the service,' he said frankly to Jervis. 'I will have
Fanny finish that country cottage and I will serve my
nation by quitting the stage before I make a greater
hash of things. I am very sorry, my lord. I have let you
and the service down badly. How will you survive this
humbling defeat?'

'Nonsense, Horatio. You look every bit the
dashing hero you are and a one-handed admiral with

your record is twice the value of most fit officers who serve me.'

'But after the court martial, what prospect will there be for me?' asked Horatio, surprised.

'Listen, Horatio, I have runs on the board, credit in the bank – call it what you will. I will have to draw down on that, but I have more than enough and so do you.'

'There won't be a court martial?'

'Why should there? You lost none of His Majesty's ships. Yes, you lost a few too many good men, among them my dear Bowen. But that is war. Those men who did return are fighting fit and ready for revenge. No more mutinous talk below deck! You will go to England on *Seahorse*. It'll give you another chance to test your skills with the newspapers! Recover yourself with Fanny and put yourself at the disposal of their lordships. I will see you again.'

CHAPTER TWELVE
August 1797

My dear Izzy,

How sad I feel that you cannot visit this summer on account of your father's sickness. Your letter arrived smelling of flowers, as if you were with me in the room. Since you are not coming, I will try to tell you everything in my heart in this letter.

Would you believe it is three years since I left Norfolk? Bath has completely captured my heart and the only thing I miss in Norfolk is Wolterton. My Bath home is neither grand nor fashionable but makes up by being very cosy and close to everything. And I have my piano, too, and am increasingly in demand to play at dinner parties.

Edmund shares the house, but I make my life quite independently of him. Edmund's work brings with it friendships at Cathedral Close. 'No one combines Godliness with cleanliness as well as the Bishop of Bath and Wells,' he says whimsically.

She put down her pen and thought about him. He was a much better father to her than the gruff Nevis judge, who drank and was always angry, had ever been. After Mother had died, they'd lived a desperately lonely life until he died too when she was seventeen.

But Edmund drank very little and was always in good spirits and his kindness was mingled with respect towards her. She enjoyed his stories about Horatio as a boy. He had been adventurous and confident then too, though he was one of the younger ones. When Edmund's wife had died, Horatio had suffered terribly. It occurred to her she and Horatio had this loss of a mother in common. It made them independent and used to taking responsibility, perhaps too much so. She picked up her pen again.

I receive visitors between ten o'clock and noon each day. The naval officers give me the latest news from the Mediterranean. I know what is happening better than most. In the late afternoon, I go to the pump room to see my women friends. We talk about everything and I feel as if I have sisters. It's great fun.

Horatio's fame and recent promotion to rear admiral

and his knighthood has raised my visibility in Bath. The tradesmen offer me credit now. It's very amusing to see how peoples' perceptions can change so quickly.

With Horatio overseas, I take care of business that can't wait. His prize agent and his solicitor write constantly. I am also sorting out my uncle's and my late husband's legacies. It's such a paper chase! It troubles me that the legacies are legally Horatio's. We women have so few rights and when we marry, we lose our property. We ought to be entitled to keep it surely?

She stopped writing and rang the bell for tea. She would finish later. She moved to the piano, warmed up with scales and practised her new sonata by Beethoven.

She returned to the letter an hour later.

As you see, I am busy with little time to be bored. But sometimes I feel sad that life is passing by without my husband and son. It's been three years and I am thirty-six. I fear it is unlikely I will have another child even if he returns soon.

At length she concluded:

Your friendship means more to me than almost anything else. Only the return of Horatio and Josiah

*would give me like happiness. Do write again very
soon.*

Your dearest friend,
Fanny

She thought about being accepted in Bath society.
When Lord Hood and Caroline had returned from
Gibraltar, they'd brought her into their circle. Indeed,
because of their kindness, she was forced to question
Horatio's dislike of his former commander. Then
Lord Howe, the hero of the 'Glorious First of June',
retired to Bath. He and his countess invited her to
their home in the Royal Crescent, the social pinnacle
of Bath society. She realised she had missed those
days in Nevis when she was the leading hostess on
the island. Slowly, she was gaining her place here. She
lit a candle and made her way to bed.

Despite the calmness of day-to-day life, the
deteriorating war situation increasingly intervened.
Newspapers said the war was 'a shambles'. The allies
were shamelessly making separate peace with France.
The French had conquered northern Italy. The
campaign in the Low Countries had collapsed in an
undignified rout. The United Irishmen had rebelled.

Every conversation mentioned the possibility of invasion and civil disturbance. The façade of being away from the war was beginning to give way to a realisation of a grave threat to everyone. People were beginning to stock up in case of shortages. Lentils and potatoes were hard to find. The war was no longer a thousand miles away. Horatio was no longer just building a successful career – through his heroism, he was now defending England.

A letter arrived, the writing scarcely recognisable. She tore it open and read the scribble as best she could. It was from Horatio.

> *My dearest Fanny,*
> *I am so confident of your affection that I feel the pleasure you receive will be equal whether my letter is by my right hand or by my left. It was a chance of war and I have great reason to be thankful and I know it will add much to your pleasure in finding that Josiah under God's providence was principally instrumental in saving my life.*

When she calmed down, her first thought was he must have had another injury. He had damaged his right hand and was writing with his left. And by the clause about Josiah, she realised Horatio must have been delivered a life-threatening blow. Was Josiah wounded too? She read on. He was expecting a pension and wanted to buy the cottage. Was he saying he would retire? Her heart rose. Then she read the news of poor Weatherhead's horrible death, which overwhelmed her with sadness. It could have been Josiah.

She put the letter down and the exciting thought sank in – Horatio would be here soon!

A month later, when days were shorter and sunny weather blessed the harvest, he arrived. She was with Edmund in the parlour discussing the news when a carriage pulled up. Before she could reach the door, the knocker pounded. Her maid opened the door and there he was. He swept her off her feet and kissed her full on the lips. He was grinning, knowing he had surprised her. He was resplendent in his admiral's coat, his hair tied loosely. But if not for his ruddy tan and broad smile, she would have mistaken him for a retired sailor. His hair was grey through and his right eye had a milky hue. He was thin and the right arm of his uniform was folded on itself and pinned. But his voice was strong.

'Fanny, my dear, my appearance shocks you!' he said, dismayed.

She took him in her arms again, hugging him and kissing his lined face with tears of happiness. 'Come and sit down, my love, put yourself at ease. You are home.' They moved into the parlour and she took off his coat and loosened the stock from his neck. 'Tell me all. How is Josiah? What has happened to your arm?'

'There's plenty of time, since this will be my last port. I am a one-armed, one-eyed sailor who has failed in battle!'

'Thank God for small mercies!' she cried, her lip quivering.

He sat next to her and put his good arm around her. 'I love you, Fanny. You have been the very rock of my existence. All these years at sea, reading your letters, knowing how you miss me and want me to come home. Now it's time to buy that cottage.'

He loves me as much as he did before he went to sea, she thought, and she felt a great load lift from her heart. But all she said was, 'I want nothing more than to spend the rest of my life with you, my darling!'

Suddenly, she noticed he had gone pale and his face was pinched.

'Are you hurting?' he asked, concerned.

He paused and swallowed, his eyes screwed shut. 'The stump is not healed, Fanny, and I have great jolts of pain. My surgeon tells me there is a trapped nerve and only when the thread they used to sew me up is gone will things get better. If it's not released, he is fearful of infection.'

'Come, let me take care of you. Let's go upstairs and I will bathe the wound and, in the morning, we will go to the Bath Hospital and have it dressed.'

Horatio noticed Edmund was still standing looking on anxiously and turned to him. 'Father, you are looking very well. I long to spend time with you.'

Edmund, trembling with pleasure, said. 'Oh, my boy, I am so very, *very* proud of you.'

Horatio gestured to his servant who had carried his sea chest into the house. Together, Horatio and Fanny slowly climbed the stairs, followed by the servant with the luggage.

Fanny's life was completely up-ended. Despite his breezy confidence, Horatio was still very ill. While he maintained he was fine, it was evident he was far from well. His stump needed new bandages every day. He was having difficulty seeing. The doctors prescribed soups and fruit, forbade alcohol and said he must cut back on laudanum as soon as possible. At the hospital, they showed Fanny how to dress the stump. She began to take pleasure in attending him. It made her feel like his wife again. Thankfully, in the week that followed, the pains in his arm were less frequent, his appetite improved and he stopped taking laudanum altogether.

Meanwhile, the news that he was in town spread and Fanny was besieged with invitations. She refused them all. People did not know the Santa Cruz story and Fanny wanted to keep Horatio from being questioned until he was ready. He began to relax and enjoy his leave. He was more talkative, cheerful and loving.

He sent a note to Lord Spencer, First Lord of the Admiralty, requesting a meeting. A carefully worded letter came by return, which he read aloud to Fanny. It conveyed greetings from the First Lord and the board, and the suggestion that Horatio stay in Bath until he was recovered.

'I will be punished,' he said.

Fanny changed the subject, reasoning he was often given to bouts of pessimism when he thought people were questioning his reputation. She was confident his achievements would win them over. To distract him, Fanny urged Edmund to take him out. They took walks beside the River Avon in the afternoons – father, tall but stooped, and son, shorter and straighter, but with a missing arm. An unlikely pair.

On the evenings Fanny and Horatio were alone, they would talk endlessly. They recalled the best of the Norfolk days and talked at great length about the house they would buy. He insisted it must be in Norfolk, 'the county of the Nelsons and the Walpoles'. He ignored her opinion that Bath had a great deal more to offer. They discussed the politics of the navy and the conduct of the war. Her knowledge of current events startled him. She saw too that his sense of destiny or ambition made the possibility of an early retirement, if he were to be reinstated, unlikely.

At the end of the second precious week, there was unwelcome news – William and Sarah were coming to visit. William's arrival was like the hurricanes that flattened the sugarcane in Nevis. He seemed to take possession of her house and dominate everything. They at least quartered themselves at a hotel but said William's income would not run to the expense. Horatio paid instead.

Soon the campaign for Horatio's assistance began.

'I have decided that a sinecure as a prebendary canon at Canterbury Cathedral will be my next goal but this will depend on your intervention with the Lord Chancellor. I also want you to help me acquire another church to supplement my Hilborough and Brandon Parva livings. I will then have adequate income to send young Horatio to Eton – as would befit your heir when you are ennobled.'

This irritated Fanny, especially as Horatio was moved by his brother's appeal. What was it about the relationship that caused Horatio to encourage him?

'My dear brother, all I am seeking is the good of the Nelson family. And, of course, now I have a male heir to consider as well.'

Horatio thought it over before speaking. 'Strictly speaking, our sister Susannah is older than you, and her son, though younger than your Horatio, may in fact be my heir.'

William cleared his throat. 'If primogeniture were not the established tradition, I would gladly remain at my post in the church, happy that Susannah's family was taking responsibility for the succession – though without the name of Nelson.'

'You know, William, you are right. We must follow precedent. Nevertheless, Susannah's boy could inherit whatever noble title I might leave if your boy Horatio has no heir. And neither of them will have anything if I have to retire from the navy, as seems likely.'

Edmund, who had been sitting quietly, piped up. 'You know, my boys, I just don't understand what this is all about. Could you tell me what we are saying?'

'It's really quite simple, Father,' Horatio explained. 'If, by any chance, I am given another chance and if I am then successful in a future battle. And if, after that, I do well and then the King makes me a peer, William wants to know who will inherit that title from me as I have no descendants. William wants to be that person.'

'My dear Horatio, if I have said anything untoward, I withdraw it. I am interested only in your needs and the family's honour!'

Later, when they were alone, Horatio spoke to Fanny. 'Of course, it's poor Maurice who actually has the best entitlement to succession, being my eldest brother, but he has no child.'

Fanny bit her tongue. What about Josiah? Didn't he count? He was not a Nelson, but Horatio could adopt him. It dawned on her Horatio's pride in his Norfolk family was a force to be reckoned with. All his life he had looked up to the Walpoles and had carried the scar of being a 'poor relation'. His goal was to rise above his origins – perhaps to father a dynasty, even if William was to be the immediate beneficiary.

The thought led her to ask herself whether she would have any role to play in settling her own future if Horatio were to be killed. It was as if the capability she had shown in managing his affairs was of little consequence. She would be a widow at the mercy of executors and lawyers and, worst of all, William Nelson. Even her own legacy might be subject to his control. For the first time, she began to harbour doubts about Horatio's judgement and even his fairness.

And when she thought it through, it became clear to her that while Horatio was doing all he could do to promote Josiah's career in the navy, he was, in the end, *her* boy. She knew she must talk to Horatio about adopting Josiah but, even as she thought this, she knew that she could not confront him now. They had been apart too long and they needed to regain the trust and devotion to each other which had been lost to distance and the length of their separation. It would have to wait a while until the time was right.

CHAPTER THIRTEEN
November 1797

One minute the old man was in bed in Gibraltar, nursing his wounds, and the next minute he shipped out to England on *Seahorse*. There was barely time to say goodbye to him! And who knew if he would return? He looked dreadful as it was: one arm, one working eye, yellow with jaundice and hair grey. In fact, he looked like he was going home to die.

A week after the *Seahorse* sailed, Josiah was ordered to the commander-in-chief's port office in Gibraltar. A warrant officer from personnel said a recommendation had been approved for Lieutenant Nisbet to be appointed to the rank of commander. Josiah was so suffused with happiness that, at first, he missed his new assignment. Then he heard 'the hospital ship, HMS *Dolphin*'. The ... *Dolphin* ... hospital ship – it was a frigate converted to a hospital ward! He'd always assumed his first command would be a sloop where he would learn the ropes and show what he could do. But a hospital ship, full of the sick and of men with addled brains and moored in a backwater? This was not what he'd been working for.

When he told his friends on *Theseus*, they congratulated him on his incredible promotion before bursting into laughter. 'The *Dolphin*!' they'd cried, shaking their heads and guffawing.

There was a farewell dinner in the wardroom of *Theseus*. The midshipmen from Norfolk were grown men now and after dinner they rowed him to the packet boat bound for Cádiz. He was completely alone.

Half a day's sail from Gibraltar was Cádiz, where the British fleet lay offshore, blockading the Spanish naval base. They came alongside the flagship where Josiah met Lord Keith, rear admiral of the Blue and second-in-command to The Earl of St Vincent. Josiah was kept waiting outside his cabin and an hour passed before the door opened and the admiral's secretary ushered him in. He stood at attention waiting for the admiral to read his papers.

'I read that your father, before departing, managed to get another a promotion for you, as well as a command.'

'Yes, your lordship,' replied Josiah.

'I am a reasonable man. This is your first command, so I will not expect much, Nisbet. You will learn how to manage a hospital ship with seventy-five hands, three warrant officers and a lieutenant.

'For a young man of ...' He ruffled through the papers on his desk. 'Good God, seventeen! For a man of seventeen, Nisbet, you will have a lot to learn. The *Dolphin* will be your nursery.' He looked at Josiah over his small spectacles, his lip curling.

Josiah flushed. 'Err, how often would you like me to report, your lordship?'

'I want no dispatches from you, Nisbet – you are the least of my responsibilities. Deal with George MacLeod, the fleet captain for auxiliary vessels. I will hear about you from him and I want to hear good news. Understood?'

Dismissed, he looked for MacLeod's cabin, and found it quite easily. MacLeod was cordial, concerned only that *Dolphin*'s books would balance and fever be kept in check. Towards the end of their meeting, he reached into a locker and pulled something out, smiling. 'I have a present for you, Josiah.' He handed Josiah a package. 'For the cold nights on the windy Tagus river, I recommend a tot of this Scotch. And a wee book.'

'*A System of Naval Tactics*? Do you think I will need that on *Dolphin*?' Josiah asked.

'It's not forever, Josiah. Now get going!'

An hour later, aboard *Bonne Citoyenne*, Josiah and its captain stood side by side on the heeling quarter-deck. The ship was travelling fast, its spanker luffing as they tacked, when Josiah opened the bottle and poured two tots.

'To your health, Captain Retalick.'

'I have the best ship in the navy, Josiah, a corvette that reaches twelve knots in a good breeze. No bull, no admirals, no bloody-minded crew. Only thirty five fellows who would die for me,' the captain replied, raising his glass to Josiah.

'I heard you had a profitable six months,' Josiah enquired.

'We took *Pleuvier*, a French privateer, nine guns and forty-three men, and *Canard*, another privateer, sixteen guns and sixty-four men, before that. We took a couple of Spanish brigs with over 9000 dollars on board a month ago.'

'How much prize money?' Josiah asked.

'We have to share with *Emerald*, who is squadron leader but my take was 10,000 pounds.'

'How I envy you!' said Josiah.

'We were at Cape St Vincent, too, so we shared in prize money there as well. I'll be able to retire when this is over.'

'One day soon I must have command of *Bonne Citoyenne*,' Josiah said to himself.

Mid-morning on the third day, they hauled around a headland and headed into the mouth of the Tagus, Lisbon before them, a tide of pink stone buildings flowing over the hills and, in its midst, golden cupolas, ramparts and noble palaces. All around were the turquoise waters of the harbour. Josiah's heart lifted.

'There she is!' The helmsman pointed ahead to three vessels silhouetted against the sun.

'Which is *Dolphin*?' Josiah asked.

'She's the one in the centre!'

An hour later, *Bonne Citoyenne* lowered her boat and Josiah was rowed to his new ship. There was no sign of life other than a marine sentry amidships, who was watching them warily.

'Ahoy! Captain Nisbet. Permission to come aboard!' Josiah called.

'Ahoy, Captain. Stay away. The ship is quarantined. We have fever,' the sentry called back.

'Is the lieutenant there?' asked Josiah.

'No. Everyone is ashore other than patients and surgeon. Row to the port –you'll find our company at the navy barracks.'

They rowed back in silence.

Josiah found the rest of the company at the barracks at the Portuguese dockyard. Being a commander, he was given a palatial room, which he shared with a Captain Foster from the supply ship, *Dromedary*.

Josiah and his roommate met for dinner later that day. A man in his late forties, hair grizzled with age and a rural English accent that marked him as an officer who had risen from the ranks, Foster was friendly enough. The dinner was cabbage soup, followed by a grilled meat and washed down by the local 'green wine'.

'Tell me about yourself, Nisbet. What are you doing here?'

'I was given *Dolphin* by Earl St Vincent. I am to learn the ropes, according to Lord Keith.'

'You'll have plenty of time to do that. There's nothing happening here. I am only in port loading supplies and then I'm back to Cádiz.'

'What's life like here?'

'There are a few British diplomats, wine merchants and others. They stick pretty much to themselves.'

'What else?' Josiah wanted to know as much as he could.

'This is not Leghorn. It's a Catholic city where locals keep us at armslength. Despite its grand buildings, it's a dirty place. If you have a taste for the low life, there are the brothels and bars to keep you happy.'

'And my Lieutenant, Kent. Do you know him?

'A troublesome man.'

'In what way?'

'Rather not say too much. Disappointed, no connections below decks or above. A loner. Drinks.'

Kent found Josiah the next day. In the transfer of command, he had been acting captain, the previous occupant having died of the fever. Foster was right. There was something strange about him. He was friendly enough, but very reserved, his thin grey hair announcing long years of service. Josiah knew the story well. Like many other lieutenants, Kent's career had ground along at a snail's pace mostly on auxiliary ships like *Dolphin*. What took some men just years to achieve had likely taken Kent decades.

The two men paced the waterfront in Lisbon, discussing *Dolphin*'s seaworthiness, its crew and its officers. Kent seemed to have no difficulty in accepting Josiah. He was beyond ambition.

'Where has *Dolphin* been over the last six months?' Josiah asked him.

'Nowhere. Just here.'

'Wouldn't it make sense to take the ship out to air out the sails and the timbers?'

'I recommended it many times, but your predecessor never wanted to take the trouble. Result is the ship stinks and the crew are idle.'

In due course, they met with the warrant officers,

and the boatswain, gunner, carpenter and surgeon. They were all quiet men who all seemed to have accepted that they could expect nothing better than *Dolphin*.

In the end, it was two full weeks before Josiah could even board *Dolphin*. It took time for the cholera to abate, the victims to recover and the ship to be purged by burning tar and careful scrubbing. When he was on board at last, the first thing he did was to muster the crew on deck where Kent introduced Josiah as the new captain and 'the son of our favourite admiral, Sir Horatio Nelson'.

Josiah searched for any hint of irony and for laughter among the men, but he didn't find it.

'Men,' he addressed them. 'I fought at Cape St Vincent. I was there and after, when we were almost destroyed, you brought bandages and supplies and helped our injured shipmates. It's noble work and I am proud to be your Captain.'

He was brief and unemotional. Recent pay increases had reduced tensions but he had no doubt that in this backwater, on this ship, there would be troublemakers. He would be fair, but he would take their measure and tolerate no insolence. He would have them flogged if necessary.

He could hear a few sniggers at the back. Kent heard them, too. He nodded to the boatswain, who strode to the rear of the group with his truncheon and hit one of the men on the back of his head. The whispers stopped. Josiah looked at Kent and ordered him to dismiss the crew. A sense of utter loneliness swept over him.

Nevertheless, Josiah immediately set about making his mark. He wanted to be a credit to Horatio, above all. Once a week, he took *Dolphin* to sea to air the sails and exercise the crew. He ordered gunnery practice over the protests of the surgeon. Morale improved and his first few weeks went quickly.

But when they were not sailing, the ship was quiet. The waves slapped the hull and the blocks creaked monotonously. There were coughs and groans. Pneumonia and bronchial infections were common. The nights were long. Josiah ate alone, wrote his captain's journal, his reports and letters and read books from his small library. Once a week, he would invite Kent for dinner and once a month he would dine in the gunroom with the other officers.

He sorely missed the companionship of fellow officers. It was his father's way of getting him the seniority that drove every promotion in the navy. If he achieved no more than that, his father would be satisfied.

But after a few weeks, the nightmares began. He was at the battle of Cape St Vincent again and they were blasting the *San José* and the *San Nicolas*. Cannonballs and grape smashed the rigging. Together with his gun crew, Josiah watched a cannonball blow the head off a sailor. The gun was reloaded and the dead man's head was rolled into the hot barrel. It was his old friend Weatherhead. He woke in a sweat. The dream returned again and again.

Then there was an epidemic of diarrhoea. Josiah lay in his bunk retching and running to the head every few minutes. The winter rains arrived and leaks in the caulking allowed streams of water to cascade into the cabin from the deck above. The carpenter was summoned.

'Our best men are assigned to the battleships and frigates. We don't have the skill to caulk the decks,' he told Josiah bluntly.

Josiah stopped shore leave and the seventy-five-man crew all became carpenters. Kent warned him the boatswain was concerned about mutinous language. Josiah ordered his first flogging: ten lashes for an inveterate troublemaker. *Dolphin* lay at her mooring, unhappiness breeding.

To dull his loneliness and the ongoing nightmares, he drank more in the evenings. A few glasses worked well. He could ease the tedium with whiskey.

On his birthday, Foster rowed over from *Dromedary*, which was in port, and invited him to dinner. His note was mysterious. It said he had arranged an evening Josiah would never forget. They met on the quay where Foster hailed a cab and a weary horse carried them up the steep hill.

'You are such a good friend.'

'Listen, your life is dull. We need a bit of fun every now and again.'

The Pink House sat behind high walls and wrought iron gates. Two ancient fig trees in the garden were home to thousands of bats. From the courtyard, a green brass-bound door opened to a high-ceilinged lobby, brightly lit by a crystal chandelier. Beyond was a drawing room and Monica, the mistress of the house. She welcomed them with glasses of Champagne.

Two handsome women served them from dishes brought in by a waiter. Mistress Monica sat at the head of the table directing everything. Party games followed dinner, the wine flowing. Then a quiet suggestive hand beckoned him. He followed, trembling, to a room with a bed and a basin and jug on a chest of drawers. A flickering candle was the only light. The woman undressed him, bathed him and took him to bed. Experienced arms held him and caresses brought him to hot firmness. Then, encouraged by her soft moans, he pounded. She laughed as they lay panting afterwards. He returned to *Dolphin* with Foster, feeling grateful and also that he had passed some sort of test.

A week later, Foster was back again and Josiah attempted to repeat the experience. No Pink House, just a low bar. Cheap drink. He came stumbling up the gangway as the first light crept over the hills.

'This ship stinks!' he yelled, swaying. 'I didn't join the navy for this!'

Kent was at his elbow. 'I have everything in control, sir. Take to your berth and rest.'

'And you, Kenty! Are you going to spend another twenty-five years on this old tub? We go to sea for glory, money or death – not to live life on this shithole.'

'Yes, sir, you are right but this is our duty. Now let me take you to your quarters.' Kent put him to bed with efficiency and gentleness.

One evening not long after, Kent returned to the episode over dinner. 'You must beware giving ammunition to your enemies,' he cautioned Josiah.

'What do you mean?'

'People would like to see you in disgrace and use that to destroy your father. Many senior men hate his success.'

'What have you learned?' Josiah asked.

'Your good friend, Captain Foster, has been the ears and eyes for Lord Keith these last eight months. Little happens here that doesn't get back to Cádiz.'

'You mean, my friend Foster is telling tales about me?' His heart sinking, Josiah tried to quell his panic.

'Foster is not your friend. He is Keith's spy. Your night out on the town, the drinking, the complaints. All gathered and carefully reported to the powers that be.'

Josiah flushed. 'And are you part of this?'

'No, sir,' Kent said firmly. 'I hate Foster. He was my Captain before I joined *Dolphin* and my lack of progress is his making. Would you pass the bottle, sir?'

Time to repent. Time to repair the damage. The crew noticed the change quickly. He cut back on his drinking. He was less hasty in ordering punishment. The doctors began to praise his consideration for the crew.

The ship was now in better order than ever. Kent was given funds to repaint her. As spring turned slowly to summer, the short cruises and the fresh air brought more invalids on deck, eager to live again. The recoveries increased and the changes were noticed in Cádiz.

Yet, even as he was able to come to terms with his loneliness and the temptations to find diversions, Josiah realised that this could not continue for long. He might have gained seniority, but it was a spurious quest. His father had gained promotion by showing courage and by being a leader of men and through battle. It was now clear to Josiah that he must take matters into his own hands.

To Admiral Lord Keith, Cádiz
From Commander Josiah Nisbet, Dolphin

Dear Sir,

I am writing to you to beg your indulgence. I have now served as Captain of the Dolphin for nine months. During this time, I have done a great deal to improve morale and to ensure that Dolphin is now in a fit state to serve the fleet in battle condition. I draw your attention to the fact that my experience in the fleet has always been in the capacity of someone who is most capable of fighting. May I strongly recommend Lieutenant Kent, a fine seaman and officer who has served on Dolphin and like ships for over thirty years, be considered to supersede me? I am willing to take an inferior position so long as I'm posted to a fighting ship. I look forward to seeing my father again soon as I hear he is returning to the Mediterranean command.

I am, sir, sincerely yours,
Josiah Nisbet, Commander, Royal Navy

CHAPTER FOURTEEN
October 1797

The house in New Bond Street which Fanny had rented for their stay in London was comfortable, as well as fashionable. She loved its tall windows, swathed in brocaded grey silk, its splendid Indian carpets which covered every floor and the mantelpiece which was crowned by a huge mirror framed in gold leaf. She had climbed another rung on the social ladder.

London made her nervous. Her instinct was to retreat to Bath. Horatio was with her, and he had connections, of course, but she had no close friends and few acquaintances. The grand people who ran everything – parliament, the City, the salons and the court – surrounded her. She would meet them all soon enough though, she supposed, as everybody wanted to meet Horatio. How would she manage? Self-doubt undermined her but she forced herself to remember she had once occupied a position of some prestige in far-off Nevis.

Marsh, the solicitor, with whom she had exchanged weekly letters for years, and Horatio's prize agent Davison were available to her if anything was needed. Davison had a magnificent home in Berkeley Square, where she and Horatio dined frequently. Davison had connections in the City and made sure the merchants knew about the rising young admiral. Horatio was also keen to develop their relationships with the Hoods, the Howes and the Elliots. They were friends with connections to both the Admiralty and parliament. Above all, Horatio was ambitious for Fanny to meet Lord Spencer's formidable wife, Lavinia, who was a cousin of the Duchess of Devonshire and a prominent arbiter in society.

Horatio was daily attended by Michael Jefferson, the surgeon and friend who had treated his eye injury in Corsica years before. This relieved Fanny of those duties and meant Horatio was under constant medical observation. She saw this as a sign that the Admiralty was considering Horatio for active duty.

Nevertheless, from Horatio's viewpoint, his career still hung in a balance. The extent of his responsibility for the disaster at Santa Cruz was not yet decided.

He had taken Lord Hood's advice to engage with the decision-makers at the Admiralty. He would take the matter to anyone who might count in making the decision about his future.

One cold morning, as they were walking along the embankment, their breath freezing in clouds of moisture, wrapped up against the winter chill, Fanny with her winter bonnet and Horatio bareheaded and wearing tweed, Horatio surprised Fanny by a sudden change of subject in the conversation.

'Fanny, about that cottage,' he said.

'My dream house?' she responded, smiling whimsically.

'Tell me about it. It's time to buy it.'

'We have talked about it for years, Horatio. Are you serious?'

'Desperately serious.'

'I have been planning our retirement and hunting for houses for ages,' Fanny began. 'I was thinking originally of being near your sister Catherine in Hampshire – it's an easy commute to Portsmouth and London with good roads and a pretty part of the Home Counties. Then you said you wanted to be near your old home in Norfolk, so I started looking there when I visited Izzy. Recently I was told about a house in Suffolk – a day's drive from Norfolk and London and by the sea. There is a community of retired admirals and officers living nearby in Ipswich and the prices in that part of the country are reasonable.'

'Let's go to visit! I want a decision before anything else happens to me. I want you settled, Fanny.'

'There's a property called Roundwood House on the market. We could take a look if you like.'

'Santa Cruz has taught me an important lesson, Fanny. Life is unpredictable. We must take it as we find it. And now we are comfortably off. The Lord Mayor of London has asked me to attend Mansion House. A pension of 1000 pounds. That's on top of my admiral's full pay of 1000 and my marine colonelcy of 500 and an award for my injury in the course of duty. It means we have an annual income of 3000 a year in addition to the prize money and your uncle's legacy.'

'What are you saying, husband?'

'Let's get on with buying that cottage!'

They both laughed, comfortable with the idea of preparing for their future together. Fanny was finally persuaded. He cared for her enough to put his money into a decent house, a place where they would put down roots at last.

Then came news of the Battle of Camperdown. The Batavian Republic, installed by the French when they overran Holland, merged Dutch and French fleets and threatened invasion. Admiral Duncan's victory over the fleet was described as the 'greatest naval battle of the war'. Immediately, fear of imminent invasion faded and once again there was an outpouring of joy and relief.

Horatio read the newspaper report to Fanny, grunting in disgust.

'Why is it bad news, dear?' Fanny asked him, noting his displeasure.

'The Santa Cruz disaster will look all the worse!' he said, still poring over the paper.

'I don't think you believe that. There will always be victories and setbacks and successful admirals. Why don't we celebrate with everyone?'

'Listen to this. The paper says there has been a coup d'état in Paris. The moderates are out. The same man I have been fighting in Italy was behind the plot – Bonaparte. He's dangerous.'

'He doesn't sound like a Jacobin,' said Fanny.

'After this, he will have a decisive role in the war.'

'Isn't that good for you? It'll mean peace will be further away!'

～

Despite assurances from his friends that the navy would now need every fighting admiral in the service, Horatio was still feeling doubtful about his future when he decided to call on Sir William Young, a member of the board of Admiralty. It had been

Gilbert Elliot's idea. Young was a swing voter on the board: highly intelligent and a former navy captain. He and Horatio knew each other slightly, having met in France years before.

'Now, whatever you do, be diplomatic,' said Fanny, helping him on with his coat and muffler against a cold and foggy October day.

'Of course I will,' he said.

'And be discreet!'

'I will be the soul of discretion, my love,' he replied, kissing her softly on the cheek before taking his leave.

While he was gone, Fanny sat down to write a letter to Izzy. In it, she described her life in London and the on-again off-again situation confronting Horatio. She wrote of her life with Horatio and the fulfilment she now enjoyed. Most important was their increased trust and intimacy and the pleasure he took in her company. She also wrote of her increasing involvement in the social life of London. After finishing Izzy's letter, she wrote to Josiah, comforting him and reassuring him of Horatio's continued interest in his career. His last letter had such a note of despondency, she was determined to cheer him up.

Having completed her letters, Fanny ordered tea and sat down at the piano. She ran through a few scales. The piano was out of tune. As she practised, she thought about Horatio. *He needs to feel at home,* she thought. An idea began to take shape – a surprise Christmas party!

There was a knock on the door. Horatio was back.

'How did it go, dear?' Fanny called out as she walked into the parlour, to find him ineffectually trying to pull off his boots with his one arm.

'I am caught in a political maelstrom between the war party and the peace party. Some people say I am impetuous. They demand I pay.'

'What was Young's advice?' she asked, as she knelt to help him with his boots.

'Continue to lobby the board,' he said, sighing.

'When will it be resolved?'

'There is a meeting at the end of October. We are going to the Middletons' on Friday, aren't we?'

'Yes – that's right.'

'Middleton has a powerful voice. Young advised me to be at my most gracious and charming.'

'What do you mean?' she asked.

'Middleton is an Evangelical, so we will probably hear about their causes – corruption, the House of Lords, the slave trade and godlessness ...' Horatio rolled his eyes.

'Can you manage to keep your opinions to yourself?' she asked him.

Horatio grunted.

After the party, Fanny wrote to Izzy.

It was a most interesting evening. The Middletons were extraordinarily welcoming. I was keeping my fingers crossed that Horatio would keep his temper. William Pitt, the first minister, was the centre of attention. He and Horatio had a long talk. Another guest was William Wilberforce, a wealthy man of quality who represents Yorkshire in parliament. You have probably heard about him as he is leader of the anti-slavery party. I was worried. Horatio has such strong feelings on that topic.

But I thought Mr Wilberforce was witty and most convincing. Horatio told me he was unimpressed, but I think he was charmed by the man's sincerity and hard work for his cause. Horatio always argues the importance of the West Indian sugar trade to Britain – he says it is more important to government revenue than America ever was. But I think of the slaves and the cruelties I saw when I lived there. The trade in slaves must be regulated or abolished. Mr Pitt was quiet, but one could see that he was firmly in favour of abolition. As the evening wore on, his consumption of claret caused him to fall asleep. His head was literally on the tablecloth and he was snoring. Everyone made bright conversation to avoid embarrassment.

I notice that these dinners in London are having an effect on Horatio. He has spent so many years aboard ship in male company and living a lonely captain's life devoid of fraternisation. I think he is beginning to see how important it is to have friends and to be sociable with women as well as men. This is the way things are done in London.

Next week, we are invited by the Elliots to a dinner with Lord Wyndham, the secretary of war. I have to say dinners would be a lot more interesting if ladies did not have to withdraw after the loyal toast. That's when the interesting matters are discussed – and we are left out! I feel better when I am playing the piano for the guests and they see I am a person with talents in my own right rather than just 'the admiral's wife'.

We will return to Bath in late December. I am planning a surprise party for Horatio. He is much better, but the inflammation and pain it causes continues. Surgeon Jefferson is confident the ligature causing all the problems will eventually come away. I cannot wait for that day – when his pain is gone – but I also dread it for, if matters are aligned once more at the Admiralty, he will be back to sea again.

The house in Suffolk was well proportioned and set in a lovely garden. Horatio liked it more than she did. From the drawing room windows, there was a magnificent view of Ipswich and its harbour a few miles away across the fields. But the house was run-down. The shabby furniture and faded curtains made it seem mean and reminiscent of the parsonage. But its smell of horse and dogs, the gun room, a breast armour which had been mounted on the staircase wall and the seasoned oak panelling immediately appealed to Horatio.

He and Fanny explored the garden – it reminded Fanny of Catherine Matcham's Hampshire home. Afterwards, as their carriage took them down the hill, they discussed what each of them liked.

Seeing Fanny had reservations about the condition of the house, Horatio pronounced, 'Fanny, you shall have as much money as you need to turn it into our home. Do what you will!'

They signed the contract and placed a deposit.

Then, everything came together. The wound healed. All Horatio's pain was gone. Then the Admiralty board met. Horatio's lobbying had paid off. The board acquitted Horatio and confirmed he would have a new Mediterranean command. In the following days, his self-confidence bounced back and he became irritable and fault-finding. Fanny realised that ambition was stirring, and he was eager to get back to sea.

In December, they both attended a service of thanksgiving for the three great naval victories of the French war – the Glorious First of June, Cape St Vincent and Camperdown. Fanny and Horatio rented a carriage. The crowds lined the streets to St Paul's Cathedral. The frosty air was free of smoke and fresh blue skies seemed a sign of divine approval. The ensigns of French, Spanish and Dutch ships taken in battle were paraded. The King followed in his golden coach.

Horatio and Fanny were loudly cheered as their open carriage passed slowly through the streets. The mood of the people had changed. They were happy to celebrate victory after months of gloomy foreboding. In his pew at the front of the nave, Horatio pointed out captains from the Mediterranean fleet.

'The best of the captains are still in Gibraltar,' he whispered to Fanny.

As they returned to New Bond Street, Horatio was quiet. Fanny chatted away to him but was unable to draw him out. It was as though he had glimpsed the future. His sense of destiny had always been strong. She knew that occasions like this stirred something in him.

Just before Christmas, they returned to Bath. Lord Spencer had told him to take the rest of his leave and join *Foudroyant* in late February.

'For he's a jolly good feeeelllllowww … And so say all of us!' It was Christmas Eve. Fanny had rented a beautiful terrace in the Circus to accommodate the whole family and celebrate Horatio's recovery. They had been separated for so long. It was the time to bring everyone together. The family, old and young, were all there. She spared no expense. The house was dressed in Christmas bunting, holly and mistletoe. There was a huge tree in the foyer. Dinner was to be served at the traditional old time of one o'clock and there was to be goose, Champagne, figgy pudding, walnuts and vintage clarets. She hired carollers to gather around the tree and sing the moment she and Horatio arrived.

Catherine and George Matcham and their seven children, Susannah and Tom Bolton with their three, William and Sarah with their two, Maurice, Horatio's older bachelor brother, and Suckling, the youngest and now a parson, were all there. There were twenty-three in all.

Horatio was easily deceived. They had first returned to New King Street, where they stayed for a few days. Then it was time. The plot began with a visit to a friend of Fanny's, living in the Circus. When Fanny revealed all, Horatio was dumbfounded. But quickly overcoming his shock, he drank the eggnog and joined in the singing.

When the singers ended with 'Good King Wenceslas', he hoisted his youngest nephew onto his shoulders and carried him into the dining room, singing and laughing. Fanny recalled the time at Montpelier when she had found Horatio on all fours playing with Josiah. She felt a wave of sadness that Josiah was the missing family member. She thought of him, passing the time cheerlessly on his hospital ship. It had been over five years and there was no sign of him returning.

At length, the family gathered and sat down around a great long table covered by a fine damask cloth decorated with sprigs of holly, candles and polished table settings. After dinner, they played parlour games and Fanny played a suite of Christmas music on the piano.

Later, lying in bed together, Fanny caressed Horatio's back, the skin scarred by cutlass wounds. *He has lost so much for his country*, she reflected. But now he was restored to health and his reputation was as strong as ever. If only he would be satisfied.

Aloud she said, 'Horatio, you give me such hope!' But he was asleep.

The family returned home, Fanny relieved at their departure. As good as it was to have family, Fanny was oppressed by their neediness and their demands. Horatio was one of the youngest of the siblings, but he was now the patron of the family. William made every effort possible to get Horatio to write to Lord Loughborough, the Chancellor whom Horatio had met at William Wyndham's house in London. He wanted a letter to support his application for an honorary doctorate at Cambridge.

He'd pressed Horatio, saying, 'After all, it is not so different from the navy where preferment always requires family connection.'

When Fanny had questioned this, Horatio explained, 'I was successful in Josiah's promotions. It's the least I can do for William.'

George Matcham had financial problems. His investments in New South Wales had not produced the expected dividends. He needed a loan. Tom, Susannah's husband, had rented a large acreage in Norfolk for his farm. But he could not afford a proper education for his son. Surely, it made sense to take care of that. And, finally, Horatio gave Suckling, his youngest brother, a decent amount to improve the parsonage at Burnham Thorpe.

Fanny waved goodbye to William and Sarah and heaved a sigh of relief as their carriage rolled out of sight. At last, some privacy. In the weeks afterwards, there was time for walks around Bath, dinners with friends, church, a ticket to the latest Sheridan farce and a Handel concert. Towards the end of February, they returned to London.

On their return, they found an invitation from Lady Spencer for both Horatio and Fanny to come to dinner – remarkable, as Lady Spencer rarely invited wives of her captains and admirals. Fanny was curious why this iron rule had been waived but took it simply as an omen of growing support for Horatio. As she prepared for the dinner, Fanny took extra care to look her best and wore a new dress for the occasion.

Before dinner, the countess spent a few minutes with Fanny, asking her about her background and about Bath. Her graciousness made Fanny feel at ease in the great house and in such company. Noticing how well the two women were getting along, Horatio showed cloying affection to Fanny as if he were trying to show what a good husband he was and how good their marriage was. It was quite out of character and more than a little embarrassing.

Fanny had practised a piece of music for the occasion. And after dinner, on Lady Spencer's new well-tuned piano, she played Bach's 'Italian Concerto' with a fluency, creativity and power that surprised everyone, including herself. Bach's great concerto never failed to captivate her audiences.

~

The end of February came, as Fanny knew it would. As the time approached to say farewell to Horatio, she summoned every ounce of self-control to not betray her feelings. It had been almost six months since

Horatio had appeared at the King Street House full of mischief and love and thinking of retirement. But now he was returning – retirement forgotten – and spoke only of his duty and his destiny. Hardened by the reality of her life, Fanny concentrated on her responsibilities, rather than succumbing to overwhelming sadness. She had to build her house. She had to be here for Josiah – when he returned. She had to deal with Marsh and Davison. She had to maintain their connections in Bath and London. She would survive. She *must* survive.

Roundwood House, Suffolk

My dear Izzy,

Horatio has left for the Portsmouth and, again, I am single. We have bought Roundwood House and I am here with Edmund to renovate it and am to live here until Horatio returns.

In the last five months, I have experienced such joy. Horatio has such vitality and is very gay company. We had such good times together. More recently, we have spent time in London and as the pressures of his career returned, I found that some distance between us also returned. It is often so with couples. The husband becomes immersed in work and is subject to great pressures. I know this and so I have tried to give him room and to forgive his tendency to be demanding and peremptory. He is a generous man and has given a goodly part of his fortune to his family who are short of money and ambitious to enjoy his new status. I sometimes wish he were more generous with me.

I have a feeling that he thinks he can take me for granted. We are a team, he and I, but I feel he forgets that I too need encouragement. Such are men. If only the world were different, and we women had greater say in the important areas of life. It would be better for everyone. Don't you agree?

I plan to visit you soon. In the meantime, keep well and let me know what is happening at Wolterton. I will keep you up to speed with my renovations!

Affectionately,
Fanny

CHAPTER FIFTEEN
March 1798

Josiah paused for breath. His hair was loosely tied, and he was wearing white cotton breeches and a singlet. He was halfway up. Green mosses clung to the boulders and yellow flowers grew amid dust-grey fescue. He stood in the shade of an ancient cork tree.

Far below was *Dolphin*, moored in the emerald Tagus, a toy beside the powerful *Vanguard* whose pennant, fluttering and flittering in the breeze, announced Horatio's presence.

Puffing up the hill behind him, Horatio said, 'Your mother covets more letters. She loves that perfect copperplate of yours. But why write so infrequently when you *know* she likes to hear from you?'

'It's so difficult,' Josiah replied.

'Why?' asked Horatio, joining him in the shade.

'I have not seen her for near five years.'

'So?'

'I can't explain this life.'

They continued up the hill in silence for some time, eventually reaching the summit and slumping on the grass. Distant bells rang across the Tagus. The British ships, anchored in lines, were like crumbs on a green tablecloth.

'This has to be one of the best walks in the world!' Horatio exclaimed.

'Yes, it is. And it is all the better with you!' Josiah turned to his father, smiling widely.

'Son, I am the happiest man in the world to hear that.'

They both sat on the stiff grass – Josiah lay on his back looking up at the white clouds drifting across the morning sky, while Horatio rested his back against a tree. As he listened to Josiah describing his achievements, Horatio remembered the little boy he had been – so dutiful, quiet and serious. Now Josiah was taller than he was. He still had spots and blemishes of puberty, but his face reflected confidence and he was happy to talk. The plan was working.

Josiah finished by telling Horatio of the letter asking to be superseded. Horatio laughed.

'What a nerve! It'll go nowhere. They'll give you another command when they are ready,' he advised.

Seeing the crestfallen look on Josiah's face, he changed tack. 'Josiah, I have something personal to ask.'

'Yes?'

'Before I left England, Fanny asked me to write a new will. I have named you both as joint executors. Naturally, Fanny is the chief beneficiary but you are, too. In the event she dies before I do, you will be my heir. You will be entitled to over 10,000 pounds.'

There was a silence while Josiah digested what Horatio said. 'Father, I am more than content to be your executor, but no more talk about dying. I cannot bear it!'

'Thank you, Josiah.'

There was a warm silence. Horatio was pleased to have the discussion out of the way – now he could enjoy the rest of the day.

Josiah returned to his theme. 'Father, when can I get another ship?'

'Are you sure you are ready for that?'

'*Dolphin* is working well.'

'I was able to get you *Dolphin* because there was an opening for a captain. Everyone is looking for action. I will talk to St Vincent, but I hope you have a good record to support your case.'

'I have done my best, but recently I discovered someone was spying for Admiral Keith and reporting my every move to him.'

'Then I hope and trust that all he had to report was worthy of you.'

'You have helped me get this far. Help me get a decent ship! A ship like *Bonne Citoyenne*. It'll bring credit to you and, if I am in your fleet, prize money.'

Horatio was startled by the gruff tone. Was Josiah hiding something?

'You are a good seaman; no one denies it. Courageous, too. But there is much for you to learn.'

Josiah stood, holding out his hand to help Horatio to his feet. 'I just need the chance,' he said soberly.

They made their way down the hill.

St Vincent's flagship was anchored off Cádiz. He could have stayed in Gibraltar, Horatio thought, as the cutter took him to the flagship. Other admirals would have let the world come to them. Not St Vincent. He liked to demonstrate that everyone had to do their share – he believed in excellence and in taking the war to the enemy. Horatio knew him to be willing to take a risk in battle – and that was partly why he needed Horatio so much. But Horatio also knew that St Vincent's need to dominate at all times and his long memory for slights made him unpopular among the men. He climbed the ladder to the deck. The pipes sounded and he paused to salute. St Vincent was waiting, his uniform thick with gold braid.

'Welcome back, Horatio! Welcome home!' His dark eyes gleamed and his craggy face split into a smile.

They walked to the great cabin of the flagship. The stern windows were open and a salty breeze swirled papers on his desk.

'My spies tell me you have been dining with the great and the good in London,' St Vincent said.

'Our friend Gilbert Elliot took care of me. I was given lessons on manners by my dear wife and did not let you down.'

'London seems elegant, but it's a pit of ambition and self-promotion – with the exception of Gilbert and one or two others. Perhaps Spencer, too.'

'Every conversation was about Camperdown. Our victory has been discounted. Duncan is the champion!' Horatio said, a bitter tang to his words.

'Yes, Duncan stayed the possible invasion. But thanks to Duncan, they have agreed to release the ships I want. How was Fanny?'

'She was steady as a rock. She took charge the moment I arrived. She pampered me, surrounded me with medical experts, insisted I rest and when I was ready, reintroduced me to society in Bath and London. Brilliant and lovely as the day we married. If only we had children, my joy would be complete.'

There was a pause. Neither he nor St Vincent had

children; however good the wife or the marriage, the ultimate gift of an heir was never guaranteed.

'Well and good. I'm glad you are back. I have plans for you. We will soon have enough ships for a powerful squadron – their best ships and my best captains. You will have command. The French have rebuilt their Toulon fleet after we destroyed it in '93 and are up to something. I want you to probe and find out what it is. You will take *Orion* and *Alexander* and a few frigates. When the other ships arrive, I'll send them to you.'

'I am to have command, my lord? What about the others?' Horatio asked.

'Humility does not become you, Horatio!' St Vincent said, chuckling. 'The others are good at blockade and administration. But you like the fight! You have Spencer, Wyndham and even Pitt's support. Don't let me down.'

Their conversation moved on to the captains, the ships, supply and communication. As they were about to part, Horatio made a final intercession. 'I met Josiah in Lisbon on the way here,' he said. 'Can we find him a corvette or a sloop?'

'I am keeping my eye on him, as I do with all my junior commanders. I see the qualities. By all accounts, he is an excellent seaman and very well organised. Writes well. He has a good heart. However, reports also tell me that he is a loner and that he drinks. I'll keep a close eye on him, never you fear.'

Had St Vincent ever been young? Horatio flared with frustration. *Or was he sixty years of age when he was sixteen?* He knew if St Vincent had his own son, he would see things differently. Horatio said, 'He's a good lad. And he needs to take a ship into action.'

'I thought I was doing you a favour by keeping him alive. Fanny can't lose both of you. Now return back to your ship and get to work.' The conversation was over.

The oarsmen rowed steadily into the rising breeze. Horatio was overwhelmed and exultant by the meeting. Then, after the excitement, came doubt. He interrogated himself. Did he still have the touch? Injury and mistakes had made him cautious. Could he win a battle against a mighty French fleet? The barge bumped gently against the hull of *Vanguard*. He bounded up the steps. He would soon find out.

Days turned into weeks as Horatio's small squadron sailed up the Spanish coast towards Toulon. Nearing the city, they captured an enemy sloop and under interrogation its crew revealed that Admiral Brueys had thirteen ships of the line in his fleet. But the news that changed everything was the report that Brueys had 300 troop transports as well. Horatio rapidly calculated that the transports could carry perhaps 50,000 troops and their supplies.

Preparations were under way to sail soon. Napoleon would be in command of the expedition.

Horatio's mind ranged over the forthcoming battle. He could take them with the reinforcements St Vincent promised. Thirteen French battleships versus his fourteen. His heart pounded as he considered destroying an army of 50,000 men. It would be the biggest victory of the war.

But his satisfaction at the prospect of the battle was soon threatened. He was still getting used to the idea of a flag captain commanding his ship. As they sailed along the coast of Catalonia towards the rendezvous, the wind freshened. The seas became a dark shade of green as the sun disappeared. The flurries of wind stirred up whitecaps. *Vanguard* was carrying all her sails, making speed to the prearranged rendezvous.

Pacing the quarterdeck, Horatio saw the crews on *Alexander* and *Orion* on the masts and the yards, taking in topsails and lowering spars. He waited for Berry to give the order, but it took ten minutes until the command was given. He frowned, knowing the ship was carrying too much sail yet not wanting to interfere with Berry's responsibilities.

By the time the topgallant yards were on the deck, he saw that Ball and Saumarez had reefed the remaining sails. Their seamanship was commendable, and he made a note to exercise the *Vanguard* crew harder.

A cigar-shaped cloud was approaching rapidly, the squall on its heels. The sea was covered in white-caps. Horatio's heart sank. *Vanguard* was off the wind, plunging and rearing, barrels breaking loose and seas smashing over the bow and sluicing the decks. The crew double-lashed the guns while others worked desperately to take in sail.

'Captain Berry, I am taking command. Lighten the ship. Dump the fresh water and stores, animals and whatever! Prepare to throw the guns overboard!'

'Yes, sir.' Berry was relieved.

Horatio called out to the first lieutenant, 'Call out all the crew, sir! Send extra men to take in sail as fast as possible! Your best men!'

Bells rang through the ship. The masts were now whipping back and forth. *Damn it!* The rigging was slack. Now he would pay the price.

With a crack of shattered timber, the main topmast broke. The crew were taking in the sails as it fell. Clinging on to the collapsing canvas and lines, down they came. The mast fell over the side. Two bodies fell, arms flailing. One fell into the sea and was gone. The other fell into a tangle of spars and sail and lay motionless. Seamen swarmed over the ship and converged in the waist, hacking away rigging and tattered sail while seas broke over the main deck.

Another crack and the mizzenmast fell in a heap on the deck, followed within the minute by the foremast and half of the bowsprit. *Vanguard* lost all steerage, rolling and careening in monstrous waves as the howling wind carried her sideways through the surf. A torrential downpour blotted out the ship from the quarterdeck. Spumes of whitewater flew across the decks. Out of control! But Horatio remained calm. He commanded a halyard be taken up the remaining mast to jury rig a sail that would give the helm some steerage, though not an awful lot.

As day turned to night, some semblance of order was restored. But Horatio had no illusion of the peril. They were being driven helter-skelter towards the Sardinian coast. Lightening the ship was a matter of survival. The 4000-ton ship with 500 men and stores and cannon for a long campaign was rolling like a log threatening to capsize. Drinking water barrels were thrown overboard together with crates of food, cattle and guns. The bow anchor was loose, swinging with every roll of the ship and splintering the forepeak. It was too dark to see. He commanded it be cut away and a few seamen, swinging axes, quickly cut through the massive hawser while the ship dipped deep in the marching rollers. Such courage.

The night wore on, the rain adding to the claustrophobic darkness. Horatio would glimpse the other ships only when lightning lit up the seas. He clung to the rigging, letting go from time to time to vomit, his great coat soaked and his hat long since gone. He felt wretched and guilty. He knew they could not survive the battering on the rocks awaiting them.

The wind abated as dawn broke but *Vanguard*, reduced to a hulk, drifted helplessly in the mountainous seas. He saw *Orion* and *Alexander* now and again as they slid to the top of a wave.

There was a brief lull and his heart stopped as he heard the sound of surf on rocks. He gathered his thoughts quickly. Five hundred souls on board. What chance did they have? He caught sight of *Alexander* a mile to the north, tattered sails hoisted, changing course and heading in their direction, signal flags fluttering as they came.

'We will give you a tow, I am coming in to your leeward,' translated the third lieutenant.

Alexander sailed to hailing distance, their yards almost touching. A strong fellow standing on her bowsprit threw a line. The crew ran it forward and pulled in the hawser. Bringing both ships into the wind took time and time was their enemy as they both approached the shore, less than a mile to larboard. They seemed to make no progress. Horatio signalled to Ball to cut them loose so that *Alexander* at least would be saved. The distance narrowed. Then, suddenly, a miracle – the wind backed and *Alexander* slowly clawed her way to sea, taking *Vanguard* with her.

Horatio gave command back to Berry and retired to his cabin, exhausted.

They arrived at San Pietro ten hours later. *Alexander* anchored, *Vanguard* alongside. There was no time to relax. The Sardinians did not welcome them, so the exhausted crew set to work, mindful of the guns guarding the bay. *Orion* cruised defensively between the fort and the anchored ships while the crew of *Alexander*, led by its carpenter, swarmed aboard *Vanguard*. They improvised, cut corners and used every scrap of timber on the three ships. At night, lanterns were rigged so work could continue through to the morning. Meanwhile, *Vanguard* men slept on the decks of *Alexander* and bivouacked on the shore. There was no let-up and within three days, restored masts and rigging rose from the decks of *Vanguard*. It was not pretty – her profile was stumpy – but she was ready to sail. Stores were transferred from the other ships and guns and sails shared between the three.

Saumarez went ashore to meet the commandant of the fort, taking with him an invitation from Horatio to have dinner on *Orion*. The commandant returned with Saumarez, and to his delight the fleet gave him a six-gun salute. Over dinner, Horatio presented a gift: a silver plate bearing the insignia of the *San Josef*. The commandant, touched by Horatio's courtesy, took a risk of French retaliation by sending live cattle and crates of local wine. Horatio was given a nine-gun salute. *Chivalry between warriors still exists*, thought Horatio.

The men crowded into the waist of the ship for a thanksgiving service. Horatio read from the Book of Psalms:

For he spoke and stirred up a tempest
That lifted high the waves.
They mounted up to the heavens and went down to the
depths
In their peril their courage melted away ...
They cried out to the Lord in their trouble and he brought
them out of their distress
He stilled the storm to a whisper; the waves of the sea
were hushed.
They were glad when it grew calm and he guided them to
their desired haven.
Let them give thanks to the Lord for his unfailing love
and his wonderful deeds for men.

He closed the book amid a murmuring of agreement from the assembled men. Then he read the articles of war, doffed his admiral's hat and placed it on the table with his Bible and prayer book.

'Men, we are grateful to almighty God to have

survived one of the greatest storms I have ever experienced. We commit to God's almighty hand our four fellows who perished and we acknowledge the work of all who kept her afloat and our comrades in *Alexander*, whose persistence in getting us a tow, persevering at their own great peril, brought us through these dangers to safe anchorage. We have been united by this perilous experience and we are humbled by coming so close to disaster.'

As he stepped back there was an upwelling of emotion from the men.

'Three cheers for Captain Berry and Admiral Nelson,' shouted the boatswain and the men responded in unison with three great shouts of 'Hurrah, hurrah, hurrah!'.

Later, writing an account for St Vincent, Horatio recalled the three days that almost ended his life. He was frank. He wrote:

It should never have happened. My desire for a faster ship and Berry's slowness brought us to destruction! It was Santa Cruz all over again. Five hundred men could have died from my mistake. I must learn from these lessons.

In the letter to St Vincent, he assigned no blame other than to himself and made positive comments about Berry, who would otherwise be blamed. He wrote compassionately to the father of poor Thomas Meek, the midshipman whom they'd lost overboard. He had been but fourteen, gone before his life at sea had begun. Then he wrote to Fanny confessing his 'unmitigated pride'. It was pride that led him to suggest Berry carry so much sail and it was senseless pride that caused him to wait too long before ordering him to take it in.

CHAPTER SIXTEEN
April 1798

Sir William Hamilton dozed as his carriage clat-
tered through the empty streets of Naples. It was
about one-thirty in the morning. Fires burned and,
in the shadows, slaves fed them with rubbish – a
practice which had been banned a hundred years ago
in London after the Great Fire burned the city to the
ground.

He asked himself again why he and Emma were
still living in Naples. It was time for him to retire.
And it was a job of limited consequence when all was
said and done. A few years ago, London had decided
that his friendship with the Italian King Ferdinand
of Naples and Sicily provided a useful backdoor to
Versailles, Ferdinand's Queen being Maria Carolina,
the sister of Marie Antoinette.

It was useful in the American war. No longer. King Louis and Marie were dead and French Jacobins were rolling up Italy. First Piedmont, then Milan, Mantua and Venice. The Royal Navy had pulled out of Tuscany and quit the Mediterranean. The game was almost up. Yet he was still here, and Emma did not want to return to England. She knew she would never be accepted there. She was too beautiful and too notorious.

A drunk staggered out of the gloom and made for the carriage, hand outstretched. The coachman flicked his whip and he retreated. Poor devils! As they continued through the empty streets, Sir William turned his mind to his vast art collection. A diplomatic career with few demands meant he could spare the time and money it took to build a collection. It had made him a rich man, a very rich man.

He looked at his reflection in the carriage window. His broad white forehead, his thinning hair covered by his wig. Emma said he had 'intelligent eyes'. Perhaps 'cunning' would be a better word. His nose was a little too long and his mouth receded as he lost his teeth. Still, he had his looks. Tonight, there was a nice little thing who had taken a genuine liking to him ... But when the others went upstairs, he stayed with her downstairs, his knowledge of the local dialect making their banter more amusing than any encounter. These parties were a good way of gathering information, but one always paid a price. It was better to drink in moderation and keep one's breeches on.

The following morning, Sir William rose before noon, and bathed and dressed. 'Good morning, my dear,' he murmured to Emma as he entered the drawing room.

She was reclining on a chaise, white cotton dress pulled up to the knees, auburn hair piled and loosely tied. Lovely. 'And how are you this morning, William? Did you get your rocks off last night or can I count on your energy for tonight?' Her accent still needed work.

'Nothing to challenge your ladyship's capabilities in that department. There are enough troubles in this world without contracting the Great Pox. How was your evening?'

'I wrote letters – to Mrs Scott, to ask after sweet Emily. It's been at least two months since I heard anything.' Emily was her bastard child. She must be at least fourteen years now. The poor child had not seen her mother in a decade.

'And how is the Queen?' William asked.

'She was on about the Royal Navy leaving Tuscany. Her Austrian brother has made peace and it worries her,' Emma replied.

'Ah, yes, the Republic of Naples. They say there are many here who would welcome it.'

'Don't joke, William. Do you think we would survive? Rape and pillage would be the order of the day,' Emma chided him.

'Do we have any tourists in town?' asked William, changing the subject.

'We have a dinner tomorrow.'

'It's good to know we are still the leading show on the grand tour. "See that doddering fool, Sir William, and his 'demi-mondaine', the voluptuous Emma. Witness her most charming breasts as she poses in the best seraglio in Europe!"'

'I know you think I am a tart. But I am what I am, and – for your information – I am the best resource you have. And I am good in bed, too.'

'Yes, dear, the best.'

❧

The afternoon of the following day, William was on Vesuvius, drawing. A guide carried a knapsack with fruit, cheese and bread, together with drawing paper and pencils.

He sat on a tuft of lava, sketching and making notes on the volcano. The midwinter sun warmed his back.

'She's getting restless, signor. She is angry,' the guide mused.

He was right. The mountain was beginning to stir. Small tremors. Two hundred yards away, vapour was rising from the rocks.

A huge explosion rocked the ground. His hat fell off. A plume of gas, rock and lava shot into the air. Pumice and rock began to fall. William gathered his papers, pencils and lunch and stuffed them into the haversack. He turned to the guide, but the chap was already a hundred yards away, running for his life. A gush of hot red lava lipped over the crater, and with a turn of speed which surprised him, he thundered down the hill. The lava followed remorselessly, burning everything in its path. He ran until he could go no further and collapsed beside the guide, gasping for breath. They looked at each other, breathing like fish newly caught. They were covered in ash and soot, and sweat ran down their faces. They raced to the carriage, which was, amazingly, still waiting for them.

Back in the city, the carriage nudged through throngs on the streets. A man in a ragged cloak was addressing the crowd.

'What is he saying? I can't hear!' asked William.

''e say Archbishop must release Saint Januarius.'

'Well, why not?'

'Archbishop say Saint Januarius no travel outside saint's day.'

In the calm of his study back at Palazzo Sezza, he

brought out his latest acquisitions. It was his way of recovering. Three magnificent pieces from the third century BC. Silhouettes of dancers and gods … He breathed in the antiquity, the elegance, the everlasting quality of the urns. He would sell them in London for a fortune.

He looked up at Emma's portrait over the fireplace; one of the early paintings by Romney: *The Spinner*. The illusion in the eyes – a sweet, butter-wouldn't-melt-in-my-mouth look. How well the master understood irony!

❧

A week later, and William was at a meeting called by King Ferdinand's first minister to discuss new initiatives against the French. They were in the throne room at the great palace at Caserta – which had been built by Charles III, the King's father, who had transformed the former grey El Escorial of Phillip II in the hills over Madrid into this even greater baroque palace, a place of immense size and style. Sir William loved to attend court at this palace, away from the heat and stink of Naples. Its grandeur made King Ferdinand seem small – he possessed not enough majesty for this most majestic of palaces. Ranged around the great room were the ambassadors to the court of Naples and Sicily. They stood in twos and threes, in formal dress. William, bewigged and in the uniform of the Foreign Service, stood alone.

It was ever thus. A summons to the palace, then a long wait as ridiculous court protocols proceeded. There were a few questions from the ambassadors, usually referred to Acton, the first minister. The outcome was always the same – procrastination or follow a path of least resistance. *This is the nature of autocracy*, William thought.

At last, Acton addressed him. 'His Majesty is most interested in the British victory at Camperdown. Does this mean the French Army will now divert its attention to this part of the world and, if so, will the British Navy re-enter the Mediterranean to support us?'

'Does your question suggest that His Majesty is willing to provide the Royal Navy with access to your port and dockyards?'

Acton translated William's question to the King, and he murmured a reply.

'His Majesty suggests that the Royal Navy occupy Malta.'

William was about to reply when the King stood up. He said something to Acton and, arm in arm with a courtier, sauntered from the room.

In the silence that followed, the Portuguese ambassador took William's arm and asked what the King had said.

'*Adesso bisogna un buono panchiata,*' William repeated. 'May I ask you to translate?'

'I have dined well and now I need a good shit!' the Portuguese ambassador replied.

Acton spoke. 'Gentlemen, I fear we have lost the King's attention. We will postpone any further discussion. In the meantime, His Majesty is hunting the stag tomorrow at Astruni. You are all invited. Please join us at daybreak, suitably attired.'

Acton drew William to the side. 'The Treaty of Campo Formio is dead. It's inevitable. Austria will create a new coalition,' Acton told him.

'Well, are you intending to join it?'

'We are deadlocked. It's the Queen – she is of two minds. Today, she is worried. Our spies tell us there is strong feeling among the middle classes and even the aristocracy that reform is necessary. The Queen sees that as revolutionary. She sees another Bastille in the offing. And who can blame her when her sister was murdered by the French Jacobins?'

'Why not consider a moderate programme of reform?' asked William.

'The Queen is mightily opposed to any sign of weakness.'

'I hope they pay you enough, Sir John,' William said affably. 'I wouldn't want your job. I'll see you in the morning.'

Bowing politely, William left the room and made his way to his carriage. His earlier indifference was overtaken by bitterness. He'd spent more than thirty years – a lifetime – in this backwater, endlessly repeating the same rituals. Insufferable! Last night, Emma had hosted a party for more British grandees: the Duke of Argyle, several elderly single ladies and two young heirs to large English estates. Rich, spoiled and boring! He hated their patronising, pompous chatter. And he knew they only came to meet Emma – the 'tart who became a lady'.

He thought about his cousin, the Duke of Hamilton. Fifty thousand acres in Scotland and 20,000 south of the border. Nothing for William except a job in the Foreign Service and 1000 pounds a year!

The next morning, he felt a little better. He loved spring days when the King was hunting. He put on his riding breeches, together with a cotton shirt and a buff coat. The carriage was waiting at the hotel for the hour's drive to the hunting lodge.

The sun had risen in a clear blue sky. There was a scent of myrtle in the air and the fir trees swayed in the gentle breeze wafting up through the valley from the sea. Carriages were parked at the edge of a large clearing paved in flagstones, where tables and benches had been set for a light breakfast. William had brought his hunter with him, attached to the carriage by a loose rein.

The groom was busy brushing him down and saddling him. His fellow huntsmen – among them the Commodore of the Naples Navy, Prince Caracciolo – stood around a brazier, eating hunks of bread and cheese and drinking a small beer. At last, the huntsmen were led off by the King, who rode a large white mare.

The hunt took them over low hills, along rough tracks and through forest glades. There were glimpses of the ocean below. William rode effortlessly. The clean air, the scenery, the comradeship and the lovely Mediterranean climate were refreshing after the smoke and filthy smells of Naples.

By three in the afternoon, the King was exhausted and the huntsman summoned them home with his horn. The dogs and horses straggled slowly back to the clearing. Servants had prepared game taken earlier. Blue smoke rose in the still air, making patterns in the fading sunlight. The smell of sizzling meat perked his appetite. They ate ravenously, toasting their adventures with red wine. It became a drinking game with the King as master of ceremonies.

'I give you three cheers for our first minister, Sir John, who never got closer than a half mile from the kill!'

To raucous cheers, Sir John drained his wineglass.

'I give three cheers for our brave admiral who fell from his horse!'

More cheers. Prince Caracciolo downed an extra-large glass of wine. The crowd began singing drinking songs.

'And now I will cut some choice pieces of meat for our patient wives and mistresses.'

Amid cheers, the King pulled his shirt over his head and threw it on the ground, revealing a huge belly which hung over his belt. Nearby was a head-height heap of offal, hooves and hornless heads surrounded by swarms of flies. He worked diligently on the resulting carcasses, his steward packing the carved flanks, sirloins and rump steaks into linen bags and distributing them.

The King as butcher-in-chief, thought Sir William. He was appalled by the absolute lack of sophistication, manners and pretension.

Rolling down the hill for the long drive back to Naples, William, tired and tipsy, did not give a damn about Scotland anymore – or anything else. 'Life is meaningless,' he muttered to himself, 'but hunting definitely makes it bearable.'

CHAPTER SEVENTEEN
May 1798

Horatio's three battleships reached the rendezvous off the Spanish coast in midMay. Captain Hardy was there in *Mutine* with St Vincent's orders – and bad news: the French had gone. Toulon harbour was deserted. The fleet and 300 troop transports and thousands of troops had vanished.

St Vincent's promised battleships showed up shortly after, the mighty fourdeckers appearing in line over the horizon, ploughing sturdily through the lumpy green seas a mile apart. *Culloden* was followed by *Goliath*, *Minotaur* and *Zealous* and then another six. Horatio surveyed them with a satisfied feeling that he was now ready. But there was no trace of the frigates that would be his eyes in the search for the French fleet. The storm had blown them hundreds of miles off course. He was irritated beyond measure these junior captains were so derelict in their duty. He feared that their failure would prove devastating in the weeks to come.

Horatio divided his commanders into two groups based on their seniority, and the more experienced group was invited to join his 'Council of War'. The mahogany dining table in his great cabin was covered by a green baize cloth and laid with glasses and silver. Familiar faces appeared one by one. Berry, Ball, Troubridge, Saumarez and then Darby. Ball had saved his life in the storm. Saumarez, the most senior of all, had shown his skills with the commander of the San Pietro fort. He felt close to them. Troubridge was St Vincent's favourite and had been Horatio's right-hand man at Santa Cruz, where his performance had been mixed. Darby was new and untested. Horatio decided then and there he would have no second-in-command.

After pleasantries had been exchanged over glasses of whiskey and plates of bread and goat's cheese, they began their meeting. Horatio looked searchingly at them and in a quiet firm voice opened the proceedings.

'Gentlemen, we must determine which way the French are headed.'

Troubridge spoke up first, with confidence. 'A landing in Ireland must be the focus of their expedition.'

Ball interrupted assertively. 'Camperdown destroyed French capabilities in the Channel.'

'Gentlemen, one at a time ...'

Saumarez detailed the case for an attack on Gibraltar. Darby responded, in his Irish brogue. 'It seems to have a higher probability than Ireland, but they would have to deal with our fleet off Cádiz.'

They agreed the target would need to be big enough to justify such a huge fleet. Horatio listened to what every man had to say, and finally said, 'I experienced the Corsican's brilliance in Toulon in '93 when he outsmarted Hood. But his attempts to invade England have all failed. He wants to achieve the next best thing: to destroy our trade with India. In the last war, the French helped to deprive us of our greatest possession – the American colonies. Today, the survival of India hangs in the balance. The intermediate target for their ambition, their staging post for taking India, must be Egypt.'

There were nods.

'And, gentlemen, time is not on our side if we are to destroy them before they get to Alexandria,' he added. Horatio studied them. St Vincent had spent time weeding out the time-serving and timid. This was the cream of his crop.

And with that, Horatio brought the meeting to a conclusion. 'Now, a toast!' Wine was poured and they all stood, chairs scraping on the wooden deck. 'A willing foe and sea room!'

He ordered the squadron to head for Naples. As they sailed, they rehearsed every aspect of the battle. Horatio scrutinised each ship, marking them for gunnery, seamanship and signalling, and commending or rebuking the captains.

Culloden had brought a batch of letters from Roundwood, where Fanny now lived. She wrote about the work on the house, about the neighbours and about Ipswich society. The letters transported Horatio home. He imagined the clip-clop of the horses as they pulled a carriage up the hill to Roundwood's sweet-scented gardens. He wrote back cheerfully, congratulating her on her work and reporting that all was well. He told her of his plans and that many of his best ideas came to him after dinner when he would sit in the great cabin, stern windows open, looking at the churning wake and the westerly sun sinking into the sea.

Fanny had a brilliant system for keeping track of everything. She had shown him her book of instructions to servants, tradesmen, solicitors, bankers and the like. She had each of them sign off on her copy to show they had received and understood what she wanted! She was a kind soul but, like him, she did not tolerate carelessness or mendacity. She was so much better organised than he was. He decided to take a leaf from her book.

Horatio's 'public order book' enlarged Fanny's idea – it was a paper trail, a way to issue commands and a way for captains to confirm that they had received and understood their orders. He knew his group were the best of captains, but each of them wanted their independence. The order book system would hold them to his strategy without destroying their ability to take initiative. He returned to his plans for the battle. He sketched out ideas to break through and 'roll up' the enemy line by teaming up his ships to outgun and destroy single enemy ships – always at close quarters.

Soon they reached Naples. Vesuvius was glowering and smoking in the orange evening sky. A message from Sir William Hamilton informed Horatio that the pro-French party was now dominant at court and that the British fleet would be denied their port facilities. *Damn him!* thought Horatio, *he's nothing but a timeserving dilettante.'*

He weighed anchor and put to sea again for Sicily, where he would join up with Hardy, who had gone ahead in *Mutine*, the only frigate in the fleet.

When they got there, Hardy provided an update. 'Two days ago we hailed a Genoese from Malta. The French have been there looting and pillaging.

The grand master has been imprisoned. There's a French garrison.'

'What about the fleet?'

'They are on their way east and in a hurry. They have to reach wherever they are going before they run out of supplies,' Hardy said.

'Great news, Hardy. I have the enemy in my sights.'

Thinking he might engage within a few days, Horatio took out his battle plan and went over the details again.

Recollecting this moment later, he saw his urgency had betrayed his better judgement. If he had considered Admiral Brueys's position more dispassionately, he might have calculated that 300 transports, frigates and battleships, weighted with men and material, would move at the speed of the slowest boat.

He had not waited for the frigates. Without their ability to range far and wide, he could see no more than fifty miles on each point of the compass. There was a strong following westerly. Horatio was in Alexandria within a week. There was no enemy fleet.

He summoned his cabinet again. The cordiality of the previous meeting had dissipated. Troubridge started, 'I warned you the French are making for Turkey. What advantage would Egypt offer Napoleon? The Indiamen use the route round the Cape. They never come near that sandy outpost.'

'And why are you so sure they are headed for Turkey?' asked Ball, angry beyond measure.

'We have no damn frigates. We should have waited until they joined us. We are like a fleet of amateurs,' groused Darby.

'Gentlemen, a show of hands whether we pursue them to the Dardanelles?' Horatio asked. A decision was soon made.

The squadron turned north. But the seas from Alexandria to the Bosporus were empty. Supplies began to run low. They had no choice. They turned around and headed back to Sicily to resupply.

The 'great search', as they termed it afterwards, was a nightmare. They were becalmed under the hot summer sun off the Greek coast, tar melting between the planks of decking and the fetid smells of animals, bilges and men living in tight quarters overpowering their senses. As the boatswain remarked in Horatio's earshot, 'It smells like a whorehouse on a hot day.'

Horatio tossed and turned at night, his wakeful mind obsessed with detail, struggling for clues. His irritability mounted. He would accept no failure. He sensed cynicism in the officers and men. There were unspoken grimaces as he passed by. Fights broke out on the lower decks and there were violent arguments in the wardroom. He gave the offending crewmen bloody backs from the cat-o'-nine-tails.

Back in Sicily at last, he restocked and reconsidered. Cattle, ship, pigs and chickens and barrels of red wine were loaded aboard.

Troubridge's temper broke. He turned to Saumarez in a gesture calculated to provoke. 'And what exactly has my friend Saumarez to say now? Empty seas and an untroubled land?'

Horatio decided that it might be best to let passions flow.

'If you are so far-seeing, perhaps you can tell us where they are?' Saumarez countered. 'I counselled a more patient, diligent search. You, sir, are too passionate for your point of view and have little evidence to commend it.'

They glared at each other.

'Gentlemen,' Horatio intervened. 'Let's be brothers and preserve the love that will save us in battle. Shake hands. I command it.'

A silent handshake.

Horatio felt his spirits sink lower and lower. *What a mess I have made of this*, he thought. *Why does God never smile on me?*

The morning after *Vanguard* arrived, there was a knock at the great cabin door. It was the first lieutenant. 'We have stopped a Greek trader and there is information. The French are in Egypt and have been there for weeks!'

Everything now changed. The temperature fell and the wind rose, driving the squadron eastwards at a pace which would have them there in days. Horationow felt only the unquenchable desire for battle. He believed that the French would be in Aboukir Bay, east of Alexandria. The transports and supply vessels would jam Alexandria Port with troops and supplies. Aboukir was nearby, protected, and had room to manoeuvre. He must catch them unprepared. He thought of Santa Cruz. Surprise lost, disaster in its wake. He calculated the right time to arrive. It must be dusk – a night attack. If he arrived too early, the French would have the upper hand.

He made careful calculations based on an earlier survey of the Bay and his plan took shape. He called his captains on board and ran through it. It was risky; he was unsure of the exact depths, but he trusted their seamanship. Without any argument, they signed off on his instructions in his public order book.

He sat and wrote a last letter to Fanny.

My dear,
This may be the last you hear from me. We will be
engaged in battle shortly and if God is gracious, he will
grant me a victory. If not, when you read this, I will be
gone. I leave you with this thought. You have been my
main stay these many years. I love and cherish you as I

did when we first met. I have raised young Josiah to be
a man. He has many of your qualities and will succeed.
And now I must leave you. If anything happens to me,
I have given my will to Marsh. He will contact you
and Josiah. Give my love to my father and my family.

Affectionately yours,
Horatio

He wrote to St Vincent outlining his plan and
confessing that it had been overconfidence that had
led to his earlier mistake. He summoned Berry and
gave him the letters. Berry tried to dissuade him from
sending the letter to St Vincent, but he insisted the
truth be told.

'I have to confess my mistakes as well as accepting
praises for success,' he told Berry, feeling the catharsis
of confession and then apprehension. St Vincent
could use it against him if things went wrong.

His final preparations were carried out efficiently.
He decided to wear his admiral's coat to show
fearlessness to the other commanders. He knelt and
humbly implored God to grant him a glorious victory
or a painless death. At last, he was ready and sat down
for dinner.

They passed Alexandria shortly after. On the
horizon, he could see the masts of the transports and

supply ships moored there. Could they reach Aboukir Bay before the French battle fleet could prepare?

The fresh easterly held, and by late afternoon a shout from the masthead passed on news from *Orion* that the French were indeed in Aboukir Bay. He nodded, confirming that his judgement was correct.

He and the cabinet had examined the anchorage on Ball's French atlas. It had defensive weaknesses. There was only one small island defending and, although the bay was shallow with sandy shoals, there was enough depth. Thank God there were no tides.

The French had the advantage of shallow water between their ships and the land on the west side. This freed their gun crews to concentrate their force on their seaward side. Their port guns would be useless, and their gun crews would be manning only the starboard guns. But Horatio quickly saw weaknesses in their plan.

His fleet would sail into the bay on a reach, parallel to the French line to its east. Then, two by two, his British ships would peel off from the column, anchor by the stern by each French battleship, concentrate fire and destroy the column, ship after ship. The British would work their way down the French line until the whole line was destroyed or captured.

By now, it was a quarter to six and the sun was sinking. They had perhaps two hours more daylight. Horatio signalled the attack.

Horatio watched the first British battleships, their ochre sails plumped by sea breeze and their battle flags fluttering as they bore down on the French line. His heart rose. He saw Foley, in *Goliath* with a better breeze, overtake Hood in *Zealous*. He sent a signal to Sam to give way. Foley then steered between the first French battleship and the shore. There was enough water between the French and the western shore! He waited for the ship to ground on a shoal, but it carried on. He realised the French had anchored too far off the shoals. There was room to pass! Their larboard gun ports were closed as they concentrated everything on their starboard where they believed the attack would come. He slapped his thigh in delight and laughed.

Everything happened slowly. The ships seemed to be coasting along. It was still quiet save for the distant thunder of guns from the leaders. The British ships were moving two by two, straddling their chosen enemy, efficiently taking in sail, anchoring by the stern, swinging around and opening fire. As each pair anchored, they were passed by the British ships following them who added their own fire to those ahead. The symmetry, the seamanship, the self-confidence were impeccable. And it was clear the French were unprepared. He had the advantage of surprise!

Vanguard was moving into the bay, stripped down

and ready for action. The sun was setting. They were close. Suddenly, he was hit. Down he went; everything stars and blazes and numbing darkness. *Thump!* He was looking up at the yards and billowing sails which were slowly returning to focus. He could barely see and knew this was his time to die. Around him, gun crews were firing broadside after broadside into the enemy. The sound, smoke and flame added to his confusion. He hauled himself to his knees, bleeding and then someone lifted him onto a stretcher, and he was carried off. He heard himself insisting he wait his turn, since he was a dead man.

Pain consumed him as the surgeon sewed up the flap of scalp that had been cut loose. The surgeon was saying he would live to see another day and Berry was insisting he be taken to the safety of the orlop deck. It was pitch dark there, but he felt better. Outside, the battle raged. The boom of *Vanguard*'s guns shook the vessel. Occasionally, there was the sound of balls striking the hull amid cries, screams and the ever-present smell of gunpowder and smoke. The laudanum reduced the pain to a dull ache, and he was half conscious. He demanded information in an unfamiliar voice and gave orders until Berry, who had been summoned, told him he was too injured to make any sense. 'Orders are not necessary,' Horatio said groggily. 'It's all in the public order book. The captains know what to do.' At last, he was carried above deck and propped in a chair in the corner where he could listen to Berry issuing commands.

It was pitch dark, the seas oily and black, the scene lit only by flashes from guns and fires burning in the sails and rigging of the battleships. The smell of powder and burning wad hung over the deck. Clouds of smoke from the guns obscured his vision. He was recovering. He was groggy, but he could think. *L'Orient*, the French flagship in the centre of the French line, was towering above nearby *Bellerophon* and blasting her to a hulk with huge broadsides from her four tiers of guns. But now *L'Orient* herself was ablaze, the fire leaping from the deck structures to the masts and rigging in jagged bursts. Clouds of smoke and sparks billowed, and flames spiralled higher and higher as the crew fought the fire. The crew were jumping overboard, their clothes ablaze.

Berry was issuing orders. 'Wet down the ship against the sparks.'

The fire reached *L'Orient*'s magazine and the thunderclap that followed was the greatest explosion Horatio had ever heard. *L'Orient* seemed to leap into the air as it disintegrated – masts, decking, guns and men hurled hundreds of feet. Then there was silence, broken by loud splashes and the patter of debris on *Vanguard*'s decks. Through the smell of burned gunpowder came a faint chorus of applause from British crews. He heard Berry order the ship's pinnace be lowered to take any survivors on board.

Then the guns opened back up and the battle continued into the early morning hours when finally the outcome was clear, with two French ships slipping their moorings and limping away, leaving eleven of their number to surrender.

By dawn, firing had ceased and the last French ship had struck its flag. Only *Gerereaux* and *Guillaume Tell* had escaped. On the British side, there was damage too. *Bellerophon* was very badly damaged. But in general, the losses were comparatively few. Troubridge's *Culloden* spent the whole battle stuck on a sandbank. A mortified Troubridge was given opportunity to salvage some honour by sailing into Alexandria harbour to set the French transports on fire and to blow up the arsenal. The army of 50,000 French was now marooned. Horatio knew it had been the greatest naval victory of the French War.

It was late in the afternoon, two days later. The cool breezes wafted through the stern windows of *Vanguard*'s cabin. The captains, the 'band of brothers' as someone named them, were summoned to dinner. Horatio's head was aching less. But something was wrong. He could ill define it. Every thought sapped his energy and mind, and his mouth struggled to keep abreast of his thoughts. He was triumphant and irritable at the same time.

My dear Fan,

I am writing to reassure you that I am still alive and well. Knowing you worry about me, let me assure you that, despite a blow to my head, I am enjoying the fruit of the greatest victory which God has granted to me. The French are destroyed and that monster, Napoleon, is marooned in Alexandria. I will soon be setting sail for Naples. There I will repair my ships before returning. Josiah joined me a few days ago. He has been given command of a small corvette and is delighted beyond words, though I fear he has earned the anger of St Vincent by his importunity and childish behaviour in Gibraltar. I will write again when I can. At this time, I am savouring this victory and giving thanks to God for my able captains and for circumstances that worked together so splendidly. You and I will now enjoy the reward for all our sacrifices. I am sure that before too long you will be a viscountess, perhaps a countess. I can think of no person who is more deserving of honour.

Yours affectionately,
Horatio.

At the victory celebration, Horatio silently enjoyed the scene. His captains were sharing their stories like young midshipmen. But he was battered and bruised and unable to enter into the fun. He had two black eyes and a bandage wrapped around the wound on his forehead. His head ached.

Darby was tearfully describing the poignant moment of *L'Orient*'s end. 'Admiral Brueys was swept off his feet early on and lost both of his legs. Tourniquets must have been applied because he sat in a chair, directing the battle. Such courage! A carronade from *Bellerophon* swept his deck and cut him in two. Then the flagship exploded!'

With some hesitancy, mischievous Captain Foley said that he had a gift for Horatio. The door to the cabin was flung open and four sailors carried in a coffin.

'It's for you, Admiral. Made up from the timbers of *L'Orient*. A memento mori! Welcome back to life!'

The captains roared.

Horatio smiled. It had been a damn close thing.

CHAPTER EIGHTEEN
May 1798

Josiah's exuberance had faded as he watched *Vanguard* haul anchor, her sails luffing as she gained way and disappeared over the horizon. The weather, which had been bright and warm, changed to heavy rain, blustery winds and scudding clouds. Life on the old hospital ship resumed its routine – keeping the ship clean, making sure the officers were doing their jobs, reviewing the patient log, questioning the surgeon and checking the calculations of the purser.

The captain of the weekly packet boat which delivered the patients to *Dolphin* told him a French fleet had been sighted in Toulon. The news plunged him into gloom.

The repetitive entries in his daily log were a constant reminder that he ought to be with Horatio, ranging the Mediterranean in pursuit. If only he had not requested a command! Horatio's patronage had given him the promotions wanted but now he would willingly have settled for a junior position on the flagship. And he knew too that winning Horatio's approval for further advancement was doubly difficult.

He decided to take matters into his own hands. There was no point in writing complaining letters. His letter to Admiral Keith asking for a change of command had been ignored. He had to get an audience with the person who might help: the commander-in-chief of the Mediterranean fleet, St Vincent. But such a meeting could take months to arrange.

He had accumulated considerable leave over the years and decided to go to Gibraltar. Approval granted, he rewrote his letter of resignation, packed his bag and said farewell to his few friends, leaving Lieutenant Kent as acting commander. On a windy day in early May, his eighteenth birthday, he arrived in Gibraltar and took a room at the naval base. Then he walked up the hill to the admiral's house to request a meeting.

Despite his low expectation of success, he was none-theless disappointed. The admiral's chief of staff icily refused to convey his request to St Vincent at all and suggested he speak to his own commander. His heart sank. Surely the great man would see Horatio's son?

As he walked back down the hill, glimpsing the admiral's great house at the bend in the road, he felt the sting of his contempt.

Without prospect of a meeting, it seemed he must return to *Dolphin*. As he procrastinated, a squadron of battleships entered port. Suddenly, Gibraltar was swarming with sailors and officers and became noisy, busy and festive. In the packed officers' mess, Josiah, name-dropping and paying for drinks, learned that the battleships had been detached from the Channel fleet to join Horatio's squadron off Toulon.

The news drove him into a frenzy. He approached the admiral's office again, but the fleet soon departed leaving him behind. Then more ships arrived – frigates this time. In the officers' mess, they told him they had separated from Horatio's three battleships in a great storm. The frigates, having failed to find the squadron at the rendezvous, returned to Gibraltar for orders.

The new arrivals welcomed Josiah to their table when he told them who he was. After dinner, he accompanied the officers into the town. Exhilarated in the company, he drank too much sweet Portuguese wine. When the captains left, a group of warrant officers arrived with their women. They delivered him back to the base leaving him on the lawn in a drunken coma. He was still there the following morning as a rear admiral arrived for breakfast at the mess.

The following day he was summoned by St Vincent.

He marched up the hill, fearing the worst. And he was not disappointed. St Vincent demanded to know why he should not be sent back to England.

'What in God's name are you doing in Gibraltar, Nesbit? My office tells me you have been badgering them! And now you have been carousing in some of the lowest dives in Gibraltar in the company of warrant officers! One of my admirals finds you asleep on the grass before the officers' mess!' St Vincent berated him sternly.

'Yes, sir. It is true, sir. I tried for a long time to give you this letter requesting that I be superseded on *Dolphin*. I want to be in the fight with the French. By my father's side, like at St Vincent and Santa Cruz. Yes, sir, I was drunk. It started like this–'

St Vincent cut in, his voice trembling with anger. 'I will not listen to your excuses, Nesbit! You have broken every rule in the book. A commissioned officer carousing with warrant officers! It is hard to believe you could breach our rules like this. I will have you know, sir, that I have a mind to court martial you!'

'I did explain my ambitions for a corvette to my father – when he was in Lisbon.'

215

'Why should I show you favour? You are already over-promoted for your years and seniority.'

'Sir, give me a ship, any ship! A sloop is enough and I will show you what I can do. The three frigates in town left my father without eyes and ears. I will get out there and help him find the French!' Josiah pleaded.

'I am not minded to do anything for you, sir,' barked St Vincent, his patience at an end. 'Now clean yourself up and report to the port admiral. You will repay the damage you have done to discipline and honour. I will let you know when and if you have any future.'

'Yes, sir. Here's my letter of supersession.'

'Get out!' roared the admiral.

The punishment was not long coming. He was again summoned by the admiral's chief of staff and was told that until further notice he would be a paper sorter – a junior clerk – in the port admiral's finance office, reporting to the chief purser. The sanction bit hard, but there was no alternative and Josiah accepted the disgrace. But within a month, his new master realised Josiah had more to offer than filing papers and put him in charge of the accounts.

His 'punishment' was educational. The money spent supplying the fleet, repairing ships, chartering vessels and maintaining the port was staggering. He ranged far and wide in headquarters, befriending forgotten petty officers and clerks and learning how they kept the huge fleet afloat and supplied. The logistics were impressive, the organisation immense – and the corruption horrific.

He studied ledgers and journals, casting his eye eagerly over rows of mind-numbing columns. With his logical mind and mathematical aptitude, he absorbed the vast data very quickly. After another three weeks' work, the purser proposed he become a permanent member of the team. Instead, Josiah wrote to St Vincent. This time he knew he would either be on the first boat to England or on a frigate bound for the squadron. It took less than a day to be summoned to the admiral's office.

St Vincent sat behind his great desk and did not stir when Josiah was shown into his office. He was reading Josiah's letter again. St Vincent raised his bushy eyebrows and Josiah saw a flicker of interest in his eyes. A second or two passed and a scowl replaced St Vincent's appraising look.

'Nisbet, I see you have wasted no time learning the affairs of the financial office.'

'Yes, sir, I thought I should write to you–'

St Vincent cut through his prepared speech with a gesture of his hand.

'You are too intelligent for your own good, Nisbet!

The navy does not run on intelligence; it runs on seniority, the articles of war, rum and the lash! I am sure you understand that. Nevertheless, your ruminations on the finances may be of some small interest to the navy board. I will forward it in due course. In the meantime, it would be best to make yourself scarce. If the contents of this letter become widely known, I would not warrant your safety and for that I am responsible to your father.'

'Does this mean that—'

'It means, Nisbet, that you will be leaving Gibraltar with tomorrow morning's tide on the frigate *L'Aigle*, commanded by Captain Tyler. You will take with you the replacement crew of the frigate *Bonne Citoyenne*. If your father agrees, you will join that corvette in Alexandria. I have confidential letters for Admiral Nelson – if you can find him.'

'As what, my lord?'

'As her commander, Nisbet. Now, remove yourself from my office. I trust when I hear of you again, the news will demonstrate that you have learned what it means to be an officer instead of a common seaman!'

'Yes, sir. Thank you, sir.'

'Here are the sealed letters for your father. Under no circumstances let them out of your sight, and if you find yourself in mortal danger, destroy the contents. Understand?'

'Yes, sir. I will endeavour to improve myself.'

The admiral had already turned away and was reading another dispatch. Josiah saluted and backed out of the room.

A strong westerly wind picked up as they left Gibraltar and with topsails and studding sails set, *L'Aigle* flew, reaching twelve knots before the Rock was even misty with distance. Josiah's offer to take a watch was refused, providing him with some time to reflect on his circumstances.

St Vincent's reaction puzzled him. He thought the admiral would be pleased with his detective work and reward him for it, but he was still angry. Yet, he promised a command. It didn't make sense unless … An idea was taking shape that would explain St Vincent's change of heart.

It took just three days to reach Tunis, where they were to pick up news of the squadron. Josiah was walking the deck, watching the city emerge from the morning haze. He idly looked on as the helmsman took his bearing from the ship's master. He looked up into the rigging. There were men aloft, adjusting the billowing sails, and he watched their fluid movements as they trimmed sheets and halyard. The sea was an azure blue, with bright sun glinting on the waves.

Spray drifted across the deck, cooling as it settled on his cheeks.

Josiah lost his balance, staggered and fell. There was a screeching, rending sound and cries of men thrown off their feet. The force of the collision brought the top gallant spars and sails crashing to the deck in a tangle of rigging and torn sail. As he picked himself up, rubbing his torn palms and bruised leg, he heard orders to take in sail and man the pumps. The crew swarmed up the ratlines and within minutes the trees were bare of sail. A hasty conference was called, the master too upset to participate.

'Men, we are on a reef. Stuck fast.'

He will never survive the court martial, thought Josiah, *he's a dead man.* Josiah hastened below to find the pouch of St Vincent's letters to Horatio. By the time he re-emerged, the carpenter was giving his report.

'We have a rock seven yards long on the starboard lower hull next to the keel which has driven through our futtocks. We are in danger of foundering, sir,' he warned.

'Can we repair it if we can get her off?' asked the captain.

'I doubt whether the pumps would be up to it, sir.'

Nevertheless, the boats were launched and effort made to tow *L'Aigle* off the rock. The sea water continued to pour in.

They tried to lighten the ship: ballast, guns, supplies and animals all went over the side. But nothing worked.

Josiah spoke up. 'Captain, we have 200 men aboard who can't swim. If *L'Aigle* slides off the rock, they'll drown. Cut down the main mast, so that it falls on the rocks. The men can then work their way along it and from there we will wait for a vessel to give us aid.'

The captain paused, weighing up what Josiah had suggested. Then he issued a terse command. It took hours for 200 men, clinging to guide ropes, to slide along the mast which lay between the stricken vessel and the rock. Drinking water was unloaded into the ship's boats and taken to the small island while two lieutenants went for help in the ship's cutter. By the time dark fell, they were all safe on the rock, the sun setting on a perfect sea. Meanwhile, the ship disintegrated as rising seas pounded her.

A cold and sleepless night on the rocky outcrop followed. But at the break of day, Josiah saw the search for help had succeeded. A large merchantman was standing-to a quarter of a mile away and launching its boats.

Safely back on dry land in Tunis, the men were housed in barracks with the officers at the British consul's house. The trading ship that had brought them to Tunis hastily made its escape. Two days later, they set sail on a merchant vessel quickly leased by the British consul, fearful that the stranded crew might be enslaved. The decks were packed with men and supplies – and everybody was accounted for, except a junior officer and the purser, who'd been left behind to stand surety for payment.

The wind was strong and steady, but the *Buona Ventura* was overloaded and under-powered and moved slowly through the seas, sturdily maintaining only six knots. It was over a thousand sea miles to Alexandria, a week's sail. Slowly, they drew nearer to Alexandria. A rumble of gunfire on the horizon announced that the British squadron was engaged. Josiah could see buildings burning and a chaotic scene as boats of every type tried to escape a cordon drawn around the port. His heart rose. He was in time, but as the day progressed and they drew closer, he saw that this was but a mopping-up operation. He had missed the battle!

They sailed on to Aboukir Bay. The British fleet was there, battered beyond belief. Crews were hard at work on every vessel. There were grotesque holes in the sides of the smoke-blackened ships. Masts were missing and stays hung loose. Bowsprits were shattered. There was only one ship undamaged, and it was off Alexandria firing on the port. A listless exhaustion attended every ship in the squadron. In its centre was *Vanguard* – more damaged than any ship other than *Bellerophon*, which was little more than a hulk. Horatio had been at the heart of the battle.

The trader discharged her passengers to the more seaworthy ships in the squadron. Eventually, Josiah was able to persuade the lieutenant of *Bonne Citoyenne* to lend him a dinghy and he rowed himself the mile or so to *Vanguard* and scrambled up the rope ladder of the four-decker.

The ship was quiet, its crews asleep or working elsewhere. The smell of smoke, gunpowder and corpses mingled and shrouded the skeleton of the flagship.

'I have messages for the admiral,' Josiah told the first man he came across.

He was ushered into Captain Hardy. Like the other officers, he was still in the torn and stained uniform he'd worn in battle.

'Your father is not well, Josiah,' the captain informed him.

'He's injured?'

'Yes. Two days ago, we won a great victory over the French. They are destroyed. Your father was hit on the head by shrapnel. You may go to him.'

Horatio was in stained breeches and was coatless, with his head bandaged and his eyes ringed by great black bruises. He stared at Josiah, and made no effort to embrace him.

'Hello, Josiah,' he managed, his voice quiet and dull, devoid of emotion.

'Father, I missed the battle!' Josiah cried, distressed by the state of Horatio.

'You are alive when so many are dead. Your mother will be grateful.'

'You are injured!'

'Yes, I have a sore head. Captain Tyler told me he was lucky to have you aboard. What have you got for me?'

'Father, you better read the mail. It will explain things.'

Horatio opened the pouch and retrieved the bundle of letters which were sealed and bound with twine. Josiah watched silently as Horatio separated them and read the orders from St Vincent. He put it aside wordlessly. Josiah scanned it quickly. He could see the letter had been overtaken by events. It ordered Horatio to return to Minorca if he was unable to find the French fleet. It recommended Josiah for command of *Bonne Citoyenne*. Josiah put down the letter. Horatio was by then reading a personal note from St Vincent. He put his hand on his brow, as if in pain. Then he wordlessly handed the letter to Josiah.

He is young for his age; ungracious in the extreme. He stayed too long at Lisbon enjoying the fleshpots ashore.

It would be a breach of friendship to conceal that he loves drink and low company; he is ignorant of manners, inattentive and wrongheaded beyond measure. In spite of all this, he is honest and truth-telling, and, I dare say, if you ask him, will agree with every word I have written.

'Well?' Horatio asked when Josiah had finished reading.

'I agree with it, but …'

'But what?'

'I can think of a dozen young commanders who have a good time when they go ashore.'

'But why would Lord St Vincent have offered you a command after this?' enquired Horatio, genuinely confused.

Josiah explained, leaving nothing out.

'You are indeed fortunate not to have been broke. You exposed weakness in the port's administration. Someone has been making a lot of money. That person will never forgive you. You have made a powerful enemy and if you get more you will be beached. It happened to me. It'll happen to you.'

'Not so long as you are for me!'

'I cannot protect you forever, Josiah.'

Horatio was scribbling a letter.

1 September 1798

To Admiral Lord St Vincent,
I am glad to think you are a little mistaken in Josiah.
He is young but I find a great knowledge of the service
in him and none better as to seamanship.

He turned to Josiah, and said, 'You shall have *Bonne Citoyenne* as soon as we reach Naples. Now leave me. I need to rest my broken head.'

CHAPTER NINETEEN
September 1798

In that semi-awake, semi-asleep languor that trav-elling induces, Fanny reflected on recent events. It was only a short time since Horatio had returned to sea, yet so much had happened. Her world had been thrown into confusion. She took out the letter that led to this journey and read it again.

10 September 1798
Spencer House, the Mall, London

My dear Lady Nelson,
I have instructed this message to be delivered to you posthaste. My husband, Spencer, was yesterday informed by Sir Horatio Nelson that the British squadron he commands has won a glorious victory over

the French at Aboukir Bay on the north coast of Egypt. He has marooned the French army there and removed all threat to our Trade and possessions in India and the Mediterranean. He has captured or destroyed eleven ships of the line. I wanted to be the first to let you know this wonderful news and to invite you to come to London to celebrate the victory at Spencer House.

Your servant,
Lavinia Spencer, Countess

As the coach rattled through the streets of Colchester, Fanny's thoughts drifted to the house-warming party she had put on just two nights earlier. Roundwood became possible when Horatio was given the generous pension from the City of London. He had given her an 'open cheque' to do whatever pleased her – though she had suspected his native thrift would reassert itself. She had been correct about that.

She recalled Montpelier on the mountainside above the steaming cane fields of Nevis. It had been shabby when she'd taken it over – redolent of her late aunt's fondness for 'Caribbean colonial'. She was still surprised at her youthful temerity in redecorating the whole house. Her uncle had begged she take the job of first lady and conceded she ought to do whatever was needed.

Men didn't understand how to create an elegant home, she reflected. They see beautiful wallpapers, carpets and furniture household as expenses rather than investments in graceful living for the years to come. Those decisions are best handled by the woman who makes the home.

At least Horatio had not been at Roundwood, injecting his half-formed ideas. She had taken possession in July. It smelt of stale cabbage and mould, and the gardens were overgrown and grass was growing between the cobbles in the yard. There were damp patches on the walls because the roof had leaked. She had wandered the empty house, buyer's remorse eating her. How could they have purchased such a run-down property?

But the driveway to the house wound through picturesque woods and fields. The house was well built, and the public rooms were spacious, with high ceilings and wood panelling. The curve of the staircase was excellent. And, brightening up, she admitted the view was marvellous. When the tide was in and the weather clear, Ipswich glittered on the sunlit estuary. The renovations had taxed her skills and ingenuity but now they were done.

She planned the house-warming party together with Louise Berry, the wife of Horatio's flag captain who lived on the London road. The smell of fresh paint lingered on after the workmen left and she had to leave the windows open all night. The house was garlanded with flowers and the table laid with her finest damask tablecloth and napkins. Crystal wine glasses and silver with the crest of the *San Josef* were produced, elegant reminders of the absent owner.

The guests were a local county family, a retired admiral with his wife, and the rector of St Margaret's. William and Sarah came down from Norfolk to join in, too. Sipping Horatio's best Champagne, the guests circled the sitting room admiring the plasterwork, the elegant curtains and carpets and the latest portrait of Horatio. In the dining room, the Chippendale mahogany chairs and elegant inlaid table were praised.

The food had been magnificent: a mushroom soup was served by Edmund from a huge silver tureen that she'd brought over from Nevis. For the main course, a shoulder of beef was carved and served with vegetables and sauces. Dessert was a flummery in her favourite Wedgwood mould, accompanied by nuts, fruit pies, cream and custard. The company drank quantities of wines from captured French and Spanish ships. It was, quite simply put, 'a triumph' and Fanny realised that whatever social demands were made once Horatio returned, she would handle them easily.

Lady Spencer's carriage met her at the coaching station in Marylebone and took her to Spencer

House. The carriage turned from Piccadilly into St James's Street and the grandly pillared façade came into view, dwarfing its neighbouring townhouses. Her pulse quickened and she gathered herself. The carriage stopped and a liveried footman, step in hand, escorted her into the great house. He handed her over to the housekeeper, who took her to her suite which overlooked St James's Park.

There was a large four-poster bed, warm carpeting and windows decorated with fine curtains and lace. The room had a sweet smell of dried flowers. On the bureau, a letter from Lady Spencer welcomed her and provided an agenda of entertainments which would occupy her week in London.

There was a knock on her door. It was the house-keeper again, stepping in to ensure everything was satisfactory and to then escort her to the parlour, a comfortable room at the back of the house where Lady Spencer was waiting. The countess was the same height as Fanny and was dressed in a white muslin gown, tied beneath the bust, her hair brushed high and held by a golden comb. Her intelligent eyes, devoid of any condescension, shone and she greeted Fanny with a warm embrace.

She spoke in a calm strong voice with a slight but unmistakable Irish brogue. 'My dear Lady Nelson – a very warm welcome to Spencer House! I wanted to be the first to congratulate you on Horatio's marvellous victory. How proud you must be! I could not bear to think of you in Suffolk while the nation rejoiced in London.'

Her voice had a steadiness that made Fanny think how nice it was to be so assured.

'Lady Spencer, I was so very moved by your invitation. To feel the warmth and kindness of someone in your station is overwhelming, especially as I know how busy you are,' Fanny responded graciously.

Lady Spencer went on. 'Dear Fanny – if I may I call you that – there is something else. I know, confidentially, your husband's victory will raise you in rank and social position. It can be very difficult to adjust to these changes, the more so if you are unready for them. So, while you are here, I want to teach you what I know about things such as protocol, dress and such other requirements you may wish to know.'

She accepts me, thought Fanny, with a sense of relief.

In the days that followed, Lavinia did her best to educate Fanny in the ways of London society. Fanny's education and her awareness of how one ought to behave made this enjoyable for both women. One day they talked about court, how to dress for such occasions and how to address the monarch and the family. Then they attended a levee at St James's Palace and a few kind words were exchanged with the King and Queen.

Another day, they visited parliament and the ministry, and Fanny learned more about the strange worlds of the Whig and Tory parties and the Pitt coalition.

There were informal, 'gossipy' discussions about who was who among the leading families. Lavinia's sister-in-law, Georgiana, came in for withering criticism from Lavinia for her morals and her risqué salon. As the week progressed and as her knowledge increased, Fanny was increasingly finding she could shed her natural reserve. She could laugh, exchange confidences and speak plainly. It was liberating for her.

She and Lavinia rode for exercise. Horses were saddled in the stables at Spencer House and together with a groom they followed a path through Green Park to Hyde Park, where they could canter on the King's drive or walk the horses on trails through woods and meadows.

One morning, overtaken by gentlemen friends of Lavinia's, Fanny found herself riding beside a great black hunter ridden by a gentleman. Tipping his hat, he asked if he could ride with her for a while. She was cautious, introducing herself as Fanny Nelson and saying she was on a short visit from Ipswich, while he introduced himself as Phillip Mountjoy, resident of Ireland and visiting friends in London.

The introductions made, they talked about the war, the subject of most conversation in at the time.

Fanny showed a becoming ignorance when the topic of Horatio's victory at the Nile came up. Thankfully, he had not noticed the common surname she shared with him. Their conversation then turned to the bête noire of wealthy persons: Mr Wilberforce and his effort to ban the slave trade. Mountjoy listened attentively when Fanny described her plantation origins and her increasing dislike of slavery. At length, they reached the park gates and said their farewells, Mountjoy exclaiming to Lavinia how enjoyable it was to have a conversation with such an intelligent and beautiful woman.

With a twinkle in her eye, Lavinia asked Fanny if she'd not been quite charmed by such an Irish ruffian and, although Fanny's feelings were moved by the genuine friendliness of the Irishman, she felt guilty. She realised London society was far freer and less 'respectable' than the circles in which she usually moved. But she acknowledged that, although she was aware of her duties as a wife, she was attracted to someone other than Horatio for the first time since they'd been married.

A visit one afternoon from Gilbert Elliot, now Lord Minto, really brought home that there would be a new title to reward the great victory Horatio had won.

'My dear Fanny, those of us who support this government will have an everlasting debt to your husband. His victory, together with Admiral Duncan's last year, has underpinned the government. Everyone from the King to the humblest person takes pride in being members of the English race,' he told her.

'I have to say that my awareness of Horatio's success is so recent that I am still discovering what happened,' Fanny replied. 'I am simply grateful that he survived. That is enough for me. Nevertheless, I am delighted to hear he has done so well.'

'But I am afraid, Fanny, that the King is being difficult about rewarding your husband suitably for his accomplishment,' Elliot warned her.

Fanny's heart sank. 'But how can that be? I am sure that whatever reward there is will match the gratitude I hear expressed.'

'Lord Spencer and I have been meeting with the King to discuss the matter. He still recalls his offer of a baronetcy to Horatio after the battle of Cape St Vincent. Horatio told His Majesty he was a man "too poor to sustain such an honour" and requested he be knighted instead – a lower degree than he could otherwise have acquired.'

'Yes, I recall that,' said Fanny. 'But I don't understand what that has to do with the present situation.'

'Well, my dear, it is complicated. The King is not minded to give Horatio any additional rank but has asked the government to come back with a proposed sum of money to address Horatio's lack of financial resources. I wanted to get a sense from you how he might respond to that? We were thinking of a cash grant of perhaps 20,000 pounds or so.'

Fanny thought quickly. She knew Horatio would want the same as St Vincent and Duncan, at least. His resentment would know no bounds if there were a lack of recognition or an implication that his family were of insufficient quality.

'I am perhaps the wrong person of whom you should ask this question, Gilbert, since I have no personal ambition except that he might return to me in one piece.'

'Fanny, I value your insight, judgement and perspective. I am also aware how this might be perceived by our allies. What I want to know are *your* feelings on the matter.'

Fanny imagined Horatio's incandescent rage at such a slight. 'I know that Horatio is extremely sensitive to the King's opinions about him. He is aware he has not forgiven him for a controversy involving the King's son when he was a captain in the West Indies. I fear it will be a great disappointment if his rank remains the same. Is there nothing that you and Lord Spencer can do?'

'This is within the King's gift. Spencer will be bound to follow the precedent. St Vincent, under whose command Horatio was operating, would be considered the admiral responsible for the victory and therefore entitled to a greater reward. Nevertheless, the public will see the matter very differently. You have convinced me that we must have another audience with the King.'

Fanny breathed a sigh of relief as she bid Elliot goodbye – it wasn't over yet.

The week in London passed quickly. In no time at all it seemed, it was the night of the victory dinner. On the guest list were Lord and Lady Minto and Lord and Lady Hood, who had travelled up from Greenwich for the occasion. The Duke of Clarence, the King's son, whose friendship Horatio and Fanny still treasured, was also to grace the evening. Duncan, now a viscount, the victor of Camperdown, and Lord Howe of the Glorious Fourth of June were also present with their wives. Fanny was treated as the guest of honour. The guests climbed the great marble staircase to be greeted by Lord and Lady Spencer. When they were all present, Lord Spencer linked his arm through Fanny's and escorted the company to the dining room.

Lord Minto winked at her across the long table – a gesture which Fanny hoped meant he had made progress. Fanny wore the gown she and Horatio had purchased late the previous year, along with her very best jewellery. It was a sapphire blue gown with long sleeves and a flattering bodice laced with braid. It matched her blue eyes and suited her pale complexion and dark hair perfectly. Her hair had been washed and set by Lavinia's personal hairdresser. She felt some anxiety at the magnificence of the occasion but steadied herself with the thought that she was representing Horatio.

She mentally compared the dinner with her own open house and was satisfied that her feast was in no way inferior – though to be sure, smaller – and her company of lesser quality. A tinkling on glass and an announcement by Spencer prayed they be upstanding for the loyal toast. Afterwards, they regained their seats and Spencer addressed Fanny, expressing his gratitude for Horatio's heroism and for Fanny's continuing support of him. He reviewed what was known about the battle. It had been a complete annihilation. The guests applauded enthusiastically when he sat down.

Fanny could not help be amazed that this was her Horatio who'd led the squadron to such victory. Six months ago, he'd thought he had no future. Now it seemed as if he had become a god. A god of war. The description of his masterful management of the battle was incredible. She knew he had to prove himself after his reverses. And she knew his implacable hatred of the French meant he would stop at nothing – even death – to destroy them. But despite his success, the description of the carnage filled her with dismay rather than pride.

She inclined her head, acknowledging the toast and

then she and the ladies withdrew. Before cards were taken out and after the men rejoined them, Lavinia tasked Fanny with playing the piano and Fanny, who had practised, obliged by playing the same sonata she had performed for her party in Ipswich just two weeks earlier. It was a bravura performance which demonstrated courage, creativity and power. It was, in a sense, her way of acknowledging the honour bestowed on her and Horatio.

Phillip Mountjoy, the mystery of Fanny's identity solved, insisted on helping turn the pages of the music – even though Fanny knew the piece by heart. As she stood to acknowledge the applause, she guiltily noticed how attractive he looked. She thanked him carefully, shaking his hand, and then moved away, knowing that she must never meet him again.

She left London the next day for Norwich to meet Horatio's family at Wolterton Park. She felt a great debt of gratitude to Lavinia. She had gained a much better knowledge of London society and the court. The behaviour of Mountjoy had reminded her of delicious flirtations of long ago. It was good to feel such a handsome man found her attractive.

Fanny also noticed how things had now changed because of Horatio's fame. For years, she and Horatio had been grateful to be invited to this great house. Now, with such a successful husband and her own house, she felt differently. While her modesty was intact, she felt she was now living at a new level in which Norfolk and Bath were correspondingly less.

She arrived at the great house late in the day, to Izzy eagerly awaiting her. She and Fanny resumed their close friendship without delay. Despite Edmund's presence, William expected to be in command of the family. Fanny ignored him and focused instead on the rest of the family. Her sisters-in-law listened raptly to her description of the work on Roundwood. The men were eager for news of the battle and her visit with the Spencers. William took her aside and talked to her earnestly about her conversation with Lord Minto. She tried to bring him to earth when he talked about Horatio becoming an earl. An unwelcome thought passed her mind, as she knew he would be the heir to any hereditary title.

Despite William's acquisition of another church living, the Matchams' East India Company dividends and the Boltons' now prosperous farm, Roundwood House signalled her own new position. Fanny saw she was viewed as wealthy, titled and very well connected. Only the question of Josiah's status stood in the way of complete happiness.

CHAPTER TWENTY
August 1798

It was five in the afternoon. Beyond the open window, pink roses waved in a sultry breeze. A madonna figurine gazed sightlessly over the rumpled bed. Carlo was in the next room, washing noisily. Emma lay back, her hand idly caressing her thigh.

Carlo – prince, playboy and extraordinary 'swordsman' – was so handsome and sweet and he paid her exquisite attention. She was so satisfied. She laughed at the thought. Carlo returned oiled and combed. He looked at her affectionately.

'Darling, what are you laughing at? It must be very amusing,' he asked, running his eyes over her.

'It was nothing, Carlo, just a passing thought.'

'You look like ripe peach which I have sucked to the stone!'

'Carlo, I would die without you!' she responded breathlessly.

He looked at her pensively and turned to the door. Then he stopped, turned and blew her a kiss. His voice changed as he remembered.

'I cannot make our rendezvous next week, Emma. I am engaged otherwise. I have to inspect a new ship that will be delivered to our navy. Shall we say two weeks? At this place?'

'Yes, my love. Save it for me. I'll see you then.'

'Ciao!'

And he was gone. She lay there for a few more minutes, her mind drifting, the breeze blowing softly on her naked breasts, the roses nodding in the breeze and the sound of voices in the distance.

Her carriage picked her up at a café in the town where she was dropped off by the farmer. Sensible discretion meant she took precautions even though Hamilton's cynical tolerance could be relied on in the last resort. As they navigated through the crowded streets, she thought about her husband.

He had grown old – in a short time. Perhaps his loss of his access to the King troubled him. A year ago, London was in constant touch to pass on messages to King Ferdinand and the Italian prime minister. Now the French party had taken over and he was sidelined. London seemed to have lost interest, and maybe even to have cut him out of diplomatic exchanges. How upsetting it was after all he had done for them over the years. To be treated as a has-been. To feel power fade.

The French had the King of Naples and Sicily where they wanted him. His army was hopeless, incapable of resistance. The aristocracy were currying favour with the French. The French were insinuating themselves with talk of 'reform' and 'time for change'. Hamilton called it self-sabotage.

They had reached Palazzo Sezza. Evening was approaching as the carriage rolled up the driveway to the grand portico. An hour later, washed and dressed, she came down for a supper set for two in the dining room. There was a screen divider to make the room and its high ceiling seem more intimate, but it was still too staid for her taste. They sat at either end of a mahogany dining table, which had had its leaves removed but still separated them by an uncomfortable distance. Around the room were his works of art collected over twenty years: clocks, paintings, bronze busts and Grecian urns. The décor was a mix of styles. She thought of it as a stage – a place for entertaining guests – rather than a home.

People used to flock here: important society people, politicians, diplomats and aristocrats. No longer. Only the river of British travellers on grand tour did not seem to slacken. An evening at Palazzo Sezza was still an important stop in Naples.

The view was unparalleled. There were few views more magnificent in all Naples. In the garden beyond the windows, she could see the climbing branches of orange bougainvillea tinted by the sun going down in the west. Hamilton liked to dine Italian style. Today, there was a pasta followed by veal and accompanied by a fine dry wine from Sicily.

'My dear, how was your day?' he asked her as they ate.

'Nothing special, William. I'd be more interested to know what is happening at the palace.'

'The French party continues in firm ascendency, Emma. Our role is negligible. I gather that should the French ambassador suspect that King Ferdinand was engaging with me, he would be threatened. The ambassador has all the local grandees in attendance who have everything to lose unless they show respect to the French. Fools!'

'And who are they?'

'Savronola, Montepercie and Di Angelos. I was surprised this morning to see your friend Carlo there as well.'

The afternoon's romp flashed across her mind and her heartbeat quickened. Did he know? Did he care? He was so detached, so ponderously involved in his job and his hobbies.

'And Prince Caracciolo, whom you call my friend, what was he up to?'

'I spoke to him and he had a lame excuse.'

'Well, perhaps he was telling the truth – why are you concerned?'

'Court gossip says that he is fucking the wife of the French ambassador,' William said harshly.

'My goodness!' she cried, flushing and struggling to keep her calm. She changed the subject. 'What are your plans to regain your influence at court?'

'I should like you to spend more time with the Queen, Emma. With the King in the hands of the French party, perhaps we would do better to cultivate her. After all, her brother is the Emperor and she's loathed the French since they murdered her sister.'

'And why would she be interested in me?' asked Emma.

'I have noticed that once you set your mind on anything, my dear,' he met her eyes, 'nothing will stop you.' He took a draught of wine and peered at her speculatively.

Could Carlo be playing a double game? she wondered. He had asked her questions about the British Navy, which at the time had seemed innocent enough. She had told him nothing that wasn't common knowledge – hadn't she? She must concentrate next time.

'She loves to gamble, you know,' added William.

'Who?' Emma asked, snapping from her reverie.

'The Queen.'

'And do we have the money for that?' she asked.

'No, I am assuming you will use your brain, drink a little less wine and concentrate on staying even!'

She didn't like his tone. 'I see your angle, William. I will make an appointment tomorrow.'

She was feeling increasingly uncomfortable. He must know about Carlo. Was he setting her up? She knew that there was no way that Carlo would be unfaithful to her. She would have known it if so, and she did not. He couldn't be.

'What else is the latest news?' she tried again.

'I heard today that Sir Horatio is still following the French fleet. A Greek trader came into port and the captain gave me letters from him. They had parlayed with him off the Peloponnese. The Greek told Horatio that the French were in Alexandria. He and the fleet set off immediately.'

'My God! It's happening!' she exclaimed.

'If he wins, our star will rise. They will want us back.'

She changed the subject for the third time. 'Hamilton, we have people coming on Friday night. I am thinking of performing my "Attitudes". What do you think?'

He looked at her pensively. 'You are very good, Emma. You could take Covent Garden by storm.

Your "Attitudes" brings the bordello into the drawing room. No wonder the great and the good visit us. Still, while they are here to see you, I get their inside stories from London which are useful.'

'I am glad to be of service, William. Shall we retire to the drawing room?' She heaved a sigh of relief. His interest in Carlo was fleeting. He was more interested in his job.

It was the third time she had been invited to the Queen's levee. She had approached the Queen's secretary with a proposal that she give the Queen and her ladies-in-waiting English lessons. To her surprise, the Queen was pleased she had found a way to meet informally.

The lessons had gone well. The Queen now refused to speak French and spoke only in Italian or English. Emma's Italian was excellent, and she had an extensive vocabulary and suitable accent. The elocutionary problem was in English pronunciation, but the Queen's knowledge of that language was so limited that it hardly mattered if she dropped her aitches and spoke with more than a trace of Cheshire.

After the lessons, Emma and the Queen and two or three other ladies would accompany the Queen to her boudoir as she changed for dinner. In these intimate moments, there was chance for more private discussion. Emma was cautious but soon realised that the Queen had an open, passionate nature. She liked to unburden herself.

'My dear Emma – may I call you that? I feel we are good friends,' Queen Maria Carolina said.

'Your Majesty, there are times when we must forsake formality for frankness,' Emma replied carefully.

'I agree, my dear Emma. I am very worried by the growing influence of the French in Naples and even in court. We are moving towards revolution. I have heard that my nephew, the dear Dauphin of France, has died of consumption after being kept in appalling conditions in a brutal prison. Poor, poor little orphan boy!' Her shoulders heaved and she shuddered. At last, she dried her tears and went on. 'Emma, placating the French is like keeping a vicious dog at bay by throwing scraps of meat. Soon he will want more and then more. And my dear children. What will become of them?'

'Your Majesty, my husband and I will do whatever we can. After the French party took over the ministry from Sir John, we have been on the outside. But perhaps you and I can talk. We women understand things in a way that the men cannot. Perhaps I can be of help as a go-between.'

'The British and my stupid brother, the Emperor, are no longer the close allies they once were.'

'We British are alone in our battle with the French. But Sir Horatio Nelson, our brave commander in the Mediterranean, is waging war in Egypt. I know the man. He will not fail us. I promise you,' Emma said in earnest.

'You know Sir Nelson personally?' asked the Queen.

'Yes, I do, and I know that he will return in triumph. I will inform him of all we have discussed. I am sure that as a man he will be the first to understand your situation. He will never permit a French revolution in Naples. He hates the French with a passion!'

'Oh, Emma, Emma, I insist you and I become the best of friends! We are at cards at the palace tomorrow with reliable people. Come to dinner. Bring Sir William. We can talk privately.'

'And the King?' Emma asked.

'Don't worry about him. He will agree. You understand?' She gave Emma a cunning wink. 'I'll see you again soon, my dear. Very soon.'

Emma was with Carlo again. Although Sir William had blighted the affair with his story of the French ambassador's wife, Emma was doing her best to forget it. At one point that afternoon, she caught him looking at her.

'Carlo, do you still love me?' she asked him.

'What sort of stupid question is that? How can I not love you?'

'I think you could perform for anyone – like Madame Valois, for example.'

He flushed as he pulled on his coat. 'I see that you have been checking up on me behind my back. Whoever told you this story is a liar and you have believed them.'

'You have been playing with me, Carlo – to discover secrets. Your innocent questions add up to a keen interest in the affairs of Britain and the navy and you are playing with the wife of the enemy ambassador. Are you passing along everything I say to the French?' she demanded to know, though she kept her voice quite light.

'That's enough, Emma! You impugn my honour! Your charms are fading and the tricks you learned in the bordello no longer arouse me. Why not return to that nonentity, your husband, and find your satisfaction with him?' he barked at her.

She was out of the bed in a flash, grabbing a water jug and throwing its contents at him. She followed with a slap that sent him reeling across the floor. Without another word, he stalked out, slamming the door behind him.

A few hours later at Palazzo Sezza, she was still fuming. How insufferable he was! His dishonesty was despicable! She stomped across the garden to the parapet. A warship was approaching, its tattered union flag fluttering from a stumpy mast. It looked as though it might have been damaged in battle. A boat was lowered and the crew pulled on the oars. A solitary figure sat in the stern.

She saw Sir William hastening to greet the figure as soon as he stepped ashore. Emma summoned the butler to make preparations. The carriage arrived at the portico and Sir William and his guest alighted. He introduced himself. Captain Berry, Sir Horatio's flag captain. His buoyant step, the hat held beneath his arm, and the way his hand smoothed his oiled hair all suggested it was good news.

Sir William broke the suspense. 'A most magnificent victory, my dear. Sir Horatio has broken the back of French sea power in the Mediterranean. We are safe!'

She felt her heart melting. *The blessed man has saved us all,* she thought. She held out her arms and embraced Berry as if he were Sir Horatio himself, hugging him to her bosom and laughing loudly with excitement. 'Come, come, Captain Berry! Take your ease. Some Champagne to celebrate this marvellous news!'

Later on that evening, after Captain Berry had returned to his ship and set sail for England, she took the carriage to the Palazzo Spontini. The Queen was waiting in the parlour and Emma was ushered in unceremoniously. Maria Carolina was sitting dressed for bed, candles extinguished and the fire banked, wearing a fine muslin cap over her hair. As the servant closed the door, the Queen stood while Emma curtseyed.

'Oh, Your Majesty, my heart is breaking with joy. I felt I must carry this news to you personally,' Emma said, taking a seat next to the dark fireplace.

'Has your husband seen the King yet?' asked the Queen without guile.

'No, I felt I should come to let Your Majesty know the news unofficially.'

'Tell me, Emma, what is happening?'

Emma felt tears filling her eyes. She flung out her arms out expressively. 'Oh, it is the most wonderful, wonderful news! Sir Horatio has challenged the French fleet and destroyed it in an amazing battle near Alexandria. The French flagship exploded, killing almost a thousand French sailors – including their admiral. Napoleon, the conqueror of Italy, is cut off from France and marooned in Egypt with his army. They have lost their power to make war on you. You and your husband and your dear children are safe!'

The Queen rushed to Emma and gave her a passionate embrace. Then she held Emma at arms-length and asked her, 'And Sir Nelson? When is he coming? We must be ready for him! We must welcome him! Oh, what a man! We must plan a victory celebration. We have a lot to do. But first, we must be rid of the French ambassador and his stooges around my husband. Leave that to me!'

A month later, when Nelson's squadron arrived in Naples Bay, the celebrations were ready. Bunting hung from public buildings, civic officials had their speeches prepared and guests had been invited to a state banquet. The French party at court was dismantled and its leaders in prison. Acton was brought back as prime minister and Palazzo Sezza had been restored to its rightful place as the centre of diplomatic influence. Emma and the Queen were in discussions about a permanent base for Horatio's squadron. The King wanted him in the Council of State. Emma heard no more from Carlo. He had disappeared and rumour had it that his affair with Madame Valois had been discovered and that she had been sent home to Paris.

The ships arrived on a bright day in mid-September, straggling one by one into port and anchoring in lines. Even without a telescope, it was clear the vessels had been fearsomely damaged in battle – patched up, but in need of serious repair. The gaping holes in the flagship, which was missing several gunports, gave it a strange gap-toothed look.

There was a flutter of signal flags and one of the vessels fired a sixteengun salute which was answered by guns at the fort, the smoke drifting lazily across the bay in the afternoon sun.

Horatio was rowed ashore with his captains and when they were all on dry land, they formed up and marched to the official reception on the mole. The King and Queen sat on a dais with Emma and Sir William. A band played martial music. Horatio approached. He was such a small creature. Emma wondered how such a puny man could command such a powerful force. Then he was among them, bowing courteously to the King and Queen and shaking hands with Acton and Hamilton. The crowd cheered. Then he was standing in front of her. Her words tumbled out, unprepared.

'My hero! God sent you to save us all! You have accomplished more than any man since Alexander the Great. Welcome. Most humbly, I bid you welcome!'

With that and with practised timing, Emma fainted, collapsing into his arm. Everyone stood to see what was happening and then Horatio was holding her and calling for smelling salts and fresh water. She recovered.

'Thank you, sir. I am such a weak woman.'

'My God, Lady Hamilton,' he said in his high-pitched, rather squeaky, voice. 'I thought I had another casualty on my conscience!'

He laughed and bowed awkwardly. Then Acton stepped forward and led him to the carriage. It was immediately surrounded by crowds reaching to touch him.

Someone shouted, 'Viva, viva Nelson!'

The crowd took up the cry. 'Viva, viva Nelson!'

The band played. Women standing in windows threw petals. Horatio's officers boarded waiting carriages, followed by Emma and Sir William.

It was glorious, and meticulously executed. The only thing that worried Emma at that moment was Horatio himself. He looked awful. A great wound on his forehead was healing. His eyes were sunk in black rings. His skin was yellowish and his hair lank and grey. Despite the jaunty smile, she could see that he was ill. She would have to nurse him back to health before he could play his new role as the defender of Naples.

CHAPTER TWENTY-ONE
October 1798

Winter was approaching and the winds were stronger and the days shorter. It took nine days to sail to Malta because of the headwind. Horatio looked up to the enormous expanses of ochre sail billowing above him. He could see a pair of midshipmen high in the crow's nest. His broad pennant fluttered from the flagstaff. A new campaign. On port and starboard were *Goliath* and *Audacious* as well as a frigate, a small sloop and two corvettes. *Bonne Citoyenne* was under the command of Josiah.

After the news from the Nile reached Malta, there had been an uprising and the French had retreated to Valletta's vast citadel. After positioning his block-ading ships, Horatio sailed north and dropped anchor in a small harbour. Then he and Josiah hiked towards Valletta to review the situation. He recalled their day on the hills above Lisbon, just six months earlier, and the taking of Bastia. But his optimism soon evaporated. Valletta's sandstone fortifications were massive, with miles of curtain walls and redoubts. It could easily withstand any attack.

Horatio called a council of war with his captains aboard *Vanguard*. Ball was to be military governor, so he was the first to speak. 'All the intelligence I have gained tells me that the French have only 3000 men in a fortress that needs 10,000 soldiers to defend it. I believe they will capitulate before long.'

Hardy chipped in, 'It all depends on how well they are supplied. They have two harbours under their control and we can't prevent every small vessel from slipping in.'

There was a murmur of agreement. This was not the council of war Horatio had expected. The 'band of brothers' were no longer as aggressive. 'Gentlemen,' he said. 'Whatever we do must be expeditious. The longer we wait, the more we deplete supplies and imperil our friends in Naples. Without Naples, we lose our base in the eastern Mediterranean. We must succeed.'

Horatio looked around the cabin. Hardy's eyes were avoiding him. Ball, he could tell, supported his position and the others were waiting. They had nothing to add. Perhaps if Saumarez and Troubridge were here, there would have been a debate, but they were back in Naples.

The squadron patrolled, day and night, wearing back and forth along the rocky coast. It was dangerous, exhausting work, and within a week little *Emerald* ran on the rocks one stormy night. *Bonne Citoyenne* and *Terpsichore* intercepted fleets of small vessels, denying the French supplies. Yet, a parley with the French defenders had given no sign they would surrender.

Horatio chafed at the inactivity. Letters from Naples arrived with dispatches from Troubridge and Saumarez. Emma's letters pleaded. The Queen was nervous. They needed him back.

Horatio paced the deck of *Vanguard* with Hardy beside him. 'This is the very devil. I have received no clear orders from St Vincent.'

'What are the priorities, sir?' asked Hardy.

'Protect Naples is my first priority. Next: capture the Malta garrison; restore Leghorn as a British base; resupply the fleet in Alexandria; help take Minorca. I am stretched.'

'I hesitate to comment, admiral. But if I were in your position, I would not commit myself to Naples. They are incompetent, corrupt and cowardly.'

Horatio fell quiet. Hardy had overstepped his mark. Horatio walked on by himself.

A packet boat arrived with mail. This time it included a packet of letters from Gibraltar and another from London. He looked casually at the seals and his heart rose: there were several from Fanny, another from Minto and a couple from the family – William and Catherine. He retired to his cabin.

My lord, began St Vincent's letter.

Thank God, he thought, his heart rising. *At last, I am a viscount.* He read on. St Vincent was suggesting he move his flag to Minorca. 'But how can I protect Naples from Minorca?' he said aloud, confused. He put the letter aside to read later and picked up a letter from Fanny.

My dear, I am sorry it has come to this, she wrote.

He put down her letter and opened Gilbert Elliot's note. Gilbert had recently been given a title and was now Lord Minto.

My dear Horatio,

Since I have been involved in the discussions around your title, I felt I should be the one to tell you what happened. The Admiralty insisted St Vincent was your commanding officer at the time of the glorious battle of the Nile and therefore must enjoy his proportionate share of the credit ...

The King, recalling your earlier complaint that you could not support the station of baronetcy, was inclined to think that the same pertained to any promotion to the peerage and was, at first, desirous of rewarding your great achievement with a large cash grant.

Knowing how you would feel about this – that it would be akin to a slight or reprimand – I was able to persuade Spencer to go into battle for your cause. The King was prevailed on – with poor grace, I might add – to promote you to the peerage with the rank of baron. Such is the prerogative of Majesty!

The rank of baron ... With Jervis an earldom for Cape St Vincent, and Duncan a viscount for Camperdown ... ? Anger overwhelmed him. A trickle of sweat ran down his neck. He picked up the silver tray, a cup and saucer on it, and hurled it at the door. It struck with a high-pitched ping and shattered pieces fell to the floor.

'Can I help, sir?' It was his servant.

'What does a man have to do to be recognised by this King?' Horatio roared.

'Sir?'

Horatio tore open Fanny's letter and read of her conversation with Minto. He put on his sea coat and boots and strode out to the quarterdeck, boiling.

But Minto's letter had come with a warning.

Horatio, I know this news will make you very unhappy. I urge you to keep quiet and leave these matters to providence and your many friends and admirers in high places. Play the game and you will win next time. I cannot conclude without saying how much help Fanny has been to your cause. No one could do better than she in such a situation and she alone charmed the King into his action.

The following morning, he rang for tea having barely slept a wink, his head aching. The shrapnel wound was better, thanks to Emma's kind attentions, this time the headache caused by his fury. The tea arrived.

Life aboard continued in the distance: shouted orders, bells, the sound of feet on the decks as sails were changed, the lapping of water against the hull, the occasional cry of a seabird. He would never go back to the life he had before. St Vincent was in awe. The great battles of Cape St Vincent and Camperdown paled compared with the Nile. Nothing would change that.

He calmed down and began to think about his situation. Immediately, he had to decide how to balance the competing demands on his resources. Should he withdraw to Minorca and concentrate on the siege of Malta? That would mean leaving a vacuum in the eastern Mediterranean, leaving Naples to the French. Betraying Emma and the Queen just as Naples broke with the French. How could he desert them now? He compared how they treated him with the disgusting parsimony of King George's reward. The reception, the military decorations, the gold pieces for his men, the repairs and supplies for the ships!

Fanny had done her best, but it had not been enough. Gilbert might apologise, but his apology was hollow. The spoils of Horatio's victory had gone to St Vincent and he was given a shilling for his troubles. Well then, he would return to Naples where he had true friends and keep a healthy distance between himself and those who had let him down.

His servant knocked and entered the cabin. 'Can I bring you something to drink, sir?'

'No!' he boomed.

The door closed.

CHAPTER TWENTY-TWO
October 1798

'Pietro's, seven o'clock.'

The puzzled midshipman on *Culloden* took the signal to Captain Thomas Troubridge. 'Sir, I don't have an explanation …' he started.

'My dear fellow, it's the best restaurant in Naples! I'm having dinner with Captain Hardy.'

Later, in his cabin, he dressed for dinner, winding a white silk stock around his neck before donning his dress jacket. He picked up the half-finished letter to his ten-year-old son, Edward, serving on the guard ship *Cambridge* in Plymouth Sound.

My dear boy,
I am deeply sorry for you losing your mama. It is a
tragedy to endure. But we take comfort that she rests

*in the arms of God. For a young man, it is a great loss
and I long to be with you. War threatens Italy and I
am here to defend the Kingdom of Naples. This great
city is the third largest in the whole of Europe and its
people are threatened by brutal French enemies.*

He paused. The ship rocked in the swell. The crew had
finished dinner and he could hear the sound of hands
cleaning up. It was almost too dark in the cabin to
write. He pressed on.

*I have been told I am to get a special medal for the
battle at the Nile and I look forward to showing it
to you.*

Why had he written that? He was one of the band
of brothers, that was true, but the gesture had a bitter
taste for Troubridge – *Culloden* had been on the damn
sandbank when the squadron won its glory.

He sighed deeply and called for his servant. 'Reilly!
I am ready to leave. Tell Lieutenant Green to man the
cutter!'

On the mole an hour later, he waited for Hardy's
barge. The sea was flecked with white and the last
rays of the sun flickered amid the clouds. Men were
lighting the street lamps. He could just make out the
lantern on Hardy's barge as it approached. He idly

kicked pebbles into the foaming water as he waited.

Hardy's barge reached the mole and he stepped ashore. Troubridge held out his hand to greet him, noticing the look of anticipation on Hardy's brave face. *What a confident man he is*, thought Troubridge.

At Pietro's they were met by Colonel Blunt, a gaunt military attaché and a school chum of Troubridge's from St Paul's. The three men made themselves comfortable.

'A bottle of your finest red wine and three glasses, *per favore!*' Hardy said.

'God, how I hate Naples!' said Troubridge. 'It's such a pigsty. Intrigue, corruption and incompetence – but I have to say the food here is incomparable.'

'Naples is our ally,' said Blunt loyally, 'and the only one willing to risk war by its friendship with us at that!'

'Blunt by name and nature,' said Hardy.

'Blunt, I hear that the army is planning to invade the Papal States and Rome. Why are we tweaking the balls of the French?'

'The King believes he has support from the Austrian Emperor – the Queen being his sister makes it a reasonable assumption. Horatio believes if he does nothing, the French will invade anyway. Taking the fight to them will force Austria to back Naples.'

'That is idiotic,' said Troubridge, picking at his ear. 'What happens when the French massacre the rabble army and march on to Naples? Will the Austrians be there or will they be hundreds of miles away?'

'Well, there you have it in a nutshell. A bluff to bring Austria into the war, which, if it fails, may cost Ferdinand his country and his life!'

Bruschetta arrived and for a while there was silence.

'Thomas, why are you so agitated?' Hardy probed.

'I am anxious that Horatio is out of his depth,' he whispered back. 'Encouraging the King to fight the French! We have a creeping commitment to a wretched regime. And for which we have no army, if we are called upon. We are also stretched over a thousand miles of sea.'

'Worse come to worst, we can withdraw to Sicily or Malta or somewhere else and regroup. No need to get so upset about it!' Hardy remonstrated with him.

'Hardy, you are a fine captain, but you know nothing of strategy. Nor does Horatio. Give him a fleet and captains like the band of brothers, and a set piece, yes. But a complicated situation like this? No. He has been beguiled by this ambassador and his wife, by the King and Queen and he is out of his depth. He has no orders to support his actions and London will not thank him if this becomes a shambles!'

Supper was served amid an embarrassed silence and for a time, the piquant pasta with a delicious meat sauce, flavoured with spices and olives, absorbed their attention. The silence continued as the waiter topped up their glasses and left to find another bottle.

Finally, Troubridge spoke again. 'What worries me more is how he has changed.'

'How?' asked Hardy.

'He always loved ranks and titles, while affecting to despise them. Now he is the centre of attention and he expects due deference. He has developed an uncommon love of the showy and the glittery. If it were anyone other than Horatio, you would say the man was becoming a popinjay or worse was going mad!' Troubridge explained.

'Well, give him credit,' reasoned Hardy. 'If anyone is entitled to show his decorations, it is Horatio.'

'He has lost his perspective. Before the Nile, he was always open, always wanted to argue the case. We used to meet around the table in his great cabin and talk endlessly through his plans. Disagree and argue. My God, how we used to argue! But now, he always has the answer and wants no opposition.'

Troubridge noticed Hardy's silence. He looked at Blunt for a moment and then asked. 'And what about Emma Hamilton? I can hardly bear to call the bitch Lady Hamilton ...'

'Careful, the walls have ears. He is besotted.'

'Is he sleeping with her?'

'He'd like to.'

'You know my wife died recently. It sickens me to think a man will indulge a fantasy with a married woman. Better pay the money and visit a clean bordello if you need that sort of comfort.'

'Well, she seems to handle him easily enough!'

They all laughed.

'And what about Sir William?'

'He's been here over twenty years. He's a collector. He finds antiques, works of art and those sorts of things and invests in them. He is very rich. He knows what is happening between his wife and Horatio and it suits him. He wants to keep your fleet here. And, if the time comes when he has to go, he wants a way to escape alive with his possessions. Horatio's loyalty to Naples suits his own interests perfectly.'

A week later, Horatio's war commenced. The Queen said farewell to her husband as he rode at the head of his troops and the column marched north in driving rain. Troubridge followed events from *Culloden* as he and the squadron sailed for Tuscany with Italian troops aboard for a pincer movement. The French retreated, evidently surprised by the plan's audacity and reluctant to bring Austria into the fight.

The council of war was held on board *Vanguard* in Leghorn harbour a few weeks later. To Troubridge,

Horatio appeared sane enough, explaining his strategy and trying to persuade them to support him. But there was no sense of unity. The battle of the Nile was history. Now the same commanders were divided and worried as Horatio presided irritably over the gathering.

'Now that we have Leghorn, we must take full advantage. There are twenty French privateers who have been raiding our shipping and the port is full of Genoese merchantmen supplying the French. We will seize them all.'

'My lord, didn't you just give your word to the Grand Duke that you would leave the operations of the port untouched?'

'I did, but in all goodness, I cannot keep my word on this. We cannot allow these supplies to reach the French and I have to stop the privateers raiding our shipping. I will take the cargoes and let the merchantmen go, but I will take the privateers. Do I have your support?'

Troubridge spoke for the rest. 'I have the gravest doubt that this campaign will achieve its goal. If it ends in embarrassment, breaking an agreement with the Duke will no doubt damage our reputation. Leghorn has always treated the Royal Navy well.'

'And earned plenty of money from us in the process, Troubridge. What about you, Hardy?'

'We must depend on Austria coming into the war,' said Hardy. 'The Tsar has already taken steps to support Naples, but we must be ready with a plan in the event that Naples is lost.'

Horatio's face darkened and the pitch of his voice rose. 'I sense, once again, that I carry the burden alone? Where is that loyalty to each other we once enjoyed? I need your support, gentlemen. The die is already cast.'

Troubridge spoke into the silence that followed. 'My lord, we will loyally support you. But my advice is that you prepare a contingency plan to evacuate the King and Queen. As like as not, they will be executed if the French break through.'

There was a pause and then Horatio said. 'As ever, Troubridge, I can rely on your good sense. I will return to Naples. They will need someone there to help make decisions. And I will make arrangements for the safety of the Royal Family in the unlikely event that the worst happens. Troubridge, you are in command in my absence. You will have Louis on *Minotaur* and *Bonne Citoyenne* and the Portuguese ships. Keep your eye on Josiah. I will see you back in Naples.'

In a matter of weeks, as Troubridge had predicted, the French counterattacked. Troubridge was patrolling the seas between Genoa and Leghorn at the time of the surge, providing supporting fire. For a while, General Naselli held, but when defeat became certain, a Neapolitan squadron supported by Troubridge plucked the troops from Leghorn in the nick of time. Now the French would take their revenge. There had never been any Austrian support. The bluff had been called.

Weeks later, at anchor in the hot sun off Alexandria where Horatio had sent him following the retreat to Naples, Troubridge learned the rest of the story from Josiah, who was conveying the new British envoy to Constantinople. Troubridge summoned him aboard. He seemed older than even a few months before; a tall and handsome young man, his wild hair tamed and conservatively dressed.

'Sit down, sit down,' Troubridge said when he came in.

'I have an apology, sir,' started Josiah.

'What for?'

'When we last met in Leghorn, I was out of line, rude and not a little intoxicated.'

'My recollection is you expressed displeasure about a certain important lady – rather well, I thought.'

Josiah's cheeks lit up. 'When I was in Naples after the Nile, in September last, she was all over me. I fell for it – the flattery, the flirting and teasing, plying me with pleasantries and drink.'

'And then?'

'As soon as she had me under her spell and had convinced my father she had changed me, I realised the whole production was purely to win his gratitude and persuade me she is harmless.'

'What is it between you and Horatio?'

'He has given me all I ever wanted.'

'What do you mean by "all"?' asked Troubridge.

'He has given me promotion – above my rightful expectations, sir.'

'And aren't you grateful?' pressed Troubridge.

'I am but he no longer shows any affection for me. He reserves that for my friends and has only harsh words for me.'

'And the lady in question – Lady Hamilton?'

'It's because of my mother. I care deeply that he is flaunting his affair before the world. He is a laughing-stock, yet when news gets to London about his relationship with another man's wife – with her husband willingly participating – my mother will be devastated. I cannot bear it, sir.'

'Calm down, calm down. I get the picture. Let's have dinner together and you can tell me what has happened since I left Naples,' Troubridge said. 'Reilly!' he called.

His manservant opened the door.

'Get some glasses and set another place for dinner.'

While they ate, Josiah told the story.

'The moment the French counterattack began, the

army in Rome began a fast retreat that quickly turned into a rout. The French troops made short work of them. The King was but a few days ahead of his army as they fell back.'

'And then?'

'After his return to Naples, my father began planning to evacuate to Palermo. The King and Queen, his friends and the Hamiltons and their valuables – works of art, jewels, the treasury bullion and other possessions – were to go and these were loaded onto our ships.'

'How did they escape the mobs?' asked Troubridge.

'Through a secret passage from the palace to the harbour. The Hamiltons accompanied the Royal Family. At an agreed signal, my father and a few officers with pistols and candles entered the palace through the tunnel and escorted the King and Queen – and the others – to the ship.'

'That's amazing! It sounds like a novel,' said Troubridge, setting his fork down in astonishment.

'It actually happened – completely in keeping with my father's sense of the dramatic!' Josiah smiled ruefully.

'And then, they sailed to Palermo? Just like that?'

'Well, not quite,' replied Josiah. 'The fleet full of the great and the good sailed into the biggest storm my father says he'd ever experienced! The Royal Family were in his great cabin, rolling on the floor and vomiting. Must have been a sight! One of the young princes actually died.'

They talked on through the afternoon and evening. Troubridge was taken with the young man. Hitherto, he had seen Josiah as surly or tongue-tied, a boy grown fat on nepotism. He was surprised by his intelligence.

'Tell me about *Bonne Citoyenne*,' Troubridge asked.

Josiah shifted uneasily in his seat. 'Well, I have learned many things,' he said. 'I dare say a young captain will always be treated with suspicion. You know, hated or patronised by his officers and even threatened with violence. The other side of this coin is that he can be very popular if he is a fighter. At first, I had to discipline and flog my troublemakers. Young Hoste on *Mutine* spent his first six months in the same situation. But I have taken more ships than any other commander of my age. You made me return a Genoan merchantman which you said should be treated a neutral – even though he was carrying supplies for the French. Do you remember?'

'I do and at the time I felt like kicking you in the arse for breaking our agreements with the Tuscans.'

'Yes, I was in the wrong,' Josiah admitted.

'Your father must be pleased with your progress, though?' asked Troubridge, though the young captain had already hinted otherwise.

'He has no time for anyone other than his mistress. He seems to have lost his mind,' Josiah said quickly, as if without thought.

'There, sir, I must stop you. There can be no disloyalty on my ship. I am pleased for you, but you must watch what you say about your father. Is that clear?'

'Yes, sir. I'm sorry. I overstepped the mark.'

As the French counterattack drove on through southern Italy, Troubridge returned to Palermo. In Syracuse, pausing to take on stores, he encountered General Stuart bolstering the defences of the city against a possible invasion of Sicily. At the same time, he heard the rumours of a guerilla priest, Fabrizio Ruffo, who'd roused the peasantry of Calabria against the French and formed the Sanfedisti, supposedly an army of the holy faith. By now, the Austrians too had entered the war.

The counterattack by the allies happened surprisingly quickly. Ruffo's men overwhelmed a thinly stretched French army, which fell back to Naples. The Austrians arrived and added to the allied strength. Troubridge was ordered to retake the islands defending Naples Bay and to prepare for the attack on the city. He was tireless in this task, successfully taking over the islands through a combination of diplomacy, threat and assault from the sea. He then ruthlessly rooted out Jacobins, traitors and spies. By June, his ships were threatening the Castel Sant'Elmo fortress in Naples and, together with Ruffo's ragamuffin army, and fresh Russian and Austrian troops, they forced the French to take refuge in forts guarding Naples Bay.

Troubridge surveyed the devastated city and the lines of French captives being marched to prison camps. He knew bitterly that his work would go unnoticed in Britain. He would be known only for his minor role in the battle of Cape St Vincent, for his part in the fiasco at Santa Cruz, for burning the French transports in Alexandria and for the attacks on these little-known islands. Mostly, he would be remembered as the man who missed the greatest battle of all time because his ship was on a sandbank!

Horatio, on the other hand, though sharing the same seniority as him in the navy, seemed to have the luck of the Irish. His failures were admired because of his boldness, and his successes were brilliant, his bumbling diplomacy produced a desired outcome – by accident – and all this while he was publicly conducting an affair with someone else's wife. Insufferable! Troubridge realised his frustration was too much to deal with. He requested leave to return to England.

CHAPTER TWENTY-THREE
April 1799

From the window of her room, Emma could see the old Norman Cathedral with its golden cupola. Tall palms in the courtyard waved in the breeze and orange bougainvillea climbed the whitewashed walls of the palazzo and peeked into her room. Some oleanders in a bowl on the table sweetly perfumed her room. She felt that at last she was home.

The move to Palermo had changed everything. It was a new beginning, with a new promise. Palazzo Sezza was the past. The shade of Sir William's first wife sanctified by her 'exemplary' character was omnipresent at the palazzo. Emma's arrival in Naples as a 'gift' from Greville to the widower Hamilton and the many years she had waited there for him to marry her added to her detestation of the place.

Now Palazzo Pelagrina was her base and Horatio the source of her new power. The Queen was uprooted and diminished – a refugee. She relied on Emma. Stirred by these thoughts, she hopped to her feet and set off to find Sir William.

He was at his desk. He looked up cheerfully.

'My dear, the winter is over. And the spring has come! I have news: Cardinal Ruffo and his peasant crusaders are relieving Naples.'

She felt a wave of relief and excitement.

'We are on the edge of victory. The French are bottled up and Troubridge is besieging the Jacobins in Castellamare.'

'We must tell Horatio!' she cried.

'I've already spoken to him and he says we sail immediately to receive the surrender,' William said.

'I shall write to the Queen this very instant.' She rushed back to her room and wrote a note, pouring out her heart.

Soon they were packed and aboard Horatio's mighty flagship *Foudroyant* for the journey to Naples. As they waited to sail, Emma took stock. It was an amazing turnaround. As recently as two weeks ago, it seemed likely the French would invade Sicily. Morale was rock bottom. The desertion by Carlo to the Jacobin cause had driven the Queen to hysterics. And now everything had changed. Naples would be recovered, and Horatio would be rewarded for his leadership. While her contribution would be known only to those close to the court, there was no doubt as to her achievement. But she must secure her gains. It was time to take the next step.

Horatio opened the door to the great cabin and sat down heavily in his chair, his face lit by the flickering candle. He was dressed in his heavy sea coat.

'Come, let me take your jacket,' Emma said, appearing out of the shadows.

He was tired. His wiry muscularity which had attracted her when she first met him in Naples five years ago was no more. Injuries such as his would usually have repelled her, but he awakened unusual feelings despite them. She knew he was ready. She tugged the blue serge from his shoulders. He had a cotton shirt beneath. He sat down and she massaged his shoulders and neck, her strong fingers seeking for tired muscles and pinched nerves.

He sighed. 'Emma, your ladyship will turn me to an invalid, ever needing your ministrations!'

'No, sir, I just want you to relax.'

'I cannot relax when I am aroused by your beauty and your attentiveness,' he said in a thick voice.

'Well then, we must talk about other things and distract you from your fantasies.' She smiled innocently. 'I have been thinking how we have become

279

a team – you, me and Sir William. You protect us, Sir William deals with the King and I with the Queen. You are the sword, Sir William is the shield and I am the belt that holds us together. We are *tria juncta in uno* – three acting as one.'

'Very nicely put!' Horatio said.

'I never worry as long as you are with us. Remember the great storm after we rescued the Royal Family? I was not seasick. I was not fearful. Because I *knew* the greatest sailor in the world was in charge of my destiny!'

'The truth is that only God commands the weather.'

The door opened again. The ship rolled and Sir William entered unsteadily.

'Sir William! Welcome! Your fair Emma has been massaging my neck to unbend me and prepare me for the trials that await.'

Emma walked to Sir William, put her arms round his neck and kissed him on the lips.

Sir William looked at her uncertainly. There was a silence that lasted too long, and then Sir William seemed to make a decision. 'I am here to talk about your authority to act for King Ferdinand, Horatio. I've spoken with Acton,' he said.

'And what did he say?'

Emma put her hand on William's shoulder. He pushed it away. 'We were discussing your powers.'

'I am a British admiral. I am not able to negotiate for Naples,' Horatio said.

'But that's what the King wants. You have to agree. There's no one else with your experience.'

'I see. What do you think?' Horatio asked him.

'If you agree, you'll have to take instruction from the King and he wants you to take a firm line with anyone who has betrayed him.'

'I don't mind negotiating a surrender,' said Horatio. 'But I'm not going to get involved in revenge killing.'

'It's up to you to decide,' William said simply.

'If you're there with me, you can advise me. If you're willing, I'll do it.'

Hours later, she came to his cabin. He was already abed and she surprised him by entering without knocking. She took the initiative, reaching for him. She moaned salaciously as he hardened. She knew what to do. And it was exciting and dark and satisfying. It didn't last long and when she lay in his embrace, she told him this belonged to both of them. Sir William wanted it too and that aroused excitement in her. She left him sleeping and returned to Sir William's bed.

Sir William had come to terms with the affair and was composed and friendly in the morning. After all, Greville had encouraged her to go to his bed the same way all those years ago.

Horatio was also reassured by Sir William's light-hearted demeanour and willingness to share Emma's attentions with him. A small cloud remained – Fanny. But it seemed less important now.

The pattern established, all three were happy to continue. Sir William stepped back, aware of Emma and Horatio's passion. He kept the cabin next to Horatio's for the sake of public consumption. But now Emma was with Horatio every night. They maintained a patina of restraint during the days when they were with Sir William and he made it his business to reassure them by remaining calm and at times jocular, as if he had settled an estate on a favourite nephew and was enjoying his gratitude. Emma felt deeply grateful and reassured him that her love for him was as strong and abiding as ever.

At length, *Foudroyant* reached Naples. The city was in the throes of a hastily patched peace. But there was tension in the air, and the constant sounds of gunfire and fires burning throughout the city. Horatio and Sir William set off for a meeting with Ruffo. Emma was waiting when they returned, and was displeased to see that Horatio was in a furious temper.

'That damn Ruffo agreed to an armistice and signed a surrender,' he spat, when she enquired how the meeting had gone.

Sir William added, 'These responsibilities were

delegated to Horatio, not to him. To make matters worse, my dear, a junior English captain, Foote, signed the surrender document on behalf of Britain.'

Horatio slammed his fist on the table. 'I will have his guts for garters.'

'The city is in mayhem – old scores settled, houses plundered, people assassinated and British traders threatened. Ruffo and Foote had no choice!' William counselled.

Emma suggested they be patient and at the next meeting Horatio backed away from his threat to repudiate the surrender. Ruffo agreed to impose tougher terms. The Jacobins were to go home or take ship for France. Horatio agreed and a new surrender document was signed. The French troops would be shipped home as soon as prisoner exchanges had been negotiated. The French left their fort.

Letters from Palermo arrived not long after. Acton wrote on behalf of the King. Sir William read the letter aloud to Emma and Horatio.

My dear Hamilton,
I am most concerned to hear that agreements on the surrender of the Jacobins have been finalised without the consent of the King. I urge you to take action to ensure those who are traitors are held for trial. His Majesty is particularly concerned about

former members of armed forces who took the side of the rebels or supported the French in the occupation. Other than in these cases, you may act as you think the circumstances warrant – if necessary with mercy and forgiveness.

Signed, on behalf of His Majesty King of Naples, by Sir John Acton, Minister.

'Listen to this, Horatio!' Emma read from the Queen's letter.

The King has heard Ruffo is pardoning Jacobins. Neither I nor my children can return to Naples. Dearest cousin, insist on behalf of a poor mother. These criminals must be killed. Please ask our dear admiral to see to it!

Maria Carolina

Emma saw Horatio's dilemma: he had agreed to a compromise and the Jacobins had given up their castles. It was a matter of honour. She thought quickly.

'The English honour system does not work here. You must understand that. It is a matter of duty. Send the Jacobins and traitors for execution. Everyone will stand by you!' she said.

Sir William intervened. 'My dear,' he said, 'you must understand there are limits – the law must be respected. We work for the British government. I will support Horatio with the King. Now let's have dinner.'

⁓

They brought Carlo aboard *Foudroyant* still dressed in civilian clothes. He was tattered and dirty, his dark hair plastered to his large head. He looked like a peasant. He was loathsome to her. He had been captured hiding at his mother's house. He stood humbly before Horatio's desk, his ankles shackled with a heavy chain. Emma thought of the last time she had seen him – debonair, bemedalled, confidently flirting with the ladies of the Palermo court.

'We have all the proof we need,' said one of the lawyers, briskly. 'He ordered our ships to fire on the Royal Navy in support of the Jacobins. He is a traitor.'

Horatio regarded the prisoner contemptuously, his face flushed. He turned to the officers crowding into his cabin. 'What man would take up a sword against a great King? He is a dishonour to naval tradition and the brotherhood of all who go to sea! Captain, are the members of your court martial all here? You shall have my great cabin. I will inspect my ship while you decide. You won't need much time for your verdict.'

The captain nodded.

Sam Hood raised his eyebrows in surprise. Horatio turned his back.

Within an hour, a messenger came to say there was a verdict and invited Horatio to hear it pronounced. He and Sam Hood, Troubridge and Emma sat at the rear of the cabin while the president of the court asked the Neapolitan captains for their decision.

Emma translated in a whisper. 'The prisoner Caracciolo is found guilty as charged.'

Caracciolo stood, ashen-faced, to hear his sentence.

'There is one penalty only for treason. You will be put to death by hanging from the yardarm. And may God have mercy on your soul!'

There was a hushed silence.

Caracciolo turned to Horatio, fell on his knees, arms outstretched, voice trembling. 'Have mercy, sir,' he begged. 'As commander acting for the King, I beg for clemency!'

'Get the bastard out of my cabin and hang him!' Horatio responded.

Emma, trying to keep out of his line of sight, wondered if Carlo would now appeal to her. No one would believe anything he said.

'Sir, sir, I beg you. Give me time,' he continued addressing Horatio.

'Within the hour.'

'Please, sir, please! Mercy! If you will kill me, at least give me the firing squad. My noble family. I plead for the firing squad.'

'Get him off my ship!' ordered Horatio.

Emma took Horatio's arm. She noticed grave looks exchanged between Troubridge and Hood.

'Dear admiral, gather yourself, I pray,' she murmured into Horatio's ear. 'Great work has been done and now let the penalty be carried out. I beg you rest and take refreshment.'

With that, she steered him out of the cabin.

A short time later, a salvo from the nearby Neapolitan battleship announced the execution. A solitary figure swung slowly to and fro from the yard.

She felt sick. Those warm afternoons. And those arms, those strong arms ... She gathered herself. Steadied her emotions. 'Thank God the traitor is dead!' she said.

Naples was in ruins and famine threatened, and Palazzo Sezza had not escaped the war. Its walls were riddled with bullet holes, its floors were torn up and its gardens overgrown.

Two weeks later, the King arrived from Palermo. It was a calmer city now, with soldiers patrolling the streets. But the palace had been ransacked, so he chose to stay aboard *Foudroyant*.

It was early in the morning, the sun barely above the

horizon. Breakfast was being prepared and the crew were holystoning the decks, polishing brass and stowing hammocks. Emma stepped out on the quarterdeck.

She watched the King strolling in the waist below, taking in the view of the city. He was studying something in the water. Suddenly, he screamed at the top of his lungs, his fat arms pumping, gasping for breath. The terrifying sound woke up the ship. Emma rushed down the companionway.

'Your Majesty! What's wrong?' Emma said.

'Look, look!' He pointed.

Emma followed the shaking finger and saw the body.

The lieutenant of the watch, Horatio and Emma crowded around the King, quelling his panic. In the water twenty yards from the port rail was a gruesome figure, bobbing in the calm sea. The black plastered hair and skull were unmistakable, the shroud had opened and the head and shoulders protruded. The eyes were gone and part of the nose. But the mouth was set in a grimace; the prince was smiling.

Horatio spoke abruptly. 'Get that thing out of the water. Now!'

He ushered the trembling King to his cabin. Emma followed.

'God has punished me for this crime! The Prince Caracciolo has returned to rebuke me. How could this happen? He came to see me, to let me know I am cursed!' The King sobbed.

Horatio looked at Emma. 'Tell the King that there is an explanation. The shroud came loose. One of the cannonballs must have fallen out and the other found its way to the body's feet and held it upright. The gases took care of the rest.'

'Horatio, I can't tell him that. What I will tell him is that we will give the prince a proper burial. Then his soul will be content and he won't haunt the King.'

'Whatever will calm him down,' said Horatio.

Emma addressed the King in his native dialect, as Horatio left the cabin.

The episode was recounted by Horatio the following day at a meeting of the captains in the great cabin on the *Foudroyant* that Emma and Sir William attended. There was an awed silence.

'I stand by my decision to execute him,' Horatio said.

'How many of the Jacobins have been executed?'

It was Sam Hood.

'As far as I know, we have had 189 executions to date.'

'Sir, I wish to be frank.'

'You can say what you damn well please, Sam. I don't suppose you like what we have done – if your tone is any indication.'

'I was here when we negotiated the surrender of those Jacobins. We guaranteed them safe passage to France and they transferred to the vessels to take them to Toulon. What we have done is break the word of the British Navy, based on which they surrendered. At the very least, if we were going to tear up the agreement, we had the moral responsibility to return them to their fort.'

There was a pregnant silence.

'Do you plan to write a report?' Horatio asked.

'There is no choice. It can't be concealed – though I doubt there will be repercussions. Sir William must also report through diplomatic channels.'

Sir William looked directly at the challenger. 'I have no knowledge of any impropriety whatsoever, young man. And I will take no instruction from you.'

Emma looked at Horatio pointedly. But he turned away contemptuously. 'This meeting is over,' he said irritably, slamming the door after they had gone.

CHAPTER TWENTY-FOUR
March 1800

Minto was waiting in the smoking room, drinking a glass of fine whiskey. An English port would send a man asleep, but a fine Scotch whisky would fire him up, rejuvenate him. He looked at the clock. They were late. His father's words – 'Punctuality is the politeness of Kings' – came to mind.

Minto was in London for a two-week assignment. Normally, he lived in Vienna, where he was the British minister at the court of the Habsburg Emperor. He was home to review developments and to bring requests for financial subsidy to underwrite Austria's war efforts. His mind went back to Vienna. It was such a lovely city, with a cultured people. His English friends couldn't understand, so immersed were they in their parliamentary business, their draughty country houses and fox-hunting. The logs in the fire burned brightly, giving off a pleasant scent of pine. The clock ticked sedately. There was a muted conversation in the vestibule. He sipped his whiskey and sighed contently. It was always such pleasure to be here at White's, in St James's. Everything was so familiar – the oak-panelled walls, the old-fashioned furniture, the oil paintings. The service was deferential and professional. And, with a few exceptions, one was among people whom one could trust. One had known them and their families since school or university.

He drank more whiskey and nodded a greeting to a gentleman as he walked by. The other thing about the club, he noted, was how useful it was for meetings like this. Friends and colleagues gathering for a drink and supper. How much easier it was to agree with one another and be merry in such convivial surroundings. No one would be taking minutes and no one would feel intimidated. A damn fine way of getting things done! And keeping things confidential, too.

A gust of wind rattled the windows and he looked up. His three companions – Grenville, Spencer and Wyndham – had arrived. They were an odd bunch: one fat and rumpled, another tall and lean and the other beautifully dressed and elegant. They handed their coats to the servant.

'Ah, Gilbert. Good to see you!' called Spencer, bowing and taking Minto's proffered hand. Grenville stood back diffidently nodding, while Wyndham shook hands next and then took his seat by the fire.

'I see you are adopting this fashion of handshaking, Gilbert,' Wyndham remarked.

'I see no reason why we should not dispense with formality,' Minto replied cordially.

The men sat with their drinks and exchanged news of their families, caught up with the latest gossip from court and discussed the prime minister's poor health.

Spencer, looking tired, explained his lateness was due to the huge load of work he was carrying. It had been a difficult week at the Admiralty. Corruption in the dockyards filled the newspapers. The budget was in disrepair and the loss of more battleships had to be explained to parliament. The news from the Mediterranean was worrisome. St Vincent, the Mediterranean commander, had returned home on sick leave, unlikely to return. That left the command in the hands of the dour Lord Keith, whom Spencer had never liked. He'd hoped that Minto would bring news that would relieve his anxiety about the war situation there.

The conversation had turned to the war and Wyndham, as minister for war, said authoritatively. 'The turn of events in Europe is simply amazing.

Just six months ago, when we last met, the French were destroying the monarchies of northern Italy, threatening the papacy and Naples. Today, only Genoa remains in France's possession. They are have withdrawn from Naples and from Rome. Amazing how quickly events change!'

Grenville added quickly, 'And that Napoleon fellow is besieged by the Turks and without a fleet to resupply him.'

Minto sighed. 'I am not convinced the French will pursue peace anytime soon. The war will ebb and flow and we may have periods of peace, but the revolutionary cork is out of the bottle and until we have a different Europe – a Europe that is neither fanatical nor absolutist – this will continue. It is really a fight to the end. The French would rather die for their republican beliefs than reach an agreement with the monarchists and the monarchists are set on revenge.'

There was a pause as each digested the unpleasant thought. A servant arrived to take them to their table, which was discreetly tucked behind a screen, out of the sight of other diners.

Over supper, Minto asked, 'How is Nelson seen by the Admiralty, Spencer?'

'Why do you ask?' Spencer replied, a terseness entering his tone.

'You and I have always been his admirers, indeed

his sponsors,' said Minto. 'Yet, you have not made Nelson acting commander of the Mediterranean fleet while St Vincent is on leave, and I wondered why not.'

'Well, that's true enough, but of course seniority meant that we had to give the role to Keith *pro tem.*'

'You could always find another job for Keith. I am not implying that Nelson *ought to* have been given the job … I am just curious why not?' Minto pressed.

'This is strictly confidential, Minto. I rely on your discretion, especially since I know how close you are to him and to Fanny,' Spencer said in a low voice.

'Of course, of course. Lips sealed!'

'He has been acting strangely since the battle of the Nile. We are not sure why. He has made many poor decisions and we are disturbed.'

'Such as? Give me examples,' urged Minto.

'The Admiralty has done its best to keep this out of the newspapers. There is a list of examples. Most disturbing is his relationship with the King of Naples. He has been acting as if he is a member of their government. There are other things, too. He definitely induced King Ferdinand to attack the French while knowing very well that Naples couldn't sustain such an attack. Then he invaded neutral Tuscany to outflank the French and broke agreements he made with the Duke. He flatly refused to support Duckworth's attack on Minorca, even when Keith ordered him to.

Most appalling to those of us who think of Nelson as a friend was his hanging of an Italian admiral to satisfy the King. There are other matters of a more personal nature, too, but I am sure you get my drift.'

'I read about the killing of prisoners following a surrender agreement that committed him to spare their lives and I was concerned,' Minto said.

Grenville interrupted. 'I have been worried about the siege of Malta. It's been over two years and we have not taken the island. The cost to us and the Maltese has been huge. Twenty thousand have died of starvation! Now the French have surrendered, and Nelson has the balls to say we must hand it over to Naples. Insanity!'

Wyndham stirred restlessly. 'The man was known for his brilliance in action, but this shows he can't manage anything much beyond a naval battle.'

There was a short silence until Minto gave voice to what they were all thinking. 'Anyone other than Nelson would have been recalled by now.'

Spencer nodded in agreement. 'No doubt you have heard that he is engaged in a relationship with the wife of the British ambassador. It is a sordid scandal and the gossip is damaging us.'

'Sir William Hamilton is causing concern to the foreign office. He has been out there far too long and has gone "local",' Grenville added. 'He is committed to the causes of the Royal Family and does their bidding. Sir William had no right to support the King attacking the French. That seems to have been cooked up between him and Nelson. Only Austrian intervention saved them, and they have a call on us very costly to the treasury. Hamilton seems to have been talked into this by his wife, who is close to Queen Maria Carolina. I hear she calls the three of them *tria juncta in uno*. I'd prefer a ménage à trois!'

They laughed.

'What in the world is going on?' asked Minto, shaking his head in disbelief. 'How has Nelson fallen so far?'

Spencer paused, considering whether to continue. 'Some at the Admiralty are asking if he has taken one too many blows to the head. Personally, I don't believe that. His letters have the hallmarks of a sound mind. However, his behaviour is troublesome, and his injuries may have affected his judgement. He has adopted a manner far beyond that appropriate to a rear admiral. He also thinks we don't appreciate his great victory. He has been given a dukedom by Naples, while we only made him a baron – and that only after a lot of effort on our part with the King, I might add.'

'I have decided to replace Hamilton,' Grenville said. 'He will retire from the service. I have his replacement, Arthur Paget, there already. He tells me

Sir William is treating him like a junior. He is in for a rude awakening!'

Spencer, as usual, summed up things very well. 'And I will have to replace St Vincent, but it won't be Nelson. I intend for him to return home where I hope someone, perhaps Fanny, can talk some sense into him. Grenville, this will mean that you will need to rely on Minto for overall political direction in the Mediterranean and I will have to trust Lord Keith with the direction of military affairs. So be it.'

They shook hands, knowing that when they met again next week, they would be in an official meeting and minutes would be kept. They knew as well that most of their business was already agreed and they would vote accordingly.

It was late afternoon and the sun had set by the time Minto walked home. He reflected sadly on the conversation about Horatio. Minto had always admired and liked the man. Minto had himself seen his early promise firsthand when he'd been Governor of Corsica and of Elba. Horatio's talents were evident. Only two years ago, Minto had been his greatest supporter in London. Indeed, he had called in favours to get Horatio his Mediterranean command. But recently, the news reaching him in Vienna worried him. Horatio's judgement was being questioned. It seemed as though he was someone different to the man he'd known. There had been the wounds and exhaustion, the sense of injustice over the rank of his peerage, the challenge of making important decisions and being second-guessed. Yes, all this was true. But it was Horatio's infidelity that worried him most. He would have to talk to him about it. Get him to reconsider before it was too late.

Before he returned to Vienna, Minto arranged to spend an afternoon with Fanny. She was in London again and he met her at the levee in St James's Palace. He steered her to a comfortable corner where they would not be disturbed.

She was dressed simply but attractively in a dark blue outfit which matched the colour of her eyes. Her peeress's tiara sparkled in her dark hair. It accentuated the gracefulness of her features.

'My dear Fanny, how wonderful to see you! I heard from Lady Spencer that you attend court from time to time, upholding dear Horatio's standard in his absence,' Minto said as she sat down.

'Gilbert, you are such a flatterer. If I did not know you better, I would think you were trying to flirt with me!' laughed Fanny.

'The last time I saw you was at the Spencers' ... That must be almost six months ago now. You had finished your house in the country and told me you planned to live there. So what are you doing in London?'

'I promised Horatio I would attend to his interests with his bankers, so I have to be in London from time to time.'

'And Horatio – how is he?'

'As ever, busy with his work and less than informative because of that. I quite miss the long letters full of news that he used to send me, frightening though they often were.'

'I'm sure he will be home soon,' Minto said kindly.

'I have trained myself not to yield to that tempting thought. It is too disheartening when he delays. The illness of Lord St Vincent has delayed any prospect of him being home before Christmas.'

'And how is Josiah?' he enquired.

'On the one hand, he seems to be very successful yet, on the other, he seems to have the severest of critics, including his father. He's a young man. He'll learn.'

'Perhaps – I hope so.'

'And you, dear Gilbert. How is Lady Minto faring in Vienna? Such an elegant capital and home to such wonderful music,' Fanny said, her eyes shining.

'We are faring very well, Fanny. The court is full of strange Germans. But it is a mighty empire. And, as you say, the music is wonderful. But such is the importance of the British alliance that I am constantly busy. I believe Horatio has a similar situation in Naples?'

Fanny paused before answering. 'If he does, I am the last person to know. I hear Lady Hamilton is much involved in his work at court – as a translator, I think. I am obliged to trust Horatio's judgement and his affection for me.'

Minto looked up sharply. The sun was pouring through the great window of the King's chamber. Fanny looked beautiful and his heart went out to her. Minto was suddenly aware of conversation around them.

'Fanny,' he managed to say. 'I am sure all will be well.'

He stood up, bowed and helped her to her feet. Then arm in arm, they rejoined the line waiting to speak with the King and Queen.

A few days after the meeting in London, Minto was in Norfolk as a guest of Mr Coke at Holkham Hall. The Palladian house was full of visitors and as his eyes travelled over the multitude, he saw how much times had changed since he was last in England. The government had urged landowners to be more inclusive of the other classes. Coke was the advance guard, as he had always been in most progressive matters. The Norfolk grandees like Walpole were there, but there were also many ordinary people present. Minto met gentry, town burgesses and successful farmers. These were the families that produced people like Horatio.

It was time for them to be recognised. 'Spoken like a true Whig,' Minto murmured to himself wryly.

As he surveyed the room, William Nelson approached. 'Ah, Lord Minto, so good to see you!' He thrust his large hands towards the fire to warm himself. 'And how long are you here? My brother told me you are the British minister in Vienna!'

'Quite right, Reverend Nelson. I am – for my sins, you might say.'

'I correspond with my brother regularly on matters and am abreast of affairs, my lord.'

Minto stirred uneasily. 'And what about you, Reverend? What are the matters that you are dealing with?'

'I now have two livings to take care of. We minister to all manner of people, keeping the peace, helping the poor and aged and ensuring the continuance of godliness and order.'

'My word, are you a magistrate as well?' asked Minto.

'No, no, I simply refer to the breadth of my responsibilities. Not unlike those of my brother. I am sure you have heard he is now a duke. Even if it is a foreign dukedom, it carries enormous precedence and authority.'

'No doubt that makes you happy,' Minto replied.

'Yes, it's a great responsibility for me as I am his heir if, God forbid, anything were to happen to him.'

'That surprises me. I would have thought that having a son of his own, the titles might pass through to him.'

'You are referring to Josiah, are you not? The son, as you call him, is an in-law, and neither a blood relative nor adopted. Quite wise, I would say. To keep everything in the family.'

The man has no finesse, thought Minto. *Next thing, he will be asking me for favours.*

'Are you familiar with the Lord Chancellor, my lord?' the reverend asked him.

'Of course, I know him passably well,' Minto answered, somewhat puzzled by the question.

'I have written to him without the benefit of a reply. Most rude! I am sure you would agree in view of my brother's social standing, it is imperative those related closely to him should also be afforded greater significance. I believe a bishopric, even a Welsh one, would be a good way of discharging that obligation. Perhaps you might be so good – when you next see him next, that is …'

'Reverend Nelson. My time is very short. I will be back in Vienna next week. I do hope you are successful in the pursuit of your goal.'

Coke approached diplomatically and took Minto by his arm. 'Excuse me, Canon Nelson,' he said smoothly. 'Lord Minto, perhaps you might come with me. So nice to see you again. I do hope you enjoy the shooting!'

Coke steered Minto away towards the windows as if to introduce him to a group standing there.

'What a bore!' Minto muttered once they were out of earshot.

'Yes, he is a complete shit,' concurred Coke. 'I invite him only because I owe Horatio a few favours. I've often reflected that he and Horatio could scarcely be more different! Now, let me introduce you to Lord Walpole.'

CHAPTER TWENTY-FIVE
May 1799

Josiah stood on the quay with his telescope. On the horizon, a frigate's sails were full with a following breeze. Its silhouette stood out against the morning sun, signal flags fluttering, a bow wave throwing a sparkling arc of spray into the bright air. He studied her with excitement. He watched as the crew reduced sail, wearing about and preparing to anchor. They were slow – too slow!

He recalled his conversation with Horatio.

'I love *Bonne Citoyenne*, sir, but she is just a corvette. I think I can handle a frigate,' he'd argued.

'Listen to you! Barely made up to post-captain!' Horatio had growled back.

'But I *am* ready!' insisted Josiah.

'Are you ready for the fall, sir!'

The sarcasm was painful.

Governor Ball sat, his fingers steepled, and contemplated the young man who stood in front of him. His headquarters were in the small town hall in a fishing port north of Valletta while the siege continued. Bottled up behind formidable castellated fortifications, 3000 hungry French soldiers defied demands for surrender and the blockade continued month after month. Horatio had assigned Josiah to take over as captain of a frigate and to join Ball's squadron enforcing the blockade.

'How old are you, Nisbet?' Ball asked.

'Almost nineteen, sir.'

'Commander of a hospital ship and a corvette. Post-captain too,' Ball added.

Josiah smiled quietly.

'*Thalia*'s captain has gone back to England on sick leave. Horatio has instructed you replace him. Will you bring any men from *Bonne Citoyenne* with you?'

'I will, Master Brierley,' he replied. Brierley had served him well as shipmaster on *Bonne Citoyenne*.

'I want you to take Lieutenant Yule as your second. He served with me on *Alexander* at the Nile. A good man. Between Brierley and Yule, you will be well supported. Colquitt, your first lieutenant, is there too.'

'Happy to oblige. I want only one thing from my officers: the willingness to die rather than surrender.'

Ball bit his lip. 'A chip off the old block, eh?'

'I was taught by him, fought with him and learned his lessons.'

Brusque, the governor thought. 'You will have enemies. People resent your father, your promotions and your bluntness. You *must* show discretion.'

Josiah thrust his hands deep in the pockets of his sea jacket, bowed his head and rocked on his heels. When would he be given the respect he had earned?

'As long as you are in my command, I expect you to obey orders and capture any enemy merchant ships that approach the coast. Do you understand?'

After a few days at sea, *Thalia*'s problem was clear. The ship was very tired and needed a refit back in England. Josiah would not have long to prove himself. Colquitt, the first lieutenant, escorted him around the gun decks, the galley and the warrant officers' mess.

'Captain Nisbet, Mr Spring, the ship's surgeon,' Colquitt said, introducing the man.

Spring was at work bandaging a sailor. He looked up and saluted casually.

'Mr Spring,' said Josiah, 'I like to see warrant

officers dressed correctly. I commanded a hospital ship so I know how standards of the navy can slip!'

Colquitt jumped in. 'Mr Spring has been with us for three years, sir. He has an excellent record for keeping our men healthy!'

'No need to defend *Mr* Spring, Colquitt. *Mr* Spring, sharpen up and we will get along very well.' The older man glowered and turned back to the grinning patient.

Punishment muster was on Sunday after the articles of war had been read. The accused were brought up and the first offender was lashed to a grating which had been set up on the forward hatch.

Josiah addressed the crew. 'We will now witness those whose behaviour endangers this ship. Brierley, carry on.'

The sailor was a bullying sort, overconfident and insolent. The usual sentence was twenty lashes, but Josiah had increased it to thirty. The man took his punishment from the boatswain's mate in silence, crying out only as the last five were given.

The second offender was hauled up and tied to the grating and a new cat was taken from its red felt bag. By the time of the fourth flogging, a hush had descended. Josiah had seen it before. The bold were cowed. Old salts would counsel caution and the fearful would pay close attention to their duties.

Josiah leant forward. 'Men, what foolishness! Do your duty and you will find me to be fair. Play hard and I will break you! For the next week, we will be improving sail handling and seamanship. And then gunnery, interception and boarding. We are going into action.'

A stony silence.

Josiah concluded, 'Take over, Colquitt.'

He returned to his cabin and threw off his coat, breathing heavily. He had done this before, and he would do it again. They would either bend or he would break them. But a feeling of loneliness overtook him as he cooled down in the silence of the cabin. *Bonne Citoyenne* with its 125 crew, its history of capturing privateers and blockade runners had been a joy to command. So different from *Thalia* with its boorish officers and sullen crew, entrenched in their ways. Managing a crew of 250 men was, he now realised, a much bigger task than he had thought. Still, he would push through. He would break those who stood in his way.

Thalia ploughed on through the soft sea driven by a kindly wind. The crew followed their routines punctiliously, knowing the captain was about. A call from the fighting top alerted the men on the quarterdeck.

'Ahoy! Ship on the starboard bow!'

Her telescopes had spotted the enemy's sails, which were lit by a full moon.

Josiah sprang onto the ratlines and sprinted aloft. He called from the masthead. 'General action! All hands on deck. No pipes or bells!'

The crew tumbled out. The studding sails were released and sheeted home. It took three hours through the silvery seas before they overhauled their quarry. It was a Frenchman and looked like a privateer. When they were within range, Josiah ordered the crew fire a round from the bow chaser.

'Close with the enemy, Colquitt!' he commanded.

'They are tacking to give us a broadside,' the lieutenant replied.

'Damn it, Colquitt. Get closer!'

The enemy ship opened fire, its balls tearing through *Thalia*'s sails.

'Colquitt, get a boarding party together. If she does not yield, we engage hand to hand.'

The privateer fired again and *Thalia* replied with two broadsides within the space of the enemy's single. Josiah nodded. Gunnery practice! Brierley rounded her up and the two ships collided, their hulls smashing together and the rigging tangling. *Thalia*'s carronades poured shot onto the enemy's deck, cutting a swathe. Josiah, sword in hand, and the marine captain, Bulkely, leapt aboard the enemy ship with his marines. He noticed Colquitt was lingering – still aboard *Thalia*. Josiah felt his blade slicing through sinew and bone. A marine fell, shot by a sniper. A short sharp battle, the weight of numbers telling, and then the enemy captain shouting an order and the crew laying down their weapons. Trembling, the French captain knelt and offered his sword to Bulkely. Josiah stepped forward.

Elbowing Bulkely out of the way, he accepted the surrender in fluent French.

Two weeks later, he rescued a British troop transport near to foundering off Malta, its sails torn to shreds and its foremast snapped off at the deck. A line was thrown to the stricken vessel and it was taken in tow. The storm raged on through the night and for most of the following day until they had her safely berthed in Malta. Eighty soldiers and a hundred crew were saved.

After that, they were back on blockade duty, tacking back and forth a few miles off the coast. Josiah noticed a change in morale; *Thalia*'s crew were becoming less resentful. Josiah was pleased. He had passed the first test. Sitting in the great cabin staring at the wake and a single gull following the ship, he thought of his next move. He had to get rid of the troublemakers among his officers. Bulkely was a drunk and a gossip. Colquitt was bitter and forward and, he knew instinctively, was waiting for the moment to discredit him. Among the older men, only Brierley was reliable and loyal.

In July, after the French surrender at Valletta, *Thalia* was posted to support Troubridge's squadron in Leghorn, visiting Palermo on the way and taking leave there.

The recapture of Naples completed, Horatio too returned to Palermo and was there when Josiah arrived. Horatio had been awarded the noble title of Duke of Bronte by the grateful king. His joy had not diminished when Josiah met him. He revelled in his elevation and was unusually jovial and kind – like the old days. Yet Josiah noticed changes. He was stooped and his white hair testified to the stress he was under. His room was untidy, the desk piled with paper like a civil servant. He seemed to have settled down in the dowdy provincial town.

Together Josiah and Horatio strolled to the harbour one afternoon to inspect *Thalia*, the experience giving Josiah an unusual sense of happiness. After they had walked over the ship and met the officers, they retired to Josiah's great cabin for supper. After dinner, they fell into somewhat stilted conversation.

'Son, I heard good things about you from Captain Ball. You have cut back your drinking,' Horatio said.

Josiah stiffened but was pleased that he had been

more careful about drinking in public. He tried to steer the conversation in a different direction.

'Since I took over *Thalia*, we stopped all commerce between the French and their Valletta garrison, father.'

'That's very commendable. I have heard too that your ship's discipline has improved and that your gunnery is good. But I am concerned that you have not yet established yourself as captain.'

Josiah blushed, his mind racing. Where had Horatio gotten his information? There was only one answer – Brierley. It had to be. Brierley was the only person who knew Horatio well enough to send messages to him. Surely not?

'Haven't you heard of our many fights? The ships we have taken, the hundreds of men on the transports whose lives we saved? We are the best of the frigates on the Malta blockade!' said Josiah, defensively.

'You are good, but not as good as Hoste,' Horatio said flatly.

He could accept criticism, censure or fatherly discipline, but not unfavourable comparison with Hoste. Josiah boiled with fury. 'Damn Hoste! He was always your favourite!' he snapped.

'Sir, be careful of your tongue,' Horatio said and stalked off. Dinner was over.

Everything changed then. Josiah's resentment fed on the injustice and spread to include the Hamiltons, who seemed to control Horatio. Emma tried to manipulate Josiah, but her flirtatiousness no longer charmed him. Her offer to arrange an assignation he rejected. He attended one more occasion – a banquet with the King and Queen. At court, Horatio was a supreme commander with ministerial rank. At the dinner, he wore a dress uniform, his many decorations brightly embroidered into the serge. He was addressed as 'Duke' this and 'His Grace' that. He sat with Emma, who diligently cut up his food. They were like a trio of clowns. Josiah's thoughts turned to his mother, living quietly at home. She was dutiful as Horatio was unfaithful, modest as Horatio was vain, and she was unaware of any of this folly. Why had he not written to her more often? He knew the answer: anything he told her would hurt her still more.

For five weeks after they left Palermo, *Thalia* patrolled the coast of Italy from Genoa to Naples as a workhorse of the fleet – carrying messages and diplomats, supporting shore operations and chasing enemy merchantmen. In August, they were transferred again – this time to Admiral Duckworth's squadron in Minorca. Horatio's affair with Emma Hamilton was now being discussed openly among the officers in the fleet. Was Josiah being transferred so as to put distance between him and the Hamiltons?

Admiral Duckworth, his new commander, was

less formal and more open to conversation than his other commanders had been. Rumour had it that Duckworth's great prize – a Spanish treasure galleon – had made him rich beyond imagining. Whatever it was, Josiah appreciated working for a kinder and more thoughtful commander who understood him. It was about time to remove the troublemakers and spies – Bulkely, Colquitt and Brierley too. To really establish himself as captain, Josiah had to rid his ship of Horatio's incongruous surveillance. The first step was to find a neutral witness and demonstrate the disloyalty of these men.

Captain Clarke of *Courageous* was invited for dinner on *Thalia*. *Courageous* was a floating barracks where the crews awaiting assignments lived and Clarke was well known as a channel for gossip to the admiral. Josiah broke out his store of fine French wine for the occasion. Dinner complete and the loyal toast given, Josiah raised his glass to Clarke.

'To wives and sweethearts!' he said with a lightness that ensured his resentment of Horatio and Lady Hamilton was well concealed.

'May they never meet!' replied Clarke.

The evening was warm and the port was passed around quickly. Bulkely, the marine captain, was already worse for wear and Josiah made sure his and Colquitt's glasses were topped up often. At length,

Bulkely became talkative and bitterly criticised the treatment of his marines. His voice raised, his manner boisterous, he gave full vent to his frustrations. 'We marines keep the scum of the focsle in their place,' he complained. 'Only last week I had a man in irons for threatening the captain! I sorted him.' He took another swallow of wine.

In the silence, while Bulkely cleared his throat and prepared for another onslaught, Josiah looked pointedly at Colquitt to see if he would intervene. Colquitt stared woodenly at the table, just as Josiah expected he would. From the corner of his eye, Josiah saw Clarke taking in the scene. He turned slowly to Bulkely. 'Bulkely, you have taken too much wine. Withdraw before you say something you'll regret,' he said evenly.

Bulkely swayed unsteadily to his feet. 'You young blackguard! If I reached over this table, I'd take you by the nose and give you a good hiding. You're too young to know a better man when you see him!'

Colquitt laughed while the other officers looked away, embarrassed.

Josiah was on his feet in a flash, but just as quickly John Yule, his second lieutenant, took his arm. While the other officers hustled Bulkely to his cabin, Yule quietly steered Josiah on deck.

'Thank you, Yule,' Josiah said. 'You are a good

fellow. Once the cabin is clear, I will retire. For too long we have played along with older disloyal men.'

Bulkely was court martialled and sent home by Duckworth shortly thereafter.

Thalia, May 1800
To Admiral Duckworth

My dear Admiral,
I am writing to add my congratulations having learned of your promotion to rear admiral of the Red. It is more than well-deserved in the eyes of the many who know what you have achieved.

I have been with Thalia for more than a year. I have recently been subject to a gross act of disloyalty and insubordination which I felt should be conveyed to you in writing. A few days ago Colquitt, our first lieutenant, a man deeply resentful of me, asked his fellow lieutenant, Yule, to fetch the sextant from his cabin. Yule made his way there and saw an open logbook on the desk. He was surprised, as the ship's logbook is in my cabin. He read a few pages and realised it was a duplicate. There was a daily entry for each page back to the day I joined the ship. He made a fair copy and gave it to me. I quote:

'13 March 1799

Wind from the south-west, freshening. Captain Nisbet came aboard this morning. Ship prepared to receive him. This log is a faithful account of the happenings on this ship under its new commander. It is necessary to keep an accurate account of all that will happen under this, a man so young and lacking in experience who has achieved command through gross nepotism ...'

Each entry was written as if Colquitt was captain, giving bearings, wind and distances together with commentary on the crew and its captain. None of it was true.

I have been careful to ensure that Colquitt does not know I have this information, but I fear if this matter is not resolved, something far worse will happen.

Sincerely yours,
Josiah Nisbet

Duckworth diplomatically arranged for Colquitt to be invalided out. It was a convenient fiction. At the same time, he permitted Josiah to send Brierley, who as acting purser was caught by Josiah enriching himself at the ship's expense, back to England.

As he left the ship, Brierley said, 'Colquitt was right about you. You let those loyal to you sink, while you swim.'

'Brierley, your sentiments might have merit were it not for the fact you are stealing from the ship and acting as my father's spy,' Josiah replied.

'How would we have won so many battles without my experience?' challenged Brierley.

'I could have handled the ship as well if you were a broomstick!' Josiah said, sharply.

After Brierley was gone, for the first time Josiah felt free; free to make his own decisions without the feeling that he was being held to another standard or being betrayed to his father. He would no longer tolerate Horatio's attempts to orchestrate command of his ship from behind the scenes. Enough was enough.

John Yule was made acting first lieutenant and Josiah, learning from his earlier mistakes, gave him more say in the day-to-day decisions. With the three older men gone, Josiah could make the other changes he wanted. In a thousand small ways, *Thalia's* morale improved. Duckworth noticed the change and gave Josiah responsibility for the southwest, the pathway of the treasure ships approaching Spain. In the gorgeous sun-filled weeks that followed, Josiah and his crew finally experienced that rare combination – good weather, good food and a happy ship.

On *Thalia*'s final return to Minorca, Admiral Duckworth congratulated him on a successful cruise and then shocked Josiah by telling him that Horatio had ordered the ship return to England forthwith. Knowing how upset Josiah was, the admiral invited the officers of *Thalia* to his house above the dockyard for a final farewell.

After dinner and the loyal toast, Admiral Duckworth asked, 'Captain, how long have you been in his part of the world? You seem like part of the furniture.'

'I came out with old 'Eggs and Bacon' in '93, sir.'

'Ah, *Agamemnon*! What a ship she was! Tell us where you have been over the last eight years.'

'I was at the battle of Cape St Vincent when we took the two great Spanish battleships. Before that at Toulon, Corsica, Santa Cruz and the blockade of Cádiz. I missed the Nile by a hair's-breadth, fought in the war against Naples, had a long cruise to Istanbul, blockaded Malta, was there when we recaptured Naples and, well, you know the rest, sir.'

The youthful faces around the table, bathed in candlelight and alcoholic bonhomie, showed amazement. He had been at sea every day of the war and fought in most of its battles.

'Gentlemen, I give you Captain Nisbet and the Thalians!' Duckworth toasted.

They raised their bumpers and gave three loud hurrahs.

The long journey home around the coast of Spain and the Bay of Biscay was uneventful. Good winds carried them up the English Channel and into the Thames Estuary. As they approached the Medway, a pilot came aboard and helped to steer *Thalia* into the Chatham dockyard that would be its home for the refit. The journey was over and the crew were paid off – only the warrant officers would remain at Chatham for the refit. The commission officers would be on leave on half-pay until the ship was ready for sea and the Admiralty reconfirmed their commissions. Josiah packed his cases knowing that he would be back when *Thalia* was ready to put to sea again.

Josiah and John Yule walked across the great expanse of the yard in a cold December drizzle. It was Sunday and no one was at work. The place was deserted, the dry docks and piers jammed with ships being readied for sea. There was cannon piled up on the quay, pyramids of spars beside bales of cord and everywhere the smell of tar and saltmarshes.

'Where are you headed, Yule?' Josiah enquired.

'I am going to Somerset, sir – to join my family for

a few weeks. I hope that when you take *Thalia* back to the Mediterranean, I can go with you again.'

'I would indeed be honoured if you would be my first lieutenant.'

'And you, sir?'

'I am going to see my mother. My father is on his way home, travelling through Europe. It will be a pleasure for the three of us to be together again.'

'Has it been eight years?'

'Yes,' Josiah said. 'Eight years since I last saw mother.'

'Captain, if I may say it, it's been a pleasure serving with you. I hope you will be successful dealing with your enemies.'

'You mean Bulkely, Colquitt and Brierley? I am sure Governor Ball and Admiral Duckworth will tell my side of the story and my father – well, I know he will side with me!'

The cab was waiting at the gates. They shook hands.

Josiah walked across the dockyard. Against the scale of the cranes and buildings and the ship, he felt small, like a rider dismounted from a great mare. The rain increased and thunder rumbled in the distance. He turned to see Yule helping the driver load his chest onto the roof of the cab and climbing aboard. He must see mother. But what would he tell her?

CHAPTER TWENTY-SIX
July 1800

The Queen of Naples was visiting her brother and so travelled to Vienna with Horatio and the Hamiltons. When they arrived, Horatio's reception by the people of Vienna overwhelmed the city. They were feted from dawn to dusk. During this time, Minto quietly returned to the embassy unannounced. He learned Horatio and the Hamiltons were staying at the 'Inn of all honest Men' in Graben Square in the elegant quarter of the city, while the Queen was staying at Schönbrunn Palace.

Minto wrote a note of welcome and then left Horatio to bask in his glory. While he still felt positively towards Horatio, his professional feelings towards Sir William were the opposite. He was troubled by what he had learned in London. He decided he must try to talk sense into Horatio before he got home.

At Horatio's reception at the embassy, Minto was nonetheless unprepared for the visible changes in him. He seemed to be as old as Sir William. There was a livid scar on his forehead, he was stooped and his cheeks were sallow. He was dressed in a navy uniform, embroidered with a multitude of decorations in silver and gold thread. He stood drinking Champagne side by side with Emma Hamilton, who was catering to his every need.

Hamilton too was a gaunt shadow of the debonair diplomat Minto had once known. Emma was in diaphanous layers which flowed around her as she moved. Her face was still lovely and, together with Horatio, she was the centre of attention. After dinner, she recited verses and verses of praise to Horatio in a theatrical voice. He choked back a laugh as her monopoly on attention irritated the other ladies while having the reverse effect on their men. At length, Minto extracted Horatio from the others and took him to the library, closing the door behind them. They sat uneasily exchanging small talk before Minto said, 'My dear Horatio. I hope you are enjoying Vienna's celebration of your great achievement.'

'The reception we have received amazes me,' Horatio said.

'Yes, Vienna is greatly relieved that the Corsican is stranded–'

'Gilbert,' Horatio interrupted. 'I was disturbed by London's treatment of Sir William. He was more or less bundled out of Naples after decades of loyal service. It was distressing to all of us and your people are to blame!'

What arrogance! Minto thought, for a moment suffused with irritation. Where was that agreeable man he'd once helped? But he said only, 'Horatio. London is awaiting you with good will, though their lordships will need to understand from you what happened in Naples.'

Later, after the guests were gone, Gilbert undressed and prepared for bed. Anna was reading. She looked at him over half-moon spectacles. She was adorable, even as she aged.

'How did you think it went this evening?' he asked her.

She put down her book. 'I don't know why you like him, Gilbert!'

'He used to be different. He was always quiet and decent but now he is … well, changed.'

'And the Hamiltons?' she said. 'What's their excuse?'

'What did you make of *her*?' Gilbert said.

'Pregnant, obviously.'

'Obviously?'

'Of course. A woman knows. The flowing dress, the high bodice, the glowing skin.'

'Poor Fanny!' he said, sitting heavily on the bed.

A few days later, the Emperor moved with the court to Baden, twenty miles outside Vienna, and Hamilton, Horatio and Minto were invited to a four-day 'fest', hosted by the wealthy Prince Esterházy. There were to be dinners, recitals and theatrical entertainments. And on the last day there would be a hunt. It was a distraction that Minto could have done without. The papers were piled high on his desk and he had a diary of appointments with ministers. Nonetheless, he cleared his time and made his way to Baden.

With Horatio at the centre of the festivities, Minto was able to witness his new demeanour. His affectations would have been laughable had Minto not understood why he was so pretentious. It was King George's snub that was behind it all.

Minto was hopeless with a musket and Horatio had only one arm, so they spent the afternoon of the hunt on foot. After an elaborate lunch, the guests, beaters and gamekeepers set off into the woods where the boar and deer were flushed towards the waiting hunters.

Minto spent the afternoon hearing Horatio's

account of the war between Naples and France. Amid sounds of the hunters' gunfire, Horatio described a bloody fight and the even bloodier aftermath. Their conversation was interrupted by the return of the hunt. While the guests slaked their thirst with foaming tankards of beer, the master of the hunt awarded Sir William Hamilton first prize for his bag of 120 animals and birds.

They resumed their conversation in the carriage taking them home to Vienna. Since the Nile, glory had been heaped on Horatio constantly and it seemed to Minto that he had come to love it – perhaps too much. He asked Horatio tactfully how becoming such a hero made him feel.

Horatio pondered. Then he said, 'I was chosen to stand in the breech to halt the godless tyrants. The praise I have received reflects the gratitude of the people for the miracle of the Nile.'

'Horatio, what happened to the man who loved the simple life?'

There was a pause. Horatio sat huddled in the corner of the coach. He seemed half dead. Yet his voice was strong.

'Minto, to people in your class I am a lowborn man with aspirations. I was not considered of sufficient *quality* to be given the same title as my peers who have won lesser battles. Countries like Russia, Turkey and Austria have lavished their highest awards on me. Naples made me Duke of Bronte. Leaders seek my opinion, granting me access reserved for only the greatest men. The common people love me. Wherever I go, I am the centre of their attention. Except among my peers in England!'

'But isn't there a danger of all this praise going to your head?' As he said this, Minto expected their friendship might end there and then.

Horatio paused. His tone did not change – as if the question were perfectly reasonable. 'I have been in the King's service for thirty years – in dangerous conditions, living like an ordinary seaman. I am drenched by storms, I board enemy vessels, and I kill and am wounded. Yet ministers underrate me and the King despises me. Thirty years, Minto! Am I not to enjoy my reward?'

'Does your reward include the wife of the British ambassador?'

There was a silence as Horatio digested Minto's implication. But his demeanour remained unchanged. 'Lady Hamilton is a good friend – indeed, more than a good friend. I admit that to you, Minto. She has earned the right to share in my honour and will continue to do so. Providence provided her for me at the right time.'

'And Fanny?'

'Fanny is my wife and I will not talk about her to you or anyone else,' Horatio said gruffly.

'Some of us worked behind the scenes to ensure you were rewarded, even though we knew you would be disappointed. Fanny has been prominent in your cause and is beloved at St James's.'

'Please don't interfere in my personal affairs if you wish to keep my friendship!' Horatio snapped.

Minto blinked. This was unpleasant. Yet he still felt he should warn Horatio of what he would face. 'Horatio, you are viewed differently in London than you are here. You will have an admiring populace but those in high places, including the King, see things differently. If I may offer advice, I suggest that when this party is over, you go home directly. Restore yourself to Fanny's bosom and be good to her. If you do, you will be shown consideration and gratitude despite your critics.'

'And if don't?'

'Your career, glorious as it is, will be endangered. Good society will avoid you.'

They rolled into Graben Square and, with a jingle of harness, stopped at the hotel. Despite the lateness of the hour, there was a crowd waiting. As soon as they saw Horatio emerge, they gave a cheer and surged towards the coach. He turned and shrugged his shoulders to Minto as if to say, 'These are my people!'

'What an arse – he always wanted to be loved more than admired,' said Minto under his breath as his carriage rolled out of the square and took him home.

H.M. British Embassy, Vienna
Personal and confidential

My dear Spencer,
I am back in Vienna and recently had opportunity to meet with Lord Nelson, who is transiting the city together with the Hamiltons. He is leaving shortly for Prague and Dresden. After our recent informal meeting at White's, I thought I would give you an indication as to what you might expect on his return.
All my fears proved correct. He is not the man he was. He has a hauteur fed by a surfeit of flattery, medals, titles and public praise. If he requires help in the feeding of his vanity, Lady Hamilton is at his elbow, singing his praises (literally as well as meta-phorically). He is no longer the man I once admired, and I fear that when he reaches London there will be a disruption. No doubt his public will adore him. But I wager the court, and the ministry, will feel differently ... It's best that you are prepared ...

CHAPTER TWENTY-SEVEN
September 1800

Louise Berry and Fanny were in the sitting room enjoying the sunny afternoon. Both were suitably dressed for the humid summer weather – Fanny in a long white muslin dress with a low square neckline and short sleeves, and Louise with a light shawl loosely draped around her shoulders to help ward off perspiration.

Louise was 'Lady Berry' now – the title had come when her husband, and Horatio's former captain, Edward, was knighted by the King after the Nile. Fanny was used to being a titled person and all it entailed – the thrill of being addressed as 'Your Ladyship' or 'My Lady' or 'Dear Lady Nelson'. Unaware of the niceties, Louise asked Fanny to explain all the delicate issues that had been revealed to Fanny by Lavinia Spencer. Their friendship meant Fanny, who might have been lonely in Suffolk, had a kindred spirit near Roundwood. Both women were about the same age and both were used to the 'waiting game' – the years they'd spent without their husbands.

Edmund was spending the summer with Fanny at Roundwood. He was now seventy-nine years old and the loss of Suckling, his youngest son, the previous year, and the illness of Maurice, his eldest, weighed heavily and he spent most of his time dozing in a comfortable chair in the sitting room. He awoke as Fanny sat at the piano and began to play a piece by Bach she had been practising.

When she had played the final chord, Fanny took a bow as Louise and Edmund applauded. Then she returned to the sofa, glancing at the view and picking up a fallen cushion. The fields of wheat below the house were swaying gently in the humid breeze. The trees at the bottom of the hill were exchanging their green leaves for the reds and yellows of autumn. A team of labourers in a distant field were scything and stooking the grain. It had been a good idea to buy this house and she no longer missed Bath. Only one thing was missing. She longed for Horatio to be here and to enjoy this place with her.

Her maid brought in a tray of tea and scones.

Edmund woke again as Louise poured the tea and Fanny passed the plates.

'Have you any more news of Horatio – is he still in Vienna?' Louise asked.

'I think he's on the move again – somewhere in Germany,' Fanny replied. She said this without any emotion and quickly asked, 'What about Edward? Any possibility of his return?'

'Nothing since we last spoke,' Louise said. 'You told me Josiah will be home soon. It will be quite the family reunion!'

'I do hope that Josiah will be here before his father returns. I want to spend time with him. If Horatio arrives first, we are bound to be called to London and we will be in great demand there.'

'Well, dear, I hope for your sake that happens. It won't be easy renewing your relationship with your dear son after almost eight years!'

They ate scones and drank their tea and Edmund added a few words to the conversation before nodding off again. When the clock chimed six, Louise rose to her feet, saying she must be home before dark. Her pony and trap were brought to the front door and the two women embraced, promising to meet again soon. Louise climbed aboard, slapped the reins on the horse's broad rump and set off while Fanny returned inside to write a letter to Horatio.

Over the last three months, she'd responded to the change in tone of his letters by adopting a less effusive style. His letters were respectful enough, but noticeably cooler, not very affectionate. Last week, she had received a note from Lavinia, saying that Spencer had heard from Horatio and 'all was well'. There was no mistaking her intent, for she'd written, *London society was curious and critical about Horatio's friendship with the Hamiltons.* Izzy's latest note was more than usually caring too, as if she were worried about Fanny. She had not mentioned anything specific, but her invitation to visit soon suggested perhaps Fanny needed to have her friend bolster her in some way. In the face of this, Fanny clung to her faith in Horatio. He had always been impatient if she expressed too much concern and she had learned to control her anxiety by now. She hoped his coolness was nothing more than moodiness. The gossip and innuendo she put down to the public's huge appetite for scandal which was fomented by Lady Hamilton's undeniably seamy history. She picked up the pen and wrote a short letter updating him on events at Roundwood and the latest news of the family.

She was shaking sand on the ink when she heard hooves clattering up the Ipswich Road. Whoever would be cantering along at this time of night? The rider slowed and she realised he was checking the house before riding up the drive. Then there were sounds of horseshoe on gravel, neighing and a thump as the rider jumped down, followed by a ring of the bell.

It must be a messenger with some news of Horatio. She heard the servant answer the door and muffled voices. She stood uncertainly. The door of the living room burst open and a tall figure dressed in a leather riding coat and boots strode in.

'Mama!'

'Is it you, Josiah?' Her tears came quickly. He was so tall! Where was the thin reedy boy? He was healthy and strong, with tousled hair and a weathered face. His voice was deep.

'Let me go, Mama! You'll crush me to death!' He laughed as he held her at arms-length, a deep chuckle.

'Take off your coat. Sit down – next to me!' She patted the sofa for him to sit down. He sat looking at her searchingly, as if to see any changes.

'Is Father back?' he asked.

'Don't worry about him. He's in German lands, coming back on a boat. He'll be here soon enough. I want to know everything. I haven't had a letter from you for three months.'

'I left my ship in Chatham and came here immediately,' he told her, his eyes warm and smiling. 'I love your house. You must show me around!'

'I'm so glad – to talk, I mean. We must catch up on all your news.' She rang the bell for her servant. 'Take Josiah's coat,' she said. Then, turning back to her son, 'Have you eaten anything? Are you hungry?'

He held her hands. 'This is a wonderful house and you are as lovely as I remember.'

'Much has changed, Josiah. Our circumstances are very different.' As she said this, she realised she was trying to cool his enthusiasm.

Supper was over and they had caught up on each other's news when Josiah turned to her and said in a soft voice, 'Mama, I have got myself into a pretty pickle. I need Father to help me.'

'What have you done?' She tried to sound calm.

'It's not easy to explain. Father gave me command of *Thalia* when its captain was sent home on sick leave. It was such an opportunity for me – to show what I could do. I moved to the next level in the captain's list,' he said.

'Yes, how good of him. He has a kind heart and loves you dearly.'

'It was. Good of him, I mean. But there were other things – not so good.'

'What happened, dear?' she asked. Fanny took his hand and stroked it. It was such a big hand, with dark hairs growing on the sunburnt skin. Like Nisbet's.

'He surrounded me with his men – his warrant

officers. They were there to keep an eye on me. They were preventing me from doing my job as captain – from taking command, properly.'

'Yes.'

'And there was another thing. There was a lieutenant, Colquitt. He was exceedingly envious of me. And he made a pact with Father's men. It was terrible. I didn't know who to trust.'

'What did you do?'

'I got rid of them all. It wasn't easy. They made mistakes and in the end Admiral Duckworth saw what was happening and took a risk of crossing Father. He put his friendship with Horatio on the line.'

'Oh dear!'

'As soon as the command situation was clear to the crew, we had three amazing months. The ship was a dream. The crew were great. We took many prizes.'

'That's good news. Then, is there a problem?'

'Yes, there is,' he said. 'Colquitt has organised a writing campaign to discredit me. He has family in politics and they have written a storm of letters. And the former warrant officer – Brierley – he has written a formal complaint as well. I was told when we were in Plymouth.'

'Well, I'm sure it will all be straightened out. Lord St Vincent is back. And he knows you. Can he be of help?'

'That's another problem, Mama. He's not an admirer of mine. I took a few liberties with him a few years ago ...'

'Josiah, you remind me of Horatio. He had so many enemies as well. That's why he was beached in Norfolk for all of those years after we married.'

'Yes, I know. That's why I need you to talk to him. Make everyone see sense. You can always talk him round.'

'Tell me. How is your father? When did you last see him?'

'He's fine. I saw him six months ago in Palermo.'

'And?'

'Do you mind if I go to bed? I'm rather tired – after my ride.'

'Is there something I should know?' she asked in a soft, steady voice.

'No. It's fine. So good to see you again, Mama. You look well and I love what you have done here!'

'By all means, darling. But in the morning, we'll have the rest of this discussion. There's so much I don't know.'

After he had gone, she returned to the living room and sat at the piano. She played a nocturne, a soft melody to soothe her heart and take her mind off the questions still demanding answers. It was good to see him again before Horatio returned.

Sleep eluded her. It was humid and the promised storm hovered without breaking. Rumbles of thunder and the occasional dim flash of sheet lightning echoed and flittered. Josiah's tale was exactly like those Horatio had told her over the years. He'd been hot-headed, talented, independent and disrespectful too, those years ago. The price he'd paid had been high: his head full of dreams but no ship. How she had struggled! At one point, he had threatened to resign his commission and join the East India Company. She'd talked him out of it and Uncle Suckling said he should be patient. The last year was the worst.

And now Josiah. He was still young enough to have another career if he wanted it. It would be difficult but not impossible. And he would be here – with her. The dawn chorus came before she fell asleep and the sun was high when she rose.

The breakfast table was cleared except for her setting and, in answer to her question, her maid said the young master had taken the trap and would be back before too long.

She had finished her breakfast by the time he returned. He strode into the room, a tall young man with wild hair and a ruddy face. Startling eyes. She reminded herself not to continue to think of Nisbet. He was Horatio's son in all but blood, moulded by him since he was a few years old. He had lived on board with Horatio for almost five years. He was Horatio's boy. The nervous energy, the reserve, the impulsiveness and the ambition. Yes, and the loving nature, the kindness and concern for her.

'Good morning, Mama!' he said brightly. He had borrowed some old clothes from Edmund while his were washed. He looked old-fashioned. Different.

'Did you sleep well?' she asked.

'Like a dog! I was exhausted after two days in the saddle.'

'And did you speak to Edmund?'

'Yes – he was up early and lent me these clothes. We had a long talk. He loves you dearly. Quite brought me back to our old life. After that, I returned the horse to the post house. Borrowed your trap. Was that right?'

'Of course, dear. I couldn't sleep until the birds started chattering – and then I slept late.'

'Mama, you wanted to talk last night but I was exhausted. I was not the best of letter writers, I know.'

'Start with the time you were in the hospital ship. Before that, Horatio was home and he told me a lot about your life on *Agamemnon* and *Captain*.'

He described his lonely year in Lisbon, the episode in Gibraltar and the journey to Alexandria. She knew the details of the battle, but she wanted to know about the return journey with Horatio to Naples.

He hesitated, not wishing to alarm her. The terrible aftermath of the battle seared them all, including those who had not fought in the battle. The repairs to the dreadfully battered ships were too extensive to describe. The treatment of the casualties among the men was more difficult. Cannonballs were the least to worry about; they killed anything in their path, but the effect of being hit by splinters of wood or shrapnel was catastrophic. Men lost limbs, eyes, ears, parts of the face and were deafened and blinded. The worst cases were those who went mad. Josiah described his own nightmares after the battles of Cape St Vincent and Santa Cruz.

Fanny listened in silent amazement. Her son, barely twenty, had experienced more in his short lifetime than men twice his age. He was articulate and sensitive as he explained how they worked with the surgeons to save the wounded and heal the sick. But the recurring thought was why he was not talking about Horatio at all as he recounted his own ordeals.

At last, she asked him directly.

'Tell me about your father. He was injured. He wrote to say that he thought the wound would be fatal, but it turned out that his head was stronger than he thought.'

'Yes. He was injured and when I saw him in Alexandria, he looked awful – black eyes, bruises, barely able to stand. He was deafened too, but his hearing recovered. He was grateful for his great victory and the seamanship and courage of his captains. Beyond that, he said that God had anointed him for this victory.'

'Had he changed at all? From his injuries, I mean.'

'If anything, those things which make him who he is were even more evident,' Josiah said.

'What are they?'

'Both good and bad things, Mama.'

'What good?' she asked.

'Ever generous to his men and those who fought with him. To me, too.'

'And bad?'

'You will have to decide, Mama,' he said quietly. 'Surely you have heard rumours?'

'Son, I need you to tell me what you know,' she insisted.

There was a pause, a silence that told her more than she wanted to know. All those things hinted at in polite company and the cartoons in the newspapers, the gossip and the sympathetic glances were true.

'I need to know!' she cried.

He was silent. Fanny saw he would not say any more.

Finally, he said impassively, 'It was nothing to do with anything you did.'

They sat silently. Then Fanny stood up. She could see he was very angry.

'Be still, Josiah dear. Whatever befalls us, we will still love him.'

After that, they stopped talking about the battle and its aftermath and never discussed Naples or the Hamiltons. They went for a walk in the cool of the late afternoon. They visited with Louise and on Sunday went to Christchurch. Then Josiah returned to London, leaving Fanny to ponder his devastating visit.

A few days after Josiah had departed, she received a letter from Alexander Davison saying that Horatio would soon be home and asking her to come to London to help him find a suitable house.

'But didn't Horatio say he was landing at Yarmouth?' Louise asked when Fanny told her as they sat together at Louise's pretty cottage near Ipswich.

'He did and I am confused. But it seems pretty clear that he wants to have a house ready when he arrives in London and Davison says he is travelling directly there.'

'But if he comes through Yarmouth, surely he will want to see the house and spend a little time with you?'

'I think it better if I get to London and get things ready.'

Fanny gave instructions to the staff to close the house for winter. They were to cover the furniture, store the bed linen, shut off the water and tidy the garden. She was organised and determined, and vowed, 'That woman will never set foot in Roundwood!' She had reached a decision. He was sick and injured. He had betrayed her and, if the rumours were only half true, he had disgraced himself. She would not be the midwife to a final disgrace. She would rather be the victim.

CHAPTER TWENTY-EIGHT
October 1800

After five weeks in Vienna, the travellers set off on the next stage of the journey home. Horatio hired two coaches to take them from Vienna to Prague, from where they would take an Elbe sailing barge to Hamburg. Horatio was in the leading coach with the guide and Sir William, while Emma, her maid, her mother and Miss Knight followed in the second. Miss Knight, Emma's companion since Palermo, was a starstruck admirer of Horatio's who wrote epic poetry celebrating his feats – good material for Emma's public performances.

The whole trip through Europe would have been unnecessary if Admiral Keith had agreed to Horatio's request for the battleship *Foudroyant* to take them home. Keith boorishly claimed the ship was needed in the Mediterranean and had offered a frigate instead. It was insulting for an officer of Horatio's stature and embarrassed him in front of the Naples establishment. Making the most of the situation, Horatio adopted Minto's suggestion that the 'hero of the Nile' would encourage the 'faint of heart' by journeying home through countries. But it also meant that Horatio would use up most of his leave. It might hurt Fanny's feelings, but his duties must be foremost in his priorities.

As he packed, Horatio thought about their magnificent reception in Vienna. He had rescued them from the barbarism of French revolutionaries. A performance by Haydn of his 'Lord Nelson Mass' at the Palais Esterházy on Wallnerstrasse had been an especially memorable highlight. Two years ago, when Haydn was writing the work, Vienna had been under threat from Napoleon's approaching army, and the mass had been performed on the very day of Horatio's victory in Aboukir Bay. To Horatio, there was no coincidence. It was God's mighty hand at work. The performance moved him deeply and Herr Haydn had given a signed libretto to Emma as a memento.

On their last day, they visited Schönbrunn to take their leave of Maria Carolina. The Emperor was elsewhere, and the Queen received them in an empty palace. She gave them presents and promised them her 'eternal' friendship, begging Horatio to return to Naples soon. Horatio felt being away from Naples had diminished her. He thought about all he had done for her over the last two years. No more. That was history and there was no room for nostalgia. It was all politics, even if Emma made it something fanciful and grand.

Boxes and trunks packed, Horatio paid the accumulated bill – over a thousand pounds. The generosity of Viennese welcome had no cash component, he reflected sourly. Then he set off for Prague, three days travel to the north.

The coaches handled nicely on the well-metalled road, stopping from time to time to refresh the horses and the travellers alike at wayside inns. Emma practised the 'Kyrie' from Haydn's mass, distant musical phrases reaching Horatio's ears in the coach he shared with Sir William. He was still full of admiration and devoted to her, and determined to continue their exciting affair.

Vienna's younger sister, Prague, was clean, efficient and prosperous. The welcome at the Hradschin Palace confirmed their 'good will' mission was working. At a lavish welcome banquet, Emma was asked to sing so, dressed in her best gown and with her auburn hair framing her pretty features, she stood at the harpsichord and sang the 'Kyrie' in her powerful soprano accompanied by court musicians.

Archduke Charles, his dukes and duchesses, army officers, ministers and monsignors and a brilliant assemblage of the great and powerful of Prague listened attentively. Momentarily, an image of Fanny crossed Horatio's mind – one of her playing the piano in Lady Spencer's drawing room, and she elegant, polished and expressive. He was lucky to have two brilliant women in his life. He looked at Emma. She was theatrical and demonstrative. He wanted both of them.

They left Prague, Horatio's purse the lighter for it, and set off through scenery, unsurpassed in charm, for Saxony. The barge drifted slowly downstream to Dresden, sails luffing in the warm breeze. Flat-topped hills, ancient castles on rocky heights and lush arable lands passed by slowly on each side of the vessel. The skies were clear and the autumn sun warmed them. Horatio felt at ease for the first time in years.

The sun was going down as Dresden appeared around a bend in the river. Their guide said it was a town of churches, guilds, a porcelain industry and a university. It looked different from Vienna and Prague. They had left the baroque Empire for austere Lutheran lands. The barge bumped the wharf. There was no one waiting. A carriage was summoned to convey them to their lodgings at the Hotel Poland. The absence of welcoming crowds was an omen.

The hotel manager gave Horatio a letter embossed with the crest of the British Embassy. It was cordial enough. Hugh Elliot – Minto's brother – welcomed the travellers, noting the uncertainty as to their arrival time meant that it was impossible to organise a welcome at the quay. They were to pay their respects to the Prince-elector at Dresden Castle the following morning. Horatio brightened.

But the following morning, no one appeared at the appointed time. The parlour smelt of stale pipe tobacco. The minutes ticked by. Emma and Sir William looked uncomfortable.

At length, Hugh Gilbert arrived red of face and out of breath. He asked Horatio to step outside. He said quickly, 'My lord, I have news from the palace. Our meeting has been cancelled. I have enquired and have to tell you that the Princess does not wish the meeting to be held.'

Horatio flushed with rage. 'What are you talking about, man? We are a British minister and an admiral in the British Navy, not to mention that I am a baron and the Duke of Bronte!'

'The Queen has her own information. Her husband is the cousin of King Ferdinand. Apparently, she feels Lady Hamilton is a woman of questionable reputation. Nothing to do with you, of course, but she is aware of her past. People here are Lutheran, very conservative.

There is an excessive sense of propriety – somewhat similar to England.'

Sir William and Emma approached. 'What's the matter, Horatio?' William asked.

'My dear Emma and Sir William, it is a foolish matter hardly worth consideration. Apparently, wives are not welcome at court.'

The party returned to the parlour to regroup. Hugh worked quickly. Mrs Elliot, Miss Knight and Emma would visit the Prince-elector's brother, whom they had met in Naples. Horatio and Sir William would meet the elector.

Horatio was not placated by the personal warmth of the monarch. An awkward discussion circled around the diplomatic situation and the precarious position of Saxony – caught in a whirlpool of French, Prussian and Polish politics. Sir William played the diplomat. Horatio listened coldly. Formalities complete, they bowed their farewells and left the grand chamber. No invitations were forthcoming.

Horatio's gut churned. He had been put in his place – like a midshipman who strayed into a great cabin. Despite his achievements, decorations and titles, he was not good enough for the Saxons. It was disrespectful. But it was not just the elector's snub. He saw the possibility that the Hamiltons would never be accepted. Emma would never overcome her low birth and her career as an 'actor'. Socially, he too was not above criticism – a lowborn captain who had made good.

The episode took the wind from Horatio's sails. He hated Dresden. Hugh escorted them around the historic castle, the cathedral, and the guild hall and arranged a breakfast with Champagne – an opportunity for Emma to give another performance of 'Kyrie'. Yet despite that, Horatio had fallen into such despondency that even Miss Knight's epic poem and Emma's soprano failed to brighten him. Quite to the contrary, they filled him with self-disgust.

Anger congealed within him and seemed to twist his outlook so that he began to find the Hamiltons irritating – Emma's histrionic mannerisms and Sir William's sardonic wit and knowledge of things cultural grew more tiresome by the day.

He no longer wanted Emma and began to wonder if his friendship with Sir William was a fiction to cover his affair. The thought sickened him. But there was more than a grain of truth in it. He recalled Minto's advice to put an end to the whole thing. For the first time since it began, he felt the stirrings of scruple. His father's hatred of vanity preyed on his mind. He wished he could go home immediately but they still had 300 miles to travel before they would reach Hamburg.

As he supervised the loading of their boxes and trunks onto the barge prior to their departure, he heard a voice cursing in French. It was Emma's black maid. The young porter who carried their bags from the Hotel Poland had dropped them casually on the deck. Horatio intervened, quietening the maid and tipping the porter. Emma's voice floated up through a skylight of the barge.

'Is there no one here who can make me stew? I'm sick of this shitty German food!' he heard her say.

'There, there, my precious, I'll scrub up some potatoes and get the pot going!' It was the cracked high-pitched voice of Mrs Cadogan – he recognised her strong northern accent.

An image of sailors and fishwives crossed his mind, followed by a thought of Fanny at Roundwood – honest, thoughtful and sane. He went below to write her a letter, sick at heart.

Days of travel carried them through Prussia towards Berlin. Horatio kept his own company, going for long solitary walks when they pulled in to moor. The scenery was magnificent, but he was conflicted. Despite his annoyance of late, he was still bound to Emma, obsessed by the unique sensual satisfaction she gave him. He was also immensely sorry for his treatment of Fanny and for his moral cowardice in failing to end the affair. He thought of his father too;

bound by his godly duty, poor as a church mouse and yet free of worldly concerns. He thought of Josiah. He would surely have heard rumours. Why were Fanny's letters still affectionate? Why did Josiah never write to him? What would happen to them all when he reached England? Palermo was far away. It seemed more and more a very strange place. And he had other questions. Why had he fallen for Emma after his victory at the Nile? Had his wound affected his judgement? He was alternately longing for Emma and hating the thought of how other people saw him.

The barges drifted through the cliff-hemmed autumn countryside, dotted with sun-dappled vineyards perching in little terraces above the river. It was quiet: the ripples of the current, the idle flap of a sail, a cheeping of birds the only sounds to disturb the awful peacefulness.

One afternoon, Horatio climbed to the top of the cliff above the right bank of the river, passing vineyards and cottages with decorated shutters. Reaching the top after an hour of climbing, he flopped under a shady tree. He sipped from his water pouch and studied the valley below. A solitary bird of prey hovered in the currents of air. He closed his eyes and soon fell asleep. At length, a gunshot woke him. He opened his eyes as a hunter in lederhosen and carrying a long musket and a satchel of game appeared from the trees with his dog. He nodded before disappearing into the woods on the other side of the clearing. The sun was setting and there was no sign of the harvesters. Purple shadows fell over the valley. A gust of wind suggested an afternoon storm. He rose and brushed leaves from his coat. He felt cleansed. He was free – of desire for Emma. Lightheartedly, he started to sing a sea shanty. He arrived at the barge feeling like a new man. Then the storm broke and rain pelted down.

Taking off his coat, he threw himself onto a bunk. At last he could free himself from Emma. And he could again share his life with Fanny.

A week later, they approached Hamburg. The inn where they were put up was, for a change, clean and warm. Sir William retired to bed, complaining of his rheumatism. Miss Knight said she had some writing to do, leaving Emma and Horatio together. Emma sat on the other side of the hearth before a roaring fire. Then, before he could gather himself, she pressed a glass of Champagne into his hand and knelt at his side.

In a quiet voice, so soft that he thought he misheard, she said, 'Take me, now!' Horatio felt his blood rush to his face and a firmness beneath his breeches. He looked at her gorgeous hair and ran his hand down the nape of her neck.

For a moment, he considered his resolution. He was torn by desire. He could not help but stare at her – she was enchanting to him. She rose to her feet and gently tugged him to the stairs. He picked up the candle. As he climbed them, the door of Miss Knight's room closed quietly.

Emma was drawing the curtains. He caught her and kissed her hungrily. Her lips were so soft. She pulled off her skirt. Beneath was a black silk chemise. He took off his jacket and she pulled off his shirt and breeches. The candle fluttered. She turned to look at him as she leant over the bed.

He awoke. The light of the early morning was seeping through the cracks in the curtains. He took a deep drink from the carafe of water. He thought about the evening. He knew it had been a mistake. Yet he'd been utterly powerless. His thoughts lingered on their lovemaking. It was deeply satisfying. Yet, as he thought back, something had changed. Her body was so soft, her belly so tight and rounded. There was a change. Could it be …?

She roused, looked up at him and murmured sleepily, 'What's wrong with you?'

'I have been thinking about us,' he said. 'And about Sir William and Fanny.'

'What about us?'

'You know I love you, Emma, but it's wrong – you, me, Sir William.'

'We are *tria juncta in uno*, remember? That means all of us, in everything. Remember?'

'That was then, in Palermo. We are in a different world now – harsh, judgemental. I have a wife.'

'The only thing that matters is our love. If we put love first, everything else will fall in place. You'll see.'

'And Sir William? Fanny?' Horatio asked.

'He needs our love and protection in his old age. That is all.'

'And us?'

'We will find the way to be together,' she told him. 'Nothing will separate us. Society will surrender before the love the people have for you.'

'I wish I believed that.' He paused, reluctant to pursue the question that filled his mind. 'Emma, are you pregnant?'

She looked down and said nothing for a moment, her hand on his shoulder. Finally, she nodded.

'Does he know?' His voice was soft, forgiving.

'Yes, he does,' Emma said. 'It's your child, Horatio.'

He paused again and then said, 'This changes everything.'

But it was not so simple. Sir William was civil but withdrew, wrapping himself in a blanket in the lee of the wheelhouse and staring blankly over the stern of the barge. The glorious weather was gone, and grey skies, freezing rain and dampness blanketed the barge. Miss Knight had also reached a decision. There were no more verses of epic poetry about sea battles. She steered clear by day and at dinner, came and went quickly.

Horatio too made his decision with customary determination. He could not possibly give up Emma now. The only question that remained was Fanny. He needed a wife who would be accepted by society, to be with him publicly. He no longer wanted inter-course with her, but was that so unusual? He would make arrangements. He would need advice. Fanny's common sense would mean they could sort this out. As the last few days of their continental journey wound down, he prepared for what lay ahead.

Amidst the turmoil of his dilemma, he overlooked an important detail. He had earlier written to Fanny instructing her to go to London and find a house. But there was a hitch. They were unable to take the London ferry because of commitments in Hamburg and would be obliged to arrive at Yarmouth instead. He dashed off a note to his agent and the Admiralty to let them know, but it was too late.

The packet boat tied up at Yarmouth docks. It was early afternoon. As the other passengers rushed to disembark, Horatio and Emma were below with Sir William, who was recovering from the rough crossing and valiantly reassuring them that he was never a good sailor. Outside were sounds of the ship settling into port – gangplanks rolling aboard, luggage being unloaded, feet tramping on the deck and, in the distance, music.

'Come, Sir William, let's get you ashore. You will feel better the instant your feet touch dry land.'

The two men – one crippled with age and the other short and one-armed – slowly mounted the steps of the companionway to the deck. The music became louder.

There was bunting and crowds as far as the eye could see. Someone spotted them. A roar erupted and swelled. Horatio was waving. Sir William had fallen behind with Emma. The mayor and aldermen were on a platform dressed in finery and gold chains. His brother William was there. Where was Fanny? He looked around. She was nowhere to be seen. Horatio approached and the mayor introduced him to the other dignitaries. The crowd was noisier now with shouts and cheers interrupting the mayor. Thank God he had put on his coat with his decorations. He gave an impromptu speech.

'People of Yarmouth. Thank you for the amazing welcome you have afforded me and my dear friends.

We have returned from a long sojourn and we defeated the French in Egypt, Malta and Naples!'

Loud cheers overpowered his words.

'I am here today to tell you that I will continue to fight until this wretched republicanism is destroyed and you no longer lie uneasily in your beds. They will never invade this country, not as long as I am alive!'

The cheering continued until at length the travellers set off for the hotel in a carriage. As the cries of welcome faded in his ears, his anger grew. Where the hell was Fanny?

CHAPTER TWENTY-NINE
November 1800

Yarmouth reminded Horatio of Wells-next-the-Sea, the port near Burnham Thorpe where he had learned to sail: flat country, long sand dunes, swooping gulls and fishing sloops. It was good to be back home. His reception had been magnificent, and he'd been besieged ever since morning to night by well-wishers of every class. Only the Admiralty had failed, as yet, to acknowledge his arrival.

He was pleased to see William, but there'd been no sign of Fanny. Not even a note! He spent time with William. He had changed: he was less pompous, less importunate and was now an ally. Horatio opened up to him about his concerns. What would Father think of his situation? Did William have any thoughts about Fanny's position? Did he have any views on his relations with Emma? The questions had been very hard to ask, but Horatio needed to know the lay of the land. William had been frank. Their father would be concerned about the friendship and fearful of scandal attaching itself to the Nelson family name. Fanny had said nothing to William – or Sarah – but would know which side 'her bread was buttered'. In regard to the larger question – how William viewed Horatio's 'friendship' with Lady Hamilton – he had been judicious in reply.

'We are all sinners,' he'd said. 'We are daily faced with temptations. But sometimes, "The Lord works in mysterious ways, his wonders to perform".' Horatio found that thought comforting. William had some risk in the matter – his standing within the church would be important to him. He must consider rewarding him. He needed to deal with the succession matter. He would call Hastlewood and get that started.

Now, onward to Ipswich, a day's journey, Horatio at last had some time to relax and to decompress. His reception in Yarmouth proved beyond doubt that his reputation with the public was stronger than ever – something for which he was extremely grateful. However, there would be a reckoning when he reached London. Of Lord Spencer, he was hopeful, but the King had already made his position clear – his elevation to lowest rank of peerage amounted to a royal reprimand. And Fanny. Their exchanges were increasingly formal. Well, he would see her today – at Roundwood – and then he would tell her how the new arrangements were to work.

The carriage rattled up the driveway and stopped in front of the portico. The place had a deserted look. The shutters were closed, but through a gap Horatio could see that drop sheets covered the furniture. The grates were empty. An elderly woman answered the knock at the door, dropping a curtsey. It was the housekeeper putting the finishing touches on preparing the house for winter.

He had anticipated, at the minimum, a warm house with fires burning and hot water for a bath and a hot meal. Horatio was dumbstruck. How could Fanny be so careless? How could she fail his friends? Was this a rebuke? He ignored the housekeeper, brushing past her into the house. She rushed after him pulling the sheets off furniture, opening shutters and saying she would put on the kettle. Horatio stalked through the house. It was cold and his anger at Fanny's insult burned. He noticed the changes – the new curtains, the wallpaper, the handsome chairs and dining table, his portrait on the wall. It was attractive, but it was the house a retired captain might have and certainly not the home of a peer and duke. It would not suffice!

'What a charming little house,' said Emma, poking into drawers, bureaus, and cupboards. 'Your Fanny is very modest in her décor. Hardly a palace!' She laughed.

Sir William said, 'Emma, I find this house much to my liking. It shows a taste that is distinctively English. I could live here – if I had my antiques.'

'And perhaps you will, Sir William. We will certainly welcome you at any time. I am mortified that Fanny has failed in her duty!' said Horatio, still reeling at Fanny's absence.

'Don't apologise, Horatio. We will all be well looked after at the inn!'

Bamford's Hotel was comfortable and had fine, though small, rooms. The joyful welcome in Yarmouth was repeated again with well-wishers crowding into their hotel and cheering loudly until he addressed them.

The following day, when they set off for London, young men detached the carriage from the horses and pulled it through the town to the London road. As Horatio passed Roundwood, he glanced up. He doubted he would be back.

Their journey to London became a procession. Local dignitaries awaited them on the steps of the town halls, bunting decorated streets and crowds of villagers and townspeople swarmed around the coach as it passed through. By now, Horatio was aware of the scale of public approval. The common man, the aldermen and mayors, the gentry and the church were all represented.

Horatio opened a pile of mail he'd picked up at their hotel in Yarmouth. There was an invitation from the Lord Mayor of London to attend a celebration at the Guildhall. A note from Lord Spencer asked him to report to the Admiralty as soon as possible. Another from the Palace bade him to attend a levee with the King and Queen – and to bring Fanny with him. Another from Lady Spencer invited him and Fanny to dinner. And mixed in with the dozen or so other letters and invitations were three or four from Fanny herself. He opened them after he had attended to his important mail. Now he realised why she was not at Roundwood. Her letter said she was obeying his instructions, passed on by Davison, to rent a house in London. She added that since he was planning to arrive there, she would close Roundwood for the winter season. The news cooled his resentment. He recalled telling Davison he would take the packet to London. Even so, he found her affectionate letter irritating. When they reached the inn on the outskirts of the city, where they changed their horses for the last time, there was another note from her asking them to go to meet at Nerot's Hotel. She did not have the house ready yet. He continued to smoulder with resentment.

Horatio's coach rolled up to the hotel late in the afternoon. A crowd waited despite heavy rain. As he stepped from the coach wearing a cocked hat and his uniform with stars and gold medals, a roar went up. Sir William and Emma alighted together with Emma's maid and then Horatio stepped onto a box. It was the same speech and the same response. The cheers and huzzas followed him into the lobby.

Standing there were his father Edmund, thin and frail-looking, and Fanny. She looked pale and drawn. Horatio kissed her politely on the cheek. His father waited with tears rolling down his cheeks and then threw his arms round his son.

Horatio was moved. He was for once comforted by Fanny's self-control. He had a momentary sense that the plan would work. Then he called Emma and Sir William and formally introduced them. While Horatio and Edmund talked with Sir William, the two women greeted each other, Emma expressing her entire *joy* at meeting Fanny *at last*, and Fanny, her eye on Horatio, circumspectly saying words of thanks for all the Hamiltons had done for Horatio. Their meeting was barely beginning when it was disrupted by the Duke of Queensbury, cousin to Sir William. He ignored the women and Edmund, and with his arm at Horatio's back steered him to a room nearby leaving Emma, Edmund and Fanny in increasingly artificial conversation.

Later that day, at the Admiralty, Lord Spencer greeted Horatio courteously. 'I am pleased to see you, Nelson. I add my thanks and congratulations on your magnificent victory at the Nile. Though much time has passed since then, I want you to understand how proud we are.'

'My lord, I am grateful that I was chosen for the mission. And the mission was, as you say, successful.'

'And now you are back. But your journey has taken you months and you scarcely have any leave left for Fanny!'

'My lord, I requested *Foudroyant*, but Keith would not part with any ship larger than a frigate. Hence our lengthy journey by land. Still, I served the nation's interests by meeting our allies along the way.'

'Yes, so I hear! I needed *Foudroyant* in the Mediterranean. She's not ready for a refit. You have returned at a time of great uncertainty. There is a peace party manoeuvring to defeat us in parliament and deal with the French, and we are worried about the Russians and the Danes. Already they are cosy with the French and our Baltic trade – so important for the supply of timber – is at some risk.'

'I am ready for service at any time. If you give me command of the Baltic fleet, I am ready, my lord!'

Spencer looked curiously at Horatio's medals. 'I say, Nelson, is that a foreign medal you are wearing?'

'Yes, it was awarded to me by the Emperor.'

'Nelson, you have to obtain the King's approval to wear foreign decorations in England! Better put those medals in a box.'

'Of course, sir.'

'And, Nelson, you might have a care that the gossips in London are examining your relationship with Lady Hamilton. Public knowledge! Now would be a good time to confound your critics by being seen out and about town with dear Fanny. You get my drift?'

Before Horatio could respond, he continued, 'And that brings me to your relations with St Vincent. Why in the world are you suing your fellow admiral? It's all over the newspapers!'

'My lord, I have a rightful claim to the prize money for the Spanish treasure ship.'

'What rightful claim?'

'I was commander of the Mediterranean "de facto" when the ships were taken. Admiral Duckworth had his share and he was reporting to me. St Vincent had been invalided home and Keith was away pursuing the French in the North Atlantic. I am convinced that the court will rule in my favour.'

'But you were never confirmed as commander-in-chief, Nelson. At best, you were acting commander.

You have made an enemy and you will likely lose your case. On a more pleasant note, I read of your reception by the people of Yarmouth. Be modest and enjoy fame while you can. Don't jeopardise your career by politicking.'

Horatio reddened. 'I look forward to meeting your charming wife again, Lord Spencer.'

'She has an invitation outstanding to you and Fanny to come to our house for dinner,' Spencer responded.

'I should like it very much if I could bring my friends Sir William and Lady Hamilton. It would be a great mark of respect to them after our many years working together in Naples.'

'I have a feeling that my formidable partner could be persuaded to invite Sir William, but I can say with certainty that she will not invite Lady Hamilton. And now farewell. I look forward to seeing Fanny at dinner.'

Smarting from the conversation, Horatio returned to the hotel. Thankfully, Fanny was asleep. He quickly disrobed and took his side of the bed without waking her. The next day, and indeed all the days before Christmas, there were more celebrations – and each more magnificent than the last. The glorious day of the Lord Mayor's procession brought more public adulation. There were crowds of cheering people and a magnificent dinner for a thousand guests at the

Guildhall. Standing to deliver his speech, Horatio recalled the night of the battle when he had lain half-senseless and later had been carried to the deck. He described the awful explosion that destroyed *L'Orient*. He brought the scene to life, painting it with vivid language. He saw that he personified virtues his audience longed for but would never experience – courage in battle, perseverance, boldness, sacrifice. They ate it up.

Fanny followed the procession with the other wives – at a distance. She was together with Horatio at the dinner, but he had little time for her amid the clamour of others eager to talk to him. Any attempts she made to draw him into conversation irritated him. He needed her to realise that he had no time to talk. He had the obligation to deal with his public, to be available to his patrons. She had yet to accept that his role had changed. If only she would also realise she must make room for Emma, then all would be well.

For several days, neither he nor Fanny talked about the tension between them. Horatio was never one to talk about feelings – he'd prefer to have his teeth pulled than have such a conversation. She knew that. As equally she knew that if she were unwilling to accept the new reality, he would break with her. He held all the cards, his only weakness being society's censure. Moreover, he was beginning to see that with the adulation of the public, the opinion of the small elite didn't matter much.

King George made his way along the receiving line, pausing here and there to talk to people he recognised. It was the following week and they were at St James's Palace for the levee. When he reached Horatio, the King paused, eyeing his uniform. He said gruffly, 'I heard that you were back, Nelson. I hope you are well. I am told you are to join the Channel Fleet. Back with your old friend St Vincent, eh?'

Without waiting for a reply, he moved to the man standing next to Horatio and talked with him for several minutes about an inconsequential matter. Horatio was crushed. Not a word about his victory.

'Good morning, St Vincent,' Horatio greeted the admiral at the reception afterwards.

'Morning, Nelson.'

'I have just been on the receiving end of a gross royal insult!'

'Are you wearing foreign medals? You haven't learned, have you?' St Vincent said in a frosty voice.

The lawsuit. Obviously, St Vincent had not seen it for what it was – a technical dispute, about prize money, between colleagues.

'What do you mean?'

'You were surprised by the King snubbing you? Just as you have ignored your obligations to me after all I did for you, you ignore His Majesty's requirement that foreign decorations and medals are not to be worn. You self-important arse!'

St Vincent strode off without another word.

On the way home, while Fanny was chattering about her conversation with the Queen, Horatio thought of St Vincent's angry remarks. Was he being disloyal? Had he made an enemy out of St Vincent? He was still in a dark mood at Lady Spencer's that evening. He sat moodily as the food was served, brooding over the King's insult. Fanny was cutting up his food. She had taken to doing it. She did not know how intensely it reminded him of Emma.

She offered him a glass. 'My dear, would you care for walnuts?'

Exasperation overcame him. 'I don't want any.' He pushed the glass away. It tipped onto its side, the nuts spilling while the glass rolled and toppled over the edge of the table, shattering on the floor.

'Damn!'

He looked up angrily. Fanny's eyes were filling with tears. He turned away and glared into the face of Lady Spencer.

'Ladies, let us withdraw and leave these *gentlemen* to their port,' she said, her voice heavy with sarcasm.

After dinner and the return of the men to the sitting room, Lavinia Spencer asked Fanny to play the piano. Fanny announced she would play a movement of a sonata by the young German composer, Herr Beethoven – the 'Sonata Pathétique'. She sat and collected herself before beginning with dramatic chords, following with a theme full of gloomy foreboding and culminating in a brilliant passage of passion and power. The company stood after she finished and there was an outcry of 'Bravo! Bravo!' and sustained applause. Fanny curtseyed.

Horatio was stunned. He had never heard her play such a difficult piece of music and with such passion. In those few moments, her music said all there was to be said about the mess of their marriage. He knew she would never concede.

At breakfast a few days afterwards, Horatio was talking about Lady Hamilton, when Fanny interrupted him and said, 'I don't want to hear about dear Lady Hamilton anymore! You will have to choose. I can't stand it any longer!'

There was a heavy silence before Horatio said firmly, 'Take care, Fanny, don't force me to make a choice!'

Fanny, a mask of anger and hurt on her face, said, 'It seems to me you have already made a choice! You expect me to accept a situation any honourable man would consider indecent!'

CHAPTER THIRTY
December 1800

Horatio had left for the Admiralty to discuss a new posting to the Channel Fleet. He would be reporting for duty in just three weeks. Sitting at her desk, Fanny took out Izzy's latest letter and re-read it. Then she picked up her pen.

> *To Lady Isobel Walpole*
> *Wolterton*
> *5 December 1800*
>
> *My dear Izzy,*

She paused to sharpen her quill.

> *My dear husband has, at least temporarily, lost his mind. He is besotted with the Hamilton woman and very careless of me. It is so obvious to all around*

*him – indeed every respectable person in London. I
am embarrassed by his intentions while devastated
by his attitude towards me. I have decided that
whatever happens I will not be induced to live in
a 'ménage à trois' with him and the Hamiltons. If
he equates me to Sir William, he does not know me.
Sir William collaborates in his wife's unfaithfulness
and although he is a man of great reputation in the
field of diplomacy and antiquities, he has the morals
of an alley cat.*

*This last week has been horrible. Horatio is
insistent that I be friends with the Hamiltons. I hate
Hamilton himself. He disgusts me. He effects not to
know what is happening and to be Horatio's friend.
She is full of artifice and obviously pregnant with
child. I mention two episodes in confidence to show
what I have had to endure: Horatio took both of us
to the theatre after Hamilton feigned sickness. How I
allowed myself to go I will regret for ever. The theatre
crowd was boisterous, cheering Horatio and making
a huge fuss of him. It was clear that the notion of
both of his 'women' together at the same time was
an exquisite farce for those who saw us. I fainted at
one point and we left the theatre before the end of
the play.*

*But that was not the worst, my dear Izzy. A few
days afterwards, the Hamiltons were at our place*

for dinner. Horatio is determined to force us into each other's company. Early in the dinner, she left the table with her servant saying she was sick. Horatio literally ordered me to see to her! I went reluctantly. I had to hold a bowl for her in the bathroom while she vomited. It was absolutely the lowest point of my life.

Even the King himself snubbed Horatio at court. But I fear Horatio is impervious to criticism. Oh, how I pray for this madness to pass!

I wait, hoping for the best.

Pray for me.

Your friend,
Fanny

When she had finished the letter and given it to the maid to post, she felt calmer and more determined to face her situation. She knew he had allotted her this short period to determine if she would play the role he had decided on – to 'share' him with Emma Hamilton. To be exiled to Roundwood and leave him to conduct his affair in London. The first shots in the battle had been fired and he was waiting for her to signal her surrender to the arrangement. If she did not, he would bring more pressure on her, perhaps by threatening her financially.

The thought of a penniless existence appalled her. His refusal to be crossed was notorious, but surely he would not cut her off? Why, oh why, was he treating her this way? What had she done to deserve such horrible treatment?

Fame could do this to a person, she knew. Society rarely admitted those of humble birth to privilege, title, wealth and responsibility. Only extraordinary courage in battle could open the door to a commoner like Horatio. But didn't he realise he would risk people's respect by engaging in a love affair with a married woman who was a former prostitute! Only the Prince of Wales seemed to have looser morals than that.

And yet, she admitted to herself, she still loved him. She knew she ought to hate him, despise him – and she wished she could. But he was still her husband whom she had vowed to love until death. She continued to love him even as she revolted against his demands.

Edmund reappeared later in the morning. He had been to visit Maurice and had returned by coach from Essex. She heard the doorbell peel and the maid open the door. She quickly looked at herself in the round hall mirror. She was pale but her hair and make-up passed muster. She watched him take off his coat. He looked old and frail. She put her arms around him.

'Father, welcome home! How was dear Maurice?'

'Not well, not well at all. His house is small and cold, and I fear for his constitution. And how are you bearing up, my dear?'

'Father, I am desolate for the reasons that you know only too well. The Horatio I knew always had a kind heart. But it is cruel to impose the company of his mistress and his cuckolded friend on me!' She felt anguish breaking through. 'I'm sorry I said that, Father. Your son is a good soul.'

'No, Fanny, you are right,' Edmund said, a grave sadness in his tone. 'He is shameless in his behaviour. I do not understand why he has changed so much. He is not the dutiful boy or the decent human being I have known these years. I brought him up in the fear of the Lord, yet he is conducting himself publicly in a way which denies his religion.'

'I do not want to get between father and son. I do not want to cause a breach in your relationship, Father,' Fanny said, tearfully.

'Fanny, you have been my mainstay these years. I do not have much time to live but I will never forsake you to please my son, no matter his eminence. Rather, I will chastise him for his unfaithfulness and impiety.'

'No matter what happens to him and to me, I will continue to love him as a faithful wife should. But I fear that he will soon make up his mind between me and that woman. He is infatuated by her. She has bewitched him with her flattery. What I need now is faith in God and courage to stand up to a man whom I have always obeyed and admired. Can I do that?'

'Where is he now?' Edmund asked.

'This morning Hastlewood was here for breakfast. I protested when he mentioned her one too many times. He warned me to obey him or he would leave me. He said as much in front of Hastlewood. Since then, he has departed. I am not sure when or where I will see him again.'

'Then let us pray for a change of heart, Fanny. If he will listen to his father, I will talk sense into him myself.'

The reply from Izzy arrived later that day.

My dearest Fanny,

Thank you for confiding your inmost thoughts. Thank you for sharing the details of the last week, hard though it would be for anyone to describe what you have been through.

Certain of our noblest and best families live shameful lives, it must be said. We all know about the Duchess of Devonshire – how the Duke's blatant affairs provoked her to take a lover. But at least the Duke does not expect the Duchess to live in a ménage with the spouse of his mistress and to be 'friendly'.

We women are so disadvantaged. There is unanimity among men that we must yield to them or go and live in a nunnery! Sometimes I think we are useful only for our dowry and for producing heirs. The men have everything and control everything. There is no prospect of divorce when a husband misbehaves, other than by act of parliament and if a divorce bill passed the House, the property and children remain with the husband who has wronged his wife.

Does this mean that we have to live in a loveless marriage, living a charade when everyone knows the truth? The alternative is also sad; to lose one's friends, to have no money, to be shunned even if we are the wronged party. It requires great courage and fortitude to embark on that course!

But sometimes the alternative is worse. To live a life that is a lie is equally sad.

If this is your choice, I know which one you will take. Be assured, dear friend, that I for one will never abandon you. You are always welcome at Wolterton. And despite Horatio's connections with this family, I promise we will always take your side.

I am praying for you as I write and will hold my breath until I hear again and trust that it will be better news.

Yours ever,
Izzy

CHAPTER THIRTY-ONE
December 1800

Horatio strode along the Strand and Fleet Street, passing the Royal Courts of Justice and then climbing Ludgate Hill. Thinking he might shelter from the rain, which had increased from a drizzle to a downpour, he entered St Paul's Cathedral and made his way to a quiet side chapel where he sat and rested.

His thoughts returned to the appalling scene that morning. He had not intended to threaten Fanny, but her rejection of Emma could not be tolerated. He had never suspected she could be so tough, so obdurate – but that was the only description he could apply to her unqualified refusal to obey. He was her husband and she had shown him no obedience. He listed the things he had done for her, the favours he had heaped on Josiah, the great leap in her social rank – and Roundwood.

He tried to see things from her point of view. A woman is so different from a man. She has responsibility for the home. She has to manage friendships and social positions while a man has to fight for position and power. He had put his life on the line for his country and for her. How could she be so narrow-minded, so cold and tough?

A clergyman approached and was about to speak. Horatio waved him away. *He will only condemn me,* Horatio thought, *and tell me I'll go to hell.* He conjured memories of days gone by: when he and Fanny met and married, Josiah as a small boy, the early years in Norfolk, the joyous return three years ago when she nursed him back to health. The letters they wrote. They must number in the thousands. The 'stuff' of marriage. The intimacies and the friendship. The image of Emma returned. Dear Emma, her boisterous nature, her beauty, generosity in bed and her loyalty to him. It was so unfair that the snobs and the straitlaced moralists were unwilling to see her as she really was. One day, possibly not until he was dead, they would understand their mistake. He could not turn his back on her after all they had been through. He would make Fanny see sense. If he had to threaten her, threaten to cut her off, he would – if it would break her will. He would have two lives. One would be the life society expected – marriage continuing but with Fanny at Roundwood. Society would accept Emma in due course – just as Vienna accepted her. So long as Fanny endorsed it. She must.

He made his way back towards Westminster. The rain had stopped and there was a damp mist. He paused in Charing Cross to slake his thirst with beer before completing the short distance to White's in St James's, where he had arranged to meet Spencer. It was almost three in the afternoon.

'Horatio, good to see you again,' Spencer greeted him in the lobby, shaking his hand in the new fashion. After Horatio shed his damp coat, they retired to the members' sitting room and were soon nursing glasses of port.

'The papers are daily full of stories about you. I can scarcely find news of the war!' Spencer said.

'My lord, the accolades from my people are more than I deserve! I am astonished to tell you the truth. Yet not everyone has treated me with such gratitude – the King, for example.'

'Yes, I heard about your encounter with His Majesty.'

'It was very hard to take, especially after I was overlooked for a viscountcy …' Horatio trailed off, looking expectantly at his friend.

'Still smarting about that?' Spencer said.

Horatio fumed. If this man had not done so much for him, he would have walked out at that instant! He changed the subject. 'I have been posted to the Channel Fleet under St Vincent – who is barely on speaking terms with me.'

'Another relationship. You do know how to make enemies, Horatio.' Lord Spencer gave a slight shake of his head.

'What is happening? I am the hero of the people, but society from the King down despises me.'

'The government will soon fall. The peace party is gaining ascendency. Fox is loathed by the King, and another man, perhaps Addison, will be appointed first minister. When that happens, there will be a new First Lord of the Admiralty. It will likely be your former commander, St Vincent.'

'Then I will be beached if a peace is made with France.'

Spencer looked at Horatio calculatingly. 'Such a peace will not hold. We need to preserve our fighting strength while we are out of government for the moment the war resumes and we are back. That means we must keep able commanders like you near at hand. But you must behave, Horatio! Don't buck the system so!'

'I will not abandon the Hamiltons,' Horatio sulked. 'They are my friends.'

'Then you will have to wear the consequences of your decisions. From our point of view, we cannot have a senior officer behaving as if he rejects the code of honour expected of our leaders. How you treat your marriage and Fanny will determine your future.'

'Like any other wife, she has to learn that her position is to obey. I cannot allow her to dictate to me.'

'I can guarantee that if you try to introduce a bill of divorce, you will be opposed by all your peers.'

'She has to learn not to stand against me. I am her lord!' Horatio exclaimed, his frustration clear.

'Nelson, don't be so pig-headed, man. You have already alienated all the women in London. You've lost that battle. Don't lose the war. Treat her respectfully. If you do, your career continues and your promotion to vice admiral will be approved by the King. I have the papers on my desk at this moment.'

'What do you mean by "respectfully"?' Horatio asked, regaining his composure.

'You will have to consider that,' Lord Spencer said. 'But she is a peeress. She will continue to be Lady Nelson. You must provide her the means to live the life of a baroness.'

'You mean I will have to set her up to be financially independent?'

'If you do that, you will be treated as a man of honour and keep your career. If you don't, then I don't want to spell out what will happen, but I think it likely that your career will not flourish – at least as long as this King is on the throne.'

'You are telling me to endow her with half of my wealth?' Horatio said, in disbelief.

'The men in town will still speak to you if you do – though I doubt their wives will, no matter what!'

Without more ado, Spencer rose and signalled to the servant to bring their coats. Then, without a backward glance, he left the club and strode to his carriage.

It was dark when Horatio returned to New Bond Street. His long walk and the conversation with Spencer had calmed him. He realised now that he would not have his way. The maid opened the door and said that her mistress was abed. Horatio handed her his cloak, which she took with a disapproving sniff before asking him if there was anything he needed.

From Fanny's room, there came the soft glow of candlelight. She was sitting up in bed, her back propped by pillows. She had a white shawl around her shoulders and her curly dark hair spread over the pillow. As he entered the room, she looked at him.

'Husband, have I not been faithful and true to you?' she asked him.

He was startled. 'You have always been faithful and true. I have no complaints in that quarter.'

He sat on the edge of the bed.

'When I lived all those years in the West Indies, our house was run by slaves. I had personal slaves. My uncle had many more working in the sugar fields.'

'Yes, I know. What is this about? Has something happened to your cousin?'

'No. I have been thinking a great deal about them ... About the slaves ...'

'Yes – a foolish mistake abolishing the slave trade!' he agreed somewhat irritably, wondering where this was going.

'All those years, I accepted their service and devotion as if they owed it to me. You see, they did love me, Horatio.'

'Yes?'

'I treated them with an ignorant, patronising disregard. Now I know how they felt.'

'I don't understand.'

She slipped out of bed and sat on its edge next to him, determined to talk after so many distractions.

'Why have you chosen Emma over me? After everything you and I have been through together? What has made you angry and upset with me? Did something happen to you in that battle?'

He stood up and put his hands on his hips. His voice was hard. 'It was not I who chose Emma. She chose me!'

'I know the temptations our men face. I understand that. But please don't treat me like this. Let's return to the friendship, love and contentment that we always enjoyed!'

There was a long uncomfortable silence. Horatio said, 'Don't you understand? You can have all those things, but you must make room for my friends.'

'For your pregnant mistress, do you mean? Is she really bearing your child or has she just made you believe it's your child? It seems you will believe anything she says! Childlessness is not as pitiful as self-deception!'

He looked at her astonished, searching her face to see if she would retract. For one moment, he seemed as though he were about to strike her. Then he picked up his hat and left, banging the door behind him.

CHAPTER THIRTY-TWO
January 1801

Christmas came and went. Fanny knew Horatio and the Hamiltons had spent their season with Beckford, Sir William's cousin, at his strange gothic house in Hampshire. Meanwhile, Fanny, Edmund and Josiah went to church and spent their Christmas day quietly, Horatio's absence keenly weighing on them.

Josiah was preoccupied. Lieutenant Colquitt had been writing to the Admiralty and navy board and working with Brierley, the former master of the *Thalia*, to register complaints against him. *Thalia*, meanwhile, was slowly being rebuilt in Chatham yard and Josiah was keen to be reconfirmed as her captain.

He tried repeatedly to reach Horatio, but the weeks dragged by. Horatio was away in the Baltic. Horatio had returned but was busy buying in Merton where he planned to live with Emma and Sir William.

As cruel January leached into damp and windy February, Horatio made his separation arrangements. Through his lawyer, he told Fanny he would give her a settlement. She would have the 4000 pounds inherited from her uncle and a generous annual allowance suitable to her status in society. Spencer would approve. There was a new will which replaced Josiah as executor with William, who would inherit Horatio's titles in the event of his death. There was provision made in the will for Fanny, too. Roundwood was to be sold.

After he had made the arrangements, Horatio received his promotion to the rank of vice admiral. To Horatio's delight, Emma gave birth in late January. Horatia was given to a wet nurse, and Horatio and Emma devised a cover story to explain her presence in their lives. What happened to the other twin born together with Horatia, Horatio never knew; nor did he attempt to find out. He had another concern. Emma, he learned, was being courted by the Prince of Wales. The Prince was collecting her paintings and voicing a desire to meet her.

Horatio became bitterly jealous, the emotion deftly fanned by Emma, shoring up her position now that he had left Fanny. His leave over, Horatio departed for Portsmouth and his new flagship, *San Josef*, which he had taken as a prize at Cape St Vincent four years earlier. He returned to the world he best understood, and where his control of events was unchallenged. He took with him painful memories of Fanny, Lady Spencer and the King, together with memories of the friendly crowds and the grand reception at the Guildhall. He had powerfully mixed feelings: obsessive love, parental pride, jealousy and resentment – each jostling for dominance in his troubled heart.

Josiah was eventually able to see him in September of that year. He was faintly encouraging, indeed pleasant, but no support was forthcoming or if it was it was ineffective. By then the government had changed and St Vincent was First Lord and Troubridge a member of the board. That seemed to cement Josiah's fate.

In 1793, Horatio had returned to sea as captain of *Agamemnon*. He had enjoyed the singular delight of being a man restored to grace with great opportunities ahead. Now he returned to high command with all its politics and complexities. He had made decisions about his wife and his lover. He had flaunted the rules of society. He knew that his future career would depend on one thing only – his ability to win battles.

CHAPTER THIRTY-THREE
September 1811

It was a bright autumn day at Wolterton Park. A party of women were walking towards the Folly – a whimsical Greek temple and statue commemorating a long dead ancestor of Izzy's – built a mile or so away on the crest of a hill. They were dressed sensibly for the uncertain weather, in capes and long flannel skirts and hats. Following them at a respectful distance was a horse-drawn jogging cart driven by Lady Isobel's butler with two footmen, picnic hampers and blankets.

Fanny walked with Izzy Walpole, arm in arm and deep in conversation. Lavinia Spencer strolled with young Jane Coke. Louise Berry and Anna Gilbert followed a few yards behind. The ladies reached the Folly and spent time admiring the splendid view.

The avenue of oak trees stretched towards the house on the horizon like long green arms. The butler set up a table and spread the rugs on the ground. There was a gentle breeze and as the sun rose overhead, they took off their capes. All was quiet except for the chatter of sparrows and finches which fluttered down from the trees to search for crumbs.

Izzy raised her glass of Champagne to Fanny. 'Congratulations on your fiftieth birthday, darling!' The friends raised their glasses. Lavinia recalled the young woman she had taken under her wing and saw how she had aged. The separation had its price. But she was the same kind person whose advice was now sought by many younger women – and some young men – and who was always available to her friends. Her musical skills meant she was always in demand at dinner parties.

'Speech, speech!' the ladies called.

'My dear friends. Thank you so much for coming here for my fiftieth birthday. I am so grateful for your friendship and all the love you have shown me since my dear husband died. I mourn him still and will do so for the rest of my days. His name will live on long after I am forgotten, a man who died to save his country.

'In my early life, when I lived in Nevis, I was always attending loved ones whose lives were soon cut short.

I helped Mother when she fell ill and died. I was only thirteen. Then it was my father, whose death left me in the care of my uncle when I was but eighteen. My first husband died a few years after we married. I lost these dear ones, but when I married Horatio, I felt those days were over and I was deliriously happy. We had five happy years together until he was called back into service. Then the waiting began. He was at sea for the next eight years, with only short periods of leave. In those years, our marriage was disrupted by the scandal about which too much has been said. Thankfully, Merton and all it stood for is history. His family and I are reconciled. Josiah rarely saw his father in the years before he died, but now he has the satisfaction of a career, and he enjoys taking me sailing on his yacht. He has yet to give me the satisfaction of grandchildren, but I am optimistic. He is only thirty so there is still plenty of time.

'All those years ago at Burnham Thorpe, I little imagined what would happen to us when Horatio's coach turned the corner and took him to London and on to his illustrious career. It forced me to take stock and to learn how to survive. I could not have done it without your friendship, especially over the last ten years. Women know we must stick together and help each other through unendurable times. Thank you all for your love.'

They surrounded her with good wishes and promises to meet again soon. The remains of the picnic were packed up and the women set off on the return walk to Wolterton. Izzy took Fanny's arm again and, as they walked down the hill, she said, 'You know, Fanny, you are a very gracious person and your continued love for Horatio is moving, given the way he treated you. Horatio had that failing found in most powerful men – the need to have their own way. If they don't get it, they are angry, resentful and vindictive. That's why I will never marry!'

Fanny squeezed her arm. They continued their walk in the warm autumn sun: accomplished women, wealthy women – and happy to be single.

AUTHOR'S NOTE
The Miniature

A recent chance discovery on eBay by Martyn Downer, author of *Nelson's Purse* and *Nelson's Lost Jewel* brought to light a lost portrait of Fanny painted in later life. Another well-known painting captures Fanny as a young woman, probably in her late teens, while a third, entitled *The Waiting Wife* by Henry Eldridge, dates to about 1800 and presents her dramatically, with a bust of Horatio in the background. The fourth belongs to me. This painting captures Fanny in middle age – after Horatio has died. The painting has similarities to *The Waiting Wife*, with the artist capturing her sadness. Yet both pictures also convey dignity and strength of character.

By the time these later pictures were painted, the myth-making around Horatio was in full swing. Fanny had to endure changes in public sentiment – usually at her expense – once the generation which supported her had passed from the scene. Especially painful was the publication of love letters between Horatio and Emma. They were leaked by Emma, who was short of money at the time. Eventually, Emma's story came to be the preferred truth. Horatio was the hero who needed a hot-blooded woman to give him the love and sensual satisfaction missing from his 'dismal' marriage. When I visited *Victory*, Horatio's flagship moored in Portsmouth Harbour, this was the account given by the guide when I enquired about Fanny and Emma. However, the publication of recently discovered documents have greatly changed informed opinion about Fanny.

I am a great-great-great-grandson of Fanny. My family is connected to the Eccles family of Plymouth, descendants on the maternal side from Fanny and Josiah. Through that family, I inherited my miniature of Fanny and various other Nelson memorabilia. We also inherited some family lore about Fanny. According to this, Fanny was a woman who loved Horatio deeply and continued to do so until she died. To the end of her life, she still found it difficult to reconcile her knowledge of him with the swift, brutal termination of their relationship. Clearly, she was either misinformed about his character or else something happened which led to the change. In recent times, much has been discovered about the effect of successive concussions on the brain and on the patient's resulting behaviour, especially in the 'executive' part of the brain, which affects judgement and inhibitions. Nelson suffered several serious injuries of this nature.

We live at a time in which society is re-examining the role of women and their treatment by men. We know much more about their lack of legal rights at the time in which this novel is set. We also know more about the dangers women faced if their husbands threatened them with divorce. A contemporary of Fanny was the Duchess of Wellington, who was treated very badly by the "hero of Waterloo". The difference was she remained in a humiliating relationship with her husband. Fanny, on the other hand, was cut out of Horatio's life and received a 'settlement'. That raises the question: why did Horatio treat Fanny so cruelly while providing for her, one might say, generously in the settlement? Horatio was not known for his willingness to part with his money. He left nothing to Emma, who died penniless, fleeing her creditors. I have dealt with the question using the freedom allowed novelists. There is no documentation to support the notion that Spencer or anyone else talked Horatio into the settlement. I have suggested that perhaps Lavinia was the instigator and Horatio's friends and employers used their leverage to ensure Fanny was well looked after financially, if not emotionally.

The historical novelist is constrained by the historical facts, but where those are unavailable it is acceptable to use his or her imagination. As my first novel – and I anticipate more to come – I have learned to reconcile my desire for facts and explanations with the essential requirements of good fiction – a satisfying plot and an exploration of the protagonists' emotions and motivations. I am unashamedly on Fanny's side. She was a woman who loved and lost and yet survived. There aren't enough people like her in our world.

My portrayal of the many characters in the story may be controversial. Some of them are ancestors of people still living. It is not my intention to be hurtful to the memories of these long-gone loved ones. Fanny's reputation was brutalised by succeeding authors who had not taken enough time to understand her and were willing to condemn her or airbrush her out of the story. As far as possible I have tried to be fair and to be faithful to the facts. If, in the eyes of my readers, I have failed to do so, I apologise.

Many people have helped me. I would like to single out a few. Emily McGuire, herself a successful author who conducted the "Novel in a Year" course at New South Wales "Writers", was always encouraging and helpful, especially as a structural editor. Emma Rafferty was a superb copy editor. My friends, Oliver Freeman, Dr Andrew Pesce and Stephen Badger, members of the "Boys Own Writer's Group" endured version after version and offered incisive advice together with some excellent wine. Ann Wilson and her team of experts have helped me produce the finished book and launch it. They are real professionals. Most of all I acknowledge my wife, Susanne, without whose advice and encouragement I would never have succeeded.

OLIVER GREEVES, a direct descendent of Fanny Nelson, lives in Sydney. He is a historian and sailor who spent many years working on Wall Street. He is currently working on a follow-on novel about Josiah Nisbet, Nelson's stepson.

Made in the USA
Las Vegas, NV
23 December 2020